SAINT DEATH

A John Milton Novel

Mark Dawson

To Mrs D, FD and SD.

"Put on the whole armour of the God, that ye may be able to stand against the wiles of the Devil / Because we wrestle not against flesh and blood, but against principalities, against powers, against the rulers of darkness of this world, against spiritual wickedness in high places."

Ephesians, Chapter 6, Verses 11 to 17

PROLOGUE

Samalayuca
South of Ciudad Juárez
Mexico

ADOLFO GONZÁLEZ lowered his AK, and the others did the same. They were stood in a semicircle, all around the three stalled trucks. There was no noise beyond the soporific buzz of the earth baking and cracking under the heat of the sun. Dust and heat shimmered everywhere. He looked out at their handiwork. The vehicles were smoking, bullet holes studded all the way across the sheetmetal. They were all shot up to high heaven. The windscreens had been staved in by the .416 calibre rounds that the snipers had fired. Some of the holes that ran across the cars were spaced and regular from the AKs, others were scattered with uneven clumps from number four buckshot. The Italians had come to the meet in their big, expensive four-wheel-drive Range Rovers. Tinted windows, leather interiors and xenon headlamps. Trying to make a big impression. Showing off. Hadn't done them much good. One of them had tried to drive away, but he hadn't got far. The tyres of the car were flat, still wheezing air. The glass was all shot out. Steam poured from the perforated bonnets.

Adolfo looked up at the hills. He knew Samalayuca like the back of his hand. His family had been using this spot for years. Perfect for dumping bodies. Perfect for ambushes. He'd put three of his best snipers up on the lava ridge. Half a mile away. They had prepared covered trenches and hid in them overnight. He could see them coming down the ridge now. The sun shone against the dark metal of their long-barrelled Barretts and reflected in glaring flickers from the glass in the sights.

He approached the nearest Range Rover, his automatic cradled at his waist. Things happened. Miracles. It paid to be careful. He opened the door. One of the Italians, slumped dead over the wheel, swung over to the side. Adolfo hauled his body out and dumped it in the dust. Bad luck, *pendejo*. There were two more bodies in the back.

Adolfo walked around the end of the truck. There was another body behind it, face up, mouth open. Vivid red blood soaked into the dirt. A cloud of hungry flies hovered over it.

He went to the second truck and looked through the window at the driver. This one had tried to get away. He was shot through the head. Blood everywhere: the dash, the seats, across what was left of the window.

He walked on to the third vehicle. Two men inside, both dead.

He walked back to the first truck to where the body lay.

He nudged the man's ribs with his toe.

The man moved his lips.

"What?"

The man wheezed something at him.

Adolfo knelt down. "I can't hear you."

"*Basta*," the man wheezed. "*Ferma.*"

"Too late to stop, *cabrón*," Adolfo said. "You shoulda thought of that before."

He put the automatic down and gestured to Pablo. He had the video camera and was taking the footage that they would upload to YouTube later. Leave a message. Something to focus the mind. Pablo brought the camera over, still filming. Another man brought over a short-bladed machete. He gave it to him.

The dying man followed Adolfo with his eyes.

Adolfo signalled, and his men hauled the dying man to his knees. They dragged him across to a tree. There was blood on his face, and it slicked out from the bottom of his jacket. They looped a rope over a branch and tied one end around the man's ankles. They yanked on the other end so that he fell to his knees, and then they yanked again, and then again, until he was suspended upside down.

Adolfo took the machete with his right hand and, with his left, took a handful of the man's thick black hair and yanked back to expose his throat.

Adolfo stared into the camera.

He went to work.

DAY ONE

The City of Lost Girls

I have fought a good fight
I have finished my course
I have kept the faith

2 Timothy 4:7

From: <redacted>
To: <redacted>
Date: Monday, September 16, 5.21 P.M.
Subject: CARTWHEEL

Dear Foreign Secretary,

At our meeting last week you requested sight of a report detailing the circumstances in which the agent responsible for the botched assassination in the French Alps has disappeared.

I attach a copy of that report to this email.

While writing, please allow me to reiterate that all efforts are being made to locate and recover this agent. He will not be easy to find, for the reasons that we discussed, but please do be assured that he will not be able to stay undetected forever.

If there is any follow-up once you have considered this report, please do, as ever, let me know.

Sincerely,

M.

>>> BEGINS

* * * EYES ONLY * * *

CODE: G15
PUBLICATION: analysis/background
DESCRIPTION: n/a
ATTRIBUTION: internal
DISTRIBUTION: Alpha
SPECIAL HANDLING: Orange

CODENAME: "Cartwheel"

Summary

Following the unsatisfactory elimination of the Iranian nuclear scientists Yehya Moussa and Sameera Najeeb, John Milton (aka G15/No. 1/ aka "John Smith"/ aka "Cartwheel"), the agent responsible, has gone AWOL. Location presently undetermined. Milton is extremely dangerous and must be recovered without delay.

Analysis

>>>extracted

Control records that Milton evinced a desire to leave the service on returning to London following the completion of his assignment in France. The meeting is said to have been heated and ended with Milton being put on suspension prior to a full assessment and review.

<redacted>

His subsequent behaviour was observed to be erratic. He began to attend meetings of Alcoholics Anonymous (almost certainly in contravention of his obligations under the Official Secrets Act). He rented a house in a poor part of Hackney, East London, and is believed to have become emotionally involved with a single mother, Sharon Warriner. Our investigations are ongoing, but it is believed that he was attempting to assist Ms. Warriner's son, Elijah, who is believed to have been on the fringes of a local gang. We suspect that Milton was involved in the death of Israel Brown (the successful rapper who performed under the *nom de plume* of "Risky Bizness"), whom we understand to have been the prime mover in the relevant gang.

The order to decommission Milton was given on Monday, 15 August. A second G15 agent, Christopher Callan (aka G15/No. 12/"Tripwire"), had located Milton at a boxing club set up for local children by a Mr. Dennis Rutherford. As Callan was preparing to carry out his orders, he was disturbed by Mr. Rutherford. In the confusion that followed, Callan killed Mr. Rutherford and shot Milton in the shoulder. This was unfortunately not sufficient to subdue him, and he was able to overpower Callan—shooting him in the knee to prevent pursuit—and then make his escape. ANPR located him driving a stolen car northwards. The last sighting was on the M62 heading into Liverpool. The working hypothesis is that he boarded a ship to leave the country.

<redacted>

Analysis of Milton's psychological assessments (attached) suggests that his mental state has been deteriorating for some time. Feelings of guilt are not uncommon in Group 15 operatives, and Milton has worked there for a decade. It is regrettable that warning signs were missed, but perhaps understandable: Milton's performance has always been superb. He was perhaps the most effective of all our operatives. Subsequent analysis has led us to the conclusion that he is suffering from insomnia, depression and possible re-experiencing of past events. PTSD is a fashionable diagnosis to make, but it is one that we are now reasonably confident is accurate.

Regardless of his mental condition, Milton is far too dangerous to be ignored. He was a key part of several key British and NATO intelligence successes, not all of which have been reported in the press, and his value to the enemy is difficult to assess. The damage that he could do by going public is similarly incalculable.

>>> ENDS

From: <redacted>
To: <redacted>
Date: Wednesday, September 19, 5.21 P.M.
Subject: Re: CARTWHEEL

Dear M.,

Thank you for the report. I have shared it with the P.M., who is not, as you might well imagine, best pleased with its contents. You are to convey his displeasure to Control personally and to remind him that it is of the highest importance that Mr. Milton is located. We simply cannot have a man with his skills and knowledge running around outside of the reservation, as our American cousins would undoubtedly say. I am not sure which grubby little euphemism our mutual friend would prefer, but let's settle on "retirement."

All due haste, please.

Regards, etc.,

James

Chapter One

JOHN MILTON got off the bus and walked into the parking lot of the first restaurant that he found. It was a hot day, baking hot, brutally hot, the noon sun battering down on Ciudad Juárez as if it bore a grudge. The sudden heat hit him like a steel-yard furnace. The restaurant was set back from the road, behind a wide parking lot, the asphalt shimmering like the water in an aquarium. A large sign, suspended from a tall pole, announced the place as La Case del Mole. It was well located, on Col Chavena, and near to a highway off-ramp: just a few miles to the border from here, plenty close enough for the place to snag daring Americans coming south for a true taste of *la vida loca*. There were half a dozen similar places all around it. Brightly painted, practically falling to bits, garish neon signs left on day and night, a handful of cars parked haphazardly in the lot. Awful places, dreadful food, and not the sort of establishment that Milton would have chosen to visit. But they churned through the staff so fast that they were always looking for replacements, and they didn't tend to be too picky about who they hired. Ex-cons, vagabonds, vagrants, it didn't matter. And there would be no questions asked so long as you could cook.

Milton had worked in places like this all the way up through Mexico. He knew that they appealed to tourists and the uncritical highway trade and that this one, in particular, was still in business for three main reasons: It was better advertised than the tumbledown shacks and chain restaurants around it, the parking lot was big enough that it would be almost impossible to fill, and the daily seafood special was just $19.95, three dollars cheaper than the seafood special of any of the nearby competitors. Milton had worked in a place in Mazatlán until he had had to move on two weeks ago, and he was willing to bet that this would be just the same.

It would do him just fine.

He crossed the parking lot and went inside. The place really was a dive, worse when viewed in the middle of the day when the light that streamed through the grime-streaked windows revealed the peeling paint, the mice holes in the skirting, and the thick patina of dust that lay over everything. It was seven hundred miles west to the Pacific and eight hundred east to the Gulf, but the owner wasn't going to let small details like that dissuade him from the nautical theme he obviously hankered after: a ship's wheel, netting draped down from the walls, fronds of fake seaweed stapled to the net, lobster pots and shrimper's buoys dangling from the ceiling, a fetid and greening aquarium that separated the bar from the cavernous dining room beyond.

A woman was sitting at the bar, running a sweating bottle of Corona against the back of her neck.

"Hello."

She nodded in response: neither friendly nor hostile.

"Do you work here?"

"I ain't here for the good of my health, baby. What you want?"

"Came in to see if you were hiring."

"Depends what you do."

"I cook."

"Don't take this the wrong way, honey, but you don't look like no cook."

"I'm not bad. Give me a chance, and I'll show you."

"Ain't me you gonna have to show." She turned to the wide-open emptiness of the restaurant and hollered, "Gomez! New blood!"

Milton watched as a man came out of the back. He was big, fat and unhealthy, with a huge gut, short arms and legs, and an unshaved, pasty complexion. The T-shirt he was wearing was stretched tight around his barrel chest, and his apron was tied right to the limit of the strings. He smelt bad, unwashed and rancid from rotting food.

"What's your name?"

"Smith."

"You cook?"

"That's right."

"Where?"

"Wherever. I've been travelling up the coast. Ensenada, Mazatlán, Acapulco."

"And then Juárez? Not Tijuana?"

"Tijuana's too big. Too Californian."

"Last stop before America?"

"Maybe. Maybe not. Are you the owner?"

"Near enough for you, *cabrón*. That accent—what is it? Australian?"

"English. I'm from London."

Gomez took a beer from the fridge and cracked it open. "You want a beer, English?"

"No, thanks. I don't drink."

Gomez laughed at that, a sudden laugh up from the pit of his gut that wobbled his pendulous rolls of fat, his mouth so wide that Milton could see the black marks of his filled teeth. "You don't drink, and you say you want to work in my kitchen?" He laughed again, throwing his head all the way back. "Hombre, you either stupid or you ain't no cook like what I ever met."

"You won't have any problems with me."

"You work a fryer?"

"Of course, and whatever else you need doing."

"Lucky for you I just had a vacancy come up. My fry cook tripped and put his arm into the fryer all the way up to his elbow last night, stupid *bastardo*. Out of action for two months, they say. So maybe I give you a spin, see how you get on. Seven an hour, cash."

"Fifteen."

"In another life, *compadre*. Ten. And another ten says you won't still be here tomorrow."

Milton knew that ten was the going rate and that he

wouldn't be able to advance it. "Deal."

"When can you start?"

"Tonight."

Chapter Two

MILTON ASKED Gomez to recommend a place to stay; the man's suggestion had come with a smirk. Milton quickly saw why: it was a hovel, a dozen men packed into a hostel that would have been barely big enough for half of them. He tossed his bag down on the filthy cot that he was assigned and showered in the foul and stained cubicle. He looked at his reflection in the cracked mirror: his beard was thick and full, the black silvered with flecks of white, and his skin had been tanned the kind of colour that six months on the road in South America would guarantee. The ink of the tattooed angel wings across his shoulders and down his back had faded a little, sunk down into the fresh nutty brown.

He went out again. He didn't care that he was leaving his things behind. He knew that the bag would be rifled for anything worth stealing, but that was fine; he had nothing of value, just a change of clothes and a couple of paperbacks. He travelled light. His passport was in his pocket. A couple of thousand dollars were pressed between its pages.

He took a scrap of paper from his pocket. He had been given it in Acapulco by an American lawyer who had washed up on the shores of the Pacific. The man used to live in New Mexico and had visited Juárez for work; he had been to meetings here and had written down the details. Milton asked a passer-by for directions and was told it was a twenty-minute walk.

He had time to kill. Time enough to orient himself properly. He set off.

Milton knew about Juárez. He knew it was the perfect place for him. It was battered and bloodied, somewhere where he could sink beneath the surface and disappear.

Another traveller had left a Lonely Planet on the seat of the bus from Chihuahua, and Milton had read it cover to cover. The town had been busy and industrious once, home to a vibrant tourist industry as Texans were lured over the Rio Bravo by the promise of cheap souvenirs, Mexican exotica and margaritas by the jug (served younger than they would have been in El Paso's bars). There was still a tourist industry but the one-time flood of visitors had dwindled now to a trickle.

That was what the reputation of being the most murderous place on the planet would do to a town's attractiveness.

The town was full of the signs of a crippled and floundering economy. Milton passed the iron girder skeleton of a building, squares of tarpaulin flapping like loose skin, construction halted long ago. There were wrecked cars along the streets, many with bullet holes studding their bodywork and their windscreens shot out. Illicit outlets—*picaderos*—were marked out by shoes slung over nearby telegraph wires and their shifty proprietors sold cocaine, marijuana, synthetic drugs and heroin. Everything sweated under the broiling desert sun.

Milton walked on, passing into a residential district. The air sagged with dust and exhaust and the sweet stench of sewage. He looked down from the ridge of a precarious development above the sprawling *colonia* of Poniente. Grids of identical little houses, cheap and nasty, built to install factory workers who had previously lived in cardboard shacks. Rows upon rows of them were now vacant and ransacked, the workers unable to pay the meagre rent now that Asian labourers would accept even less than they would. Milton saw one street where an entire row had been burnt out, blackened ash rectangles marking where the walls had once stood. Others bore the painted tags of crack dens. These haphazard streets had been built on swampland, and the park that had been reserved for children was waterlogged; the remains of a set of swings rusted in the sun, piercing the muddy sod like the broken bones of a skeleton. Milton paused to survey the wide panorama: downtown El Paso just over the border; burgeoning breeze-block and cement housing slithering down into the valley to the south; and, in the *barrio*, dogs and children scattered among the streets, colourful washing drying on makeshift lines, radio masts whipping in the breeze, a lattice of outlaw electricity supply cables and satellite dishes fixed to the sides of metal shacks.

He reached the church in thirty minutes. It was surrounded by a high wire fence, and the gate was usually locked, necessary after thieves had broken in and made off with the collection one time too many. The sign hanging from the mesh was the same as the one Milton had seen around the world: two capitalised letter A's within a white triangle, itself within a blue circle. His first meeting, in London, seemed a lifetime ago now. He had been worried sick then: the threat of breaching the Official Secrets Act, the fear of the unknown, and, more, the fact that he would have to admit that he had a problem he couldn't solve on his own. He had dawdled for an hour before finding the guts to go inside, but that was more than two years ago now, and times had changed.

He went inside. A large room to the left had been turned into a crèche, where parents with jobs in the factories could abandon their children to listless games of tag, Rihanna videos on a broken-down TV and polystyrene plates divided into sections for beans, rice and a tortilla. The room where the meeting was being held was similarly basic. A table at the front, folding chairs arranged around it. Posters proclaimed the benefits of sobriety and how the twelve steps could get you there.

It had already started.

A dozen men sat quietly, drinking coffee from plastic mugs and listening to the speaker as he told his story. Milton took an empty seat near the back and listened.

When the man had finished, the floor was opened for people to share their own stories.

Milton waited for a pause and then said, in his excellent Spanish, "My name is John, and I'm an alcoholic."

The others welcomed him and waited for him to speak.

"It's been 870 days since my last drink."

Applause.

"Why can't we drink like normal people? That's the question. It's guilt for me. That's not original, I know that, but that's why I drink. Some days, when I remember the things I used to drink to forget, it's all I can do to keep away from the bottle. I spent ten years doing a job where I did things that I'm not proud of. Bad things. Everyone I knew then used to drink. It was part of the culture. Eventually I realised why—we all felt guilty. I was ashamed, and I hated what I'd become. So I came to these rooms, and I worked through the steps, like we all have, and when I got to step four, "make a searching and fearless moral inventory," that was the hardest part. I didn't have enough paper to write down all the things that I've done. And then step eight, making amends to those people that you've harmed, and well, that's not always possible for me. Some of those people aren't around for me to apologise to. So what I decided to do instead was to help people. Try to make a difference. People who get dealt a bad hand, problems they can't take care of on their own, I thought maybe I could help them.

"There was this young single mother—this was back in London before I came out here. She was struggling with her boy. He was young and headstrong and on the cusp of doing something that would ruin the rest of his life. So I tried to help, and it all went wrong—I made mistakes, and they paid the price for them. That messed me up even more. When the first people I tried to help end up worse than when I found them, what am I supposed to do then?"

He paused, a catch in his throat. He hadn't spoken

about Rutherford and Sharon before. Dead and burned. He blamed himself for both of them. Who else was there to blame? And Elijah. What chance did the boy have now after what had happened to him? He was the one who had found Rutherford's body.

"You can't blame yourself for everything," one of the others said.

Milton nodded, but he wasn't really listening. "I had to get out of the country. Get away from everything. Some people might say I'm running away from my problems. Maybe I am. I've been travelling. Six months, all the way through South America. I've helped a few people along the way. Small problems. Did my best, and by and large, I think I made a difference to them. But mostly it's been six months to think about things. Where my life's going. What I'm going to do with it. Do I know the answers yet? No, I don't. But maybe I'm closer to finding out."

Milton rested back in his chair: done. The others thanked him for his share. Another man started with his story. The meetings were meditative, a peaceful hour where he could shut out the clamour of the world outside.

Ignore his memories.

The blood on his hands.

He closed his eyes and let the words wash across him.

Chapter Three

THE MAN they called El Patrón was in his early seventies, but he looked younger. There had been a lot of plastic surgery in the last decade. That pig Calderon would have paid handsomely for his capture—the bounty was ten million dollars the last time he had checked—and it had been necessary for him to change the way he looked. The first few operations had been designed to do that: his nose had been reshaped, new hair had been transplanted onto his scalp, his teeth had been straightened and bleached. The recent operations were for the sake of vanity: wrinkles were pulled tight with a facelift, bimonthly Botox injections plumped his forehead, filler was injected into his cheeks. In a profession such as his, when Death was always so close at hand, it gave him a measure of satisfaction to be able—at least superficially—to thumb his nose at the passing of time.

His name was Felipe González, although no one outside of his family used it any more. He was El Patrón or, sometimes, El Padrino: the Godfather. He was of medium height, five foot eight, although he added an inch or two with Cuban-heeled boots. He had a stocky, powerful build, a bequest from his father, who had been a goatherd in the Sierra Madre Mountains, where he still maintained one of his many homes and where he had learned how to cook methamphetamine, cultivate the opium poppy crop, and move cargos without detection. He had large, labourer's hands, small dark eyes, and hair coloured the purest black, as black as ink or a raven's feathers.

He opened the door to the laboratory. The work was almost done. The equipment that he had been acquiring for the better part of six months—bought carefully, with discretion, from separate vendors across the world—had all been installed. The room was two thousand square feet, finished with freshly poured concrete floors and walls, everything kept as clean as could be. The largest piece of equipment was the 1200-litre reaction vessel, a huge stainless steel vat that had been positioned in the middle of the large space. There were separate vats for the other processes and a hydraulic press to finish the product. The top-of-the-line filtration system had been purchased from a medical research company in Switzerland and had cost a quarter of a million dollars alone. There were large tanks for the constituent parts: ephedrine, red phosphorous, caustic soda, hydrogen chloride, hydrochloric acid, ammonia hydroxide, and other chemicals that Felipe did not recognise nor was interested in understanding. The actual operation of the lab was not his concern. He had hired a chemist for that, a man from a blue-chip pharmaceutical company who felt that he was not receiving a salary commensurate with his talents. Felipe could assuage all doubts on that score. He would make him a millionaire.

Felipe considered himself an expert in the tastes and preferences of his clientele, and so far as he was concerned, meth was the drug of the future. He had been a little slow in getting into it, but that would all change now.

He had seen enough and went back outside. They were high in the mountains. The lab was stuffy, but the air was fresh and clean. It was a perfect spot for the operation: the only way to get to the lab was along a vertiginous road that wound its way around the face of the mountain, slowly ascending, an unguarded drop into a ravine on the right-hand side as the road climbed. There were shepherds and goatherds all along the route, each of them furnished with a walkie-talkie that Felipe had provided. In the unlikely event that an unknown vehicle attempted to reach the summit, they would call it in, and the *sicarios* who provided security for the laboratory would take to their posts and, if necessary, prevent further progress. The government made all the right noises about closing down operations like this one, but Felipe was not concerned. He knew the rhetoric was necessary for the public's consumption, but there would always be the cold, hard impracticality of putting those fine words into action. They would need helicopters and hundreds of men. It wasn't worth the effort.

His second-in-command, Pablo, was behind him. The man was as loyal as a dog, perhaps a little too enamoured of the white powder, but very dependable.

"It is done, El Patrón," he said.

"You have spoken to Adolfo?"

"I have."

"It was straightforward?"

"Apparently so. They killed them all. One of them was still alive. Adolfo cut off the man's head and posted the footage on YouTube."

Felipe tutted. His son had a weakness for the grand gesture. There was a time and a place for drama—it was practically de rigueur among the younger narcos these days—but Felipe preferred a little more discretion.

Pablo noticed his boss's disapproval. "It will be a message for the Italians."

"Yes," Felipe said shortly.

Pinche putas. Traitors. They had it coming.

La Frontera had been doing business with them for five years, and until recently, it had been a fruitful and mutually beneficial relationship. The Italians needed his drugs and his ability to get them over the border; he needed their distribution. In recent months, they had overestimated how much he needed them and underestimated how much they needed him. He had tried to make them understand, but they were stubborn and wrong-headed and kept asking for more. In the end, he had had to withdraw from the arrangement. It had to be final, and it needed to provide an idea of the consequences that would flow should they not accept his decision. For all his son's drama, at least that had been achieved.

"What about the gringos?"

"It is in hand," Pablo said. "The plane will collect them tomorrow morning. They will be in Juárez by the evening. I thought you could conclude the business with them there and then fly them here to see all this."

"They will be impressed, yes?"

"Of course, El Patrón. How could they not be?"

"Is there anything else?"

"There is one other thing, El Patrón. Your son says that they have located the journalists."

"Which? Remind me."

"The bloggers."

"Ah, yes." He remembered: those irritating articles, the ones that promised to cast light on their business. They had started to get noticed, at home and abroad, and that was not something that Felipe could allow to continue. "Who are they?"

"A man and a woman. Young. We have located the man."

"*Estúpido!* Take care of them, Pablo."

"It is in hand."

Chapter Four

CATERINA MORENO stared out into the endless desert, grit whipped into her face by the wind. It was just past dawn, and she was on the outskirts of Lomas de Poleo, a shanty that was itself in the hinterland of Ciudad Juárez. They had passed through a fence marked PRIVATE PROPERTY and out onto land that was known to have connections with La Frontera cartel. There were rumours that there was an airstrip here for the light planes that carried cocaine north into America and roads used by no one except the *traficantes*.

Caterina looked up into the crystal-clear blue sky and searched for the buzzards that would be circling over a possible cadaver.

She was standing with a group of thirty others, mostly women but a handful of men, too. They were from *Voces sin Echo*—Voices Without Echo—an action group that had been established to search for the bodies of the girls who were disappearing from the streets of Juárez. She was young and pretty, with her finely boned face and jet black hair just like her mother's, long and lustrous. Her eyes were large and green, capable of flashing with fire when her temper was roused. Her eyes were unfocussed now; she was thinking about the story she was halfway through writing, lost deep within angles and follow-ups and consequences.

She already had the title for the post.

The City of Lost Girls.

That was what some people were calling Juárez these days. It was Murder City, too, and people were dying in the drug wars every day, more than seven hundred this year already and not yet Easter. Caterina was obsessed with the drug wars; it was the bread and butter of Blog del

Borderland: post after post about the dead, mutilated bodies left in plain sight on the city's waste ground, drive-by shootings with SUVs peppered with hundreds of bullets, babies boiled in drums of oil because their parents wouldn't do what they were told, bodies strung up from bridges and lamp posts. Grave pits were being dug up all around the city, dozens of bodies exhumed, the dead crawling out of their holes. And all the awful videos posted to YouTube and Facebook showing torture and dismemberment, warnings from one cartel to another, messages to the government and to the uncorrupted police and to the people of Mexico.

We are in control here.

We own this city.

Caterina reported on all of it, three thousand posts that had slowly gathered traction and gathered pace, so much so that Blog del Borderland was attracting a hundred thousand visitors every day. She had an audience now, and she was determined to educate it.

People had to know what was happening here.

The City of Lost Girls.

She kept coming back to it. The drug war was Juárez's dominant narrative, but there were other stories, too, drowned out in the static, stories within the story, and the one Caterina had found was the most compelling of them all. They were calling it *feminicidio*—femicide—the mass slaughter of women. In the last five years, three hundred women and girls—mostly girls, fifteen, sixteen years old—had been abducted as they made their way home from the *maquiladoras* that had sprung up like mushrooms along the southern banks of the Rio Bravo. The multinationals had hurried in under the auspices of one-sided trade agreements to exploit wages a fraction of what they would have to pay their workers north of the border. Sweatshops and factories staffed by young women who came from all over the country for the chance of a regular pay check and a better life. Women were favoured over men: their fingers were nimbler and more dextrous, and they could be paid even less.

These girls were nobodies, anonymous ghosts who moved through the city, barely disturbing its black waters. The kind of women who would not be missed. Some of them were abducted from the streets. Others were taken from bars, lured to hotels and clubs and other rendezvous, promised work or money or romance or just an evening when they could forget the mind-numbing drudgery of their workaday lives.

No one ever saw them alive again.

Their bodies were dumped without any attempt to hide them: on patches of waste ground, in culverts and ditches, tipped out of cars and left in the gutters. The killers did not care and made no attempt to hide their handiwork. They knew that they would not be caught. Not all of the missing were found, and desperate parents glued posters to bus shelters and against walls.

Caterina photographed the posters, published them all, noted down the names.

Alejandra.

Diana.

Maria.

Fernanda.

Paulina.

Adriana.

Mariana.

Valeria.

Marisol.

Marcella.

Esperanza.

Lupe.

Rafaela.

Aciano.

She had a notebook full of names, ages, dates.

This one was called Guillermina Marquez. She had worked for Capcom, one of the large multinationals who made transistors for Western appliances. She would normally have walked home from the bus stop with her friends, but the company had changed her shift, and she had walked alone. It was dusk; there should have been plenty of people to intervene, and police officers were around, including a special downtown patrol. But Guillermina disappeared. After she failed to return home, her mother went to the police. They shrugged and said that there was nothing they could do. Her mother made a thousand flysheets and posted them around the neighbourhood. Caterina had seen the posters and had interviewed the mother. She had posted an appeal for information on the blog, but nothing had come of any of it. And this was two weeks ago.

Caterina knew that they wouldn't find her this morning. Her body would appear, one day, in a place very much like this. She was here to write about the search. She took photographs of the participants scouring the dirty sand and the boiling rocks for anything that might bring some certainty to the idea that they must already have accepted: that the girl was dead.

Because only a handful of them ever came back alive.

They gave up the search for the morning and headed back to the place where they had parked their cars. Young women were emerging from their shacks and huts, huddling by the side of the road for the busses that would take them to the factories. As they passed through the fence again, Caterina watched a dirt-biker cutting through the dunes to intercept them, plumes of dust kicked up by his rear wheel. He rolled to a stop fifty feet away and removed his helmet. He was wearing a balaclava beneath it. He gunned the engine two times, drawing attention to himself, a reminder that they were trespassing and that they needed to get out.

Chapter Five

SIX HOURS LATER, Caterina sat in front of her laptop, willing a response to her last message. She bit her lip anxiously, but the cursor carried on blinking on and off, on and off, and the message did not come. She ran her fingers through her long dark hair, wincing as she stared at the screen. She had scared the girl off. She had pushed too hard, gone too fast, been too keen for her to tell her story, and now she had lost her.

Damn it. Damn it all. She kicked back, rolling her chair away from the desk a little, and stretched out her arms above her head. She was tired and stiff. She had spent eight hours at her desk, more or less, just a five-minute break to go and get lunchtime gorditas and quesadillas from the take-out around the corner, bringing them back and eating them right here. The papers were still on the floor, next to the overflowing bin where she had thrown them. Yesterday had been the same, and there had been little sleep during the night, either. When she was in the middle of a story like this, she allowed it to consume her. She knew it was a fault, but it was not one that she was prepared to correct. That was why she didn't have a boyfriend or a husband. It would take a very particular type of man—a very patient, very understanding man—to put up with a woman who could become so single-minded that she forgot to wash, to eat properly, to go out, to do anything that was not in the service of furthering the story.

But that was just how it had to be, she reminded herself.

The story was the most important thing.

People had to know.

The world had to know what was happening in Ciudad Juárez.

She did her work in the living room of her one-bedroom flat. The walls had been hung with large sheets of paper, each bearing scribbled ideas for stories, diagrams that established the hierarchy of the cartels. One sheet was a list of three hundred female names. There was a large map to the right of the desk, three hundred pins stuck into the wall to mark where the bodies had been found. Caterina's second-hand MacBook Pro sat amidst a whirlwind of papers, books and scrawled notes. An old and unreliable iMac, with an opened Wordpress document displayed, was perched on the corner of the desk. Minimised windows opened out onto search results pages and news stories, everything routed through the dark web to ensure that her presence was anonymous and untrackable. Caterina didn't know whether the cartels themselves were sophisticated enough to follow the footprints from the Blog del Borderland back to this flat in the *barrio*, but the government was, and since most of the government was in the pocket of the cartels, it did not pay her to be blasé. She was as sure as she could be: nothing she wrote could be traced, and her anonymity—shielded behind a series of online pseudonyms—was secure. It was liaisons like this one, with a frightened girl somewhere in the city, that were truly dangerous. She would have to break cover to write it up, and all she had to go on with regard to the girl's probity was her gut.

But the story was big. It was worth the risk.

She checked the screen.

Still nothing.

She heard the sound of children playing outside: "*Piedra, papel, tijeras, un, dos, tres!*" they called. Scissors, paper, stones. She got up and padded to the window. She was up high, third floor, and she looked down onto the neighbourhood. The kids were playing in front of the new church, the walls gleaming white and beautiful new red tiles on the domed roof. The money to build it came from the cartels. Today—and yesterday, and the day before that—a row of SUVs with tinted windows had been parked in front of the church, a line of men in DEA windcheaters going to and from the garden at the back of the house three doors down from her. She could see all the gardens from her window: the backs of the whitewashed houses, the unused barbeques, rusted satellite dishes, the kids' trampoline torn down the middle. The third garden along was dominated by pecan trees and an overgrown creosote bush. The men in the windcheaters were digging a deep pit next to the bush. Cadaver dogs sat guard next to the pit, their noses pointing straight down, tails wagging. Every hour they would pull another body out.

Caterina had already counted six body bags being ferried out.

Like they said.

Ciudad Juárez.

Murder City.

The City of Lost Girls.

She pulled her chair back to the desk and stared absently at the computer.

"I am here."

The cursor blinked at the end of the line.

Caterina sat bolt upright, beginning and deleting responses until she knew what to say.

"I know you're scared."

There was a pause, and then the letters tapped out, one by one, slow and uncertain: "How could you know?"

"I've spoken to other girls. Not many, but a few. You are not the first."

"Did they tell you they could describe them, too?"

"They couldn't."

"Then the stakes are much higher for me."

"I accept that."

"What would I have to do?"

"Just talk."

"And my name?"

"Everything is anonymous."

"I don't know."

"You're right to be scared. I'm scared, too. These men are dangerous. But you can trust me."

The cursor blinked on and off again. Caterina found she was holding her breath.

"If I come, it would just be to talk?"

"It would be whatever you want it to be. But talking is fine."

"Who would be there?"

"Me and my partner—he writes, too. You can trust him."

Another pause and Caterina wondered whether she should have said that it would just be her alone. Leon was a good man, but how was she to know that? A fear of men whom she did not know would be reasonable enough after what Delores had been through.

The characters flickered across the screen again. "I can choose where?"

"Wherever you want—but somewhere public would be best, yes?"

"La Case del Mole—do you know it?"

Caterina swept the papers from the iMac's keyboard and typed the name into Google. "The restaurant on Col Chavena?"

"Yes."

"I know it."

"I could meet you there."

"I'll book a table. My name is Caterina Moreno. I will be there from 8PM. Okay?"

There was no immediate reply.

And then, after a pause, three letters: "Yes."

Chapter Six

LIEUTENANT JESUS PLATO stopped at the door of his Dodge Charger police cruiser and turned back to his three-bedroom house on the outskirts of Juárez. His pregnant wife, Emelia, was at the door, with their youngest—Jesus Jr—in her arms. She was calling him.

"What is it?"

"Come here," she said.

He tossed his shoulder holster, the Glock safely clipped within it, onto the passenger seat, and went back to the house. "What did I forget?"

"Nothing," his wife said, "I did." She stood on tiptoes, and he bent a little so that she could plant a long kiss on his lips. "Be careful, Jesus. I don't want to hear about you taking any risks, not this week. Lord knows you've done enough of that."

"I know. I won't—no risks."

"You got a different life from next Monday. You got me and this one to think about, the girls, and the one on the way. If you get into trouble on your last week, it's going to be much worse as soon as you get back, all right? And look at that lawn—that's your first job, right there, first thing, you hear me?"

"Yes, *chica,*" he said with an indulgent grin. The baby, just a year old, gurgled happily as Plato reached down and tickled him under the chin. He looked like his mother, lucky kid, those same big dark eyes that you could get lost in, the slender nose and the perfect buttery skin. He leant down again to kiss Emelia on the lips. "I'll be late back tonight, remember—Alameda and Sanchez are taking me out for dinner."

"They're just making sure you're definitely leaving. Don't go getting so drunk you wake the baby."

He grinned again. "No, *chica*."

He made his way back down the driveway, stopping where the boat he was restoring sat on its trailer. It was a standing joke between them: there he was, fixing up a boat, eight hundred miles from the coast. But it had been his father's, and he wanted to honour the old man's memory by doing a good job. One day, when he was retired, maybe he'd get to use it. Jesus had been brought up on the coast, and he had always hoped he might be able to return there one day. There would be a persuasion job to do with his wife, but when his job was finished, there would be little to hold them to Juárez. It was possible. He ran the tips of his fingers along the smooth wooden hull and thought of all the hours that he had spent replacing the panels, smoothing them, varnishing them. It had been his project for the last six months, and he was looking forward to being able to spend a little more time on it. Another week or two of good, hard work—time he could dedicate to it without having to worry about his job—that ought to be enough to get it finished.

He returned to the cruiser and got inside. He pulled down the visor and looked at his reflection in the vanity mirror. He was on the wrong side of fifty now, and it showed. His skin was old and weathered, a collection of wrinkles gathered around the corners of his eyes. His hair was salt-and-pepper where it had once been jet black, and his moustache was almost entirely grey. Age, he thought, and doing the job he had been doing for thirty years. He could have made it easier on himself, taken the shortcuts that had been offered, made the struggle of paying the mortgage a little easier with the backhanders and bribes he could easily have taken. He could have avoided getting shot, avoided the dull throbbing ache that he felt in his shoulder whenever the temperature dipped. But Jesus Plato wasn't made that way, never had been and never would. Honour and dignity were watchwords that had been driven into him by his father, a good man who had also worked for the police, shot dead by a *sicario* around the time that it all started to go to hell, the time that dentist was shot to death. The rise of El Patrón and La Frontera. Plato had been a young cadet then, and while he had been green, he had not been blind. He could see that plenty of his colleagues had already been bought and sold by the narcos, but he vowed that he would never be the same as them, and thirty years later, he still wasn't.

He looked down and saw that Emelia was laughing at him, watching him stare at his own reflection. He waved her away with an amused flick of his hand and gunned the Dodge's big engine. One more week, he thought, flipping the visor back against the roof. He reversed off the drive and onto the street, his eye drawn to the overgrown lawn, and wondered if he could justify buying that new sit-down mower he had seen in The Home Depot the last time he had crossed over the bridge into El Paso. A retirement present for himself; he deserved it. Just five more days and then he could start to enjoy his life.

Chapter Seven

THE CALL had come through as Plato was cruising down the Avenida, Juárez's main drag. The street had two-storey buildings on each side, the once garish colours bleached out by the sun, the brickwork crumbling and broken windows sheltering behind boards that had themselves been daubed with graffiti. The shops that were still open catered to the baser instincts: gambling, liquor, whores. East of the main street was the red-light district, a confusing warren of unlit streets where if the unwary escaped after being relieved just of their wallets, then they were lucky. Plato had seen plenty of dead bodies in those dirty, narrow streets and the rooms with single bare light bulbs where the hookers turned their tricks. But then he had seen plenty of dead bodies, period.

The call had been a 415, just a disturbance, but Plato was only a couple of blocks away, and he had called back to say that he would handle it. He knew that if he took it, there would be less chance he would be assigned one of the day's 187s or 207s. Those were the calls you didn't want to get, the murders and the kidnappings that always turned into murders. Apart from the risk that the killers were still around—first responders had been shot many times—they were depressing, soul-sickening cases that were never really resolved, and the idea of having one or two of them on his docket when he finally hung it up wasn't the way he wanted to go out.

No, he reminded himself as he pulled the Dodge over to the kerb. Taking this call wasn't cowardice. It was common sense, and besides, hadn't he had more than his fair share of those over the years? He had lost count, especially recently.

The disturbance was on the street outside one of the

strip clubs. Eduardo's: Plato knew it very well. Two college boys were being restrained by the bouncers from the club. One of the boys had a bloody nose.

Plato looked at the dash. Inside was sixty degrees. Outside was one hundred and ten. He sighed and stepped out of the air-conditioned cool and onto the street. The heat on his body hit him like a hammer.

"What's going on?" Plato asked, pointedly addressing the nearest bouncer first. It was a man he knew, "Tiny" Garcia, a colleague from years ago who had been chased out of the force for taking a cartel's money. Plato abhorred graft and despised the weakness in the man, but he knew that treating him respectfully was more likely to get him back to the station with the information that he wanted with the minimum of fuss.

"*Teniente*," the big man said. "How you doing?"

"Not bad, Tiny."

"You still in?"

"Only just. Coming to the end of the line. This time next week and I'll have my pension and I'm done."

"Good for you, brother. Best thing I ever did, getting out."

Plato looked at him, his shabby dress and the depressing bleakness of the Avenida, and knew that that was his pride talking.

"So—these two boys. What have we got?"

"A little drunk, a little free with their hands with one of the girls, you know what I mean, not like it's the first time. We ain't got many rules back in there, but that's one of them, no touching none of the girls at no time. She calls me over, and I say to them, nice and polite like you know I can be, I says to them that it's time to leave."

The boys snorted with derision. "That's not what happened," one of them said.

Plato nodded to the boy's bloodied face. "And his nose?"

"He didn't want to go, I guess. He threw a punch at

me, I threw one back. I hit, he didn't."

"Bullshit!" the boy with the bloody nose spat out.

Plato looked at the two of them more carefully. They were well dressed, if a little the worse for wear. They had that preppy look about them: clothes from Gap, creases down the trousers, shirts that had been ironed, deck shoes that said they would be more at home crewing up a regatta schooner. Plato recognised it from the university at El Paso. A little too much money evident in their clothes and grooming, the supercilious way they looked at the locals. He'd seen it before, plenty of times. A couple of young boys, some money in their pocket and a plan to take a walk on the wild side of the border. They usually got into one sort of scrape or another. They'd end up in a rough, nasty dive like this, and then they didn't like it when they realised that they couldn't always get their own way. On this occasion, Plato knew that the boys had just been unlucky or tight. There was plenty of touching in Eduardo's, and a lot more besides that, if you were prepared to pay for it.

He shepherded them towards the Dodge. As they reached the kerb, one of them—blond, plenty of hair, good looks and a quarterback's physique—reached out and pressed his hand into Plato's. He felt something sharp pricking his palm. It was the edge of a banknote. He turned back to the boy and grasped it between thumb and forefinger.

"What is this?" Plato asked, holding up the note.

"It's whatever you want it to be, man."

"A bribe?"

"If you want."

"You've got to be kidding me. You're trying to buy me off?"

"It's a Benjamin, look! Come on, man! There's no need for all of this, right? A hundred bucks makes it all go away. I know how things work round here. I been here before, lots of times. I know the way the land lies."

"No," Plato said grimly. "You don't. You just made

things worse. Turn around, both of you."

Garcia gave out a deep rumble of laughter. "They don't know who they're talking to, right, Jesus? You dumb fucks—I know this man, I worked with him. I doubt he's ever taken so much as a peso his whole life."

"Come on, man. I know we fucked up. What do we have to do to make it right? Two notes? Come on, two hundred bucks."

"Turn around," Plato said, laying his hand on the butt of the Glock.

"Come on, man—let's say three hundred and forget all about this."

"Turn around now."

The boy saw Plato wasn't going to budge, and his vapid stoner's grin curdled into something more malevolent. He craned his neck around as Plato firmly pressed him against the bonnet of the car. "What's the point of that? If you won't take my money, I know damn straight one of your buddies will. You *federales* are so bent you can't even piss straight; everyone knows it. You're turning down three hundred bucks bonus for what, your fucking *principles*? We all know it won't make a fucking bit of difference, not when it comes down to it. We'll be out of here and on our way back to civilisation before you've finished your shift and gone back to whatever shithole you crawled out of."

"Keep talking, son." Plato fastened the jaws of his cuffs around the boy's right wrist and then, yanking the arm harder than he had to, snapped the other cuff around the left wrist, too. The boy yelped in sudden pain; Plato didn't care about that. He opened the rear door, bounced the boy's head against the edge of the roof, and pushed him inside. He cuffed the second boy and did the same.

"Later, Garcia," he said to the big man as he shut the door.

"Keep your head down, Jesus."

"You too."

Chapter Eight

THE LEACH HOTEL in Douglas, Arizona, was a handsome relic from a different era. It had served an important purpose in the frontier years, the best place to stay in the last town before the lawlessness and violence of the borderlands. The hotel, built at the turn of the century, bore the name of the local dignitary for whom it was a labour of love. Mr. Robert E Leach was a southern nationalist, a supporter of slavery and, in later years, the US Ambassador to Mexico. It was Leach who, in 1853, had overseen the purchase of all land, including southern Arizona, south of the Gila River for the United States from the Mexicans. His hotel, a last beacon of respectability among the gun stores and bike repair shops of hard scrabble Cochise County, was the only monument to him now. It was still a fine building; it had seen better times, perhaps, but the Italian marble columns in the lobby and the marble staircase that curled up to the first floor were still impressing newcomers as they made their way to the reception desk to check in. The place was a relic of the Wild West, of Wyatt Earp and Geronimo, and the sounds of that time still echoed around the wood-panelled walls.

Beau Baxter knew everything there was to know about the Leach. He had a fondness for history, and the faded glamour of the hotel, the sense of a place caught out of time, appealed to him. This area of Cochise County had been frequented by desperados, including celebrities like Clay Hardin, who had killed forty men by the time he was forty years old, and Billy the Kid, who had laid twenty-one men in their graves by the time he was twenty-one. Local outlaws who had stayed in the hotel included Clay Allison, Luke Short, Johnny Ringo and Curly Bill Brocius. Beau had read up on all of them. And the great Pancho Villa was reputed to have ridden his horse right up the marble staircase.

He often met his clients here—those who didn't require him to travel to Houston or Dallas, anyway—and he had been pleased that the man who had asked to see him today had been conducting business on the border and had not been averse to coming to him.

Beau was in his early sixties, although he looked younger. His face was tanned and bore the traces of many dust storms and rancorous barroom brawls. He was wearing a light blue suit, nicely fitted, expensive looking. He wore a light blue shirt, a couple of buttons open at the throat, and snakeskin boots. He was sitting at a table in the lobby, his cream Stetson set on the table in front of him. The light was low, tinted green and blue by the stained-glass skylights that ran the length of the lobby.

A man was at the door, squinting into the hotel. He recognised his client: he was a man of medium height, heavy build, olive brown skin and quick, suspicious eyes. His hair was arranged in a low quiff, a dye job with delicate splashes of silver on each side that made Beau think of a badger. He often dressed in bright shirts that Beau found a little distasteful. He did not know the man's full name—it wasn't particularly important—and he referred to himself just as Carlo. He was Italian, of a certain vintage, and belonged to a certain family of a certain criminal organisation. New Jersey. It was the kind of organisation about which one did not ask too many questions, and that suited Beau fine, too. They always paid their debts on time, and their money was just as good as anyone else's, as far as he was concerned.

He stood and held out his hand. "Carlo."

"Baxter. This is a nice place. Impressive. Is it authentic?"

"Been here nigh on a hundred years. I know they make a big play of it, but the history here's the real deal."

"Can't believe, all this time we been working together, you've never once brought me here."

Beau shrugged. "Well, you know—never had the opportunity, I guess."

They sat on a sofa in the corner of the lobby, and the man took out a brown envelope and set it on the table. "That's yours," he said. "Good job."

Beau took the envelope and opened it a little. He ran his finger against the thick bundle of notes inside. "Thank you." He folded the envelope and slipped it into the inside pocket of his jacket. "I hope you got what you wanted from our friend."

"We did. How did you find him?"

"What difference does it make?"

"I'm curious."

"You don't have to worry about that. That's why you pay me."

"A trade secret, Baxter?"

"Something like that." Beau smiled at him. "All right, then. You said you had something else?"

"Yes. But it's not easy."

"Ain't never easy, else anyone could do it. Who is it?"

Carlo took out his phone and scrolled through his pictures to the one that he wanted. He gave the phone to Beau. "You know him?"

He whistled through his teeth. "You ain't kidding this ain't going to be easy."

"You know him?"

"Unless I'm much mistaken, that's Adolfo González. Correct?"

"Correct. Know him by sight?"

"I believe so."

"Have you come across him before?"

"Now and again. Not directly."

"But you know his reputation?"

"I do."

"Is that a problem?"

"Not for me, maybe for you. A man like that's going to be mighty expensive."

"Go on."

Beau sucked air through his teeth as he thought. "Well, then, there's how difficult it'll be to get to him, and with the connections he has, I got to set a price that takes into account how dangerous it'll be for me both now and in the future if they ever find out it was me who went after him. That being said—I'd say we're looking at an even fifty, all-in. Half now, half later."

Beau found his eye drawn to the scruffy bush of chest hair that escaped from between the buttons of Carlo's patterned shirt. "Fifty?"

"Plus expenses."

"Fine."

"As easy as that?"

"You think you should have asked for more?"

"The price is the price."

"You can have the first twenty-five by two thirty."

"You got a hurry-up going on for this fellow, then?"

"How well do you know him?"

"I knew him when he was younger. Busted him coming over the border this one time."

"And what do you think?"

"If he was bad then, he's worse now."

"How bad?"

"I'd say he's a mean, psychopathic bastard. Want to tell me what he's done so that you want him so bad?"

"We had an arrangement with his old man—the buying and selling of certain merchandise. But then we had a problem: he changed the terms, made it uneconomic. We went to discuss it, and Señor González murdered six of my colleagues."

Beau remembered. "That thing down south of Juárez?"

Carlo spread his hands wide. "Let's say we would like to discuss that with him."

"Alive, then?"

"If you can. There'll be a bonus."

"Understood." Beau didn't need to enquire any more than that. He'd been working bounties long enough to reckon that revenge came in a lot of different flavours.

"Do you need anything else?"

"No, sir," Beau said. "That's plenty good enough."

"Then we're done." He rose. "Happy trails."

Beau followed him to his feet and collected his Stetson from the table. "You know what they call our boy over the border?"

Carlo shook his head.

Beau brushed the dust from his hat. "Oh yeah, this man, on account of his reputation, he's made quite the impression. Last time I heard anything about him they were calling him Santa Muerte."

"The wetbacks are superstitious fucks, Baxter."

"Maybe so. Fifty thousand? For a man like that, my friend, I'd say you've got yourself a bargain."

Chapter Nine

THE BORDER. They called it The Reaper's Line. Beau Baxter edged forward in the Cherokee. The checkpoint was busy today in both directions: trucks and cars and motorbikes heading south and a longer, denser line coming north. He looked at the trucks coming out of Juárez with a professional eye. How many of them were carrying drugs? Every tenth truck? Every twentieth? Vacuum-packed packets of cocaine dipped in chemicals to put the dogs off the scent. Packets stacked in secret cavities, stuffed in false bumpers, hidden amongst legitimate cargo. Billions of dollars.

Beau regarded the high fence, the watchtowers and the spotlights. It had changed a lot over the years. He had been working the border for all of his adult life. He had graduated from the Border Patrol Academy in 1975 and had been stationed in Douglas. His work had taken him across the continent and then to the Caribbean in the immigration service's anti-drugs task force, eventually returning him full circle. For two decades, he had been a customs special agent in this wild and untamed corner of the frontier, patrolling the border on horseback, a shotgun strapped onto his saddle.

He looked out at the guards circulating between the cars and trucks. Those boys doing the job today would have thought he was an anachronism, relying on a horse when he could have had one of the brand-new Jeeps they were driving around in.

But Beau was a realist, too, and he knew that time had moved on. A man like him was from a different era. He'd fought regular battles with the narco traffickers of Agua Prieta over the border. During his career, he had seen the territory between Nogales and Arizona's eastern border with New Mexico become known as "cocaine alley" and then quickly get worse. Juárez was the worst of all. The dirty little border *pueblo* was a place where greed, corruption and murder had flourished like tumbleweed seeds in souring horse manure. Now, with the cartels as vast and organised as multinationals, with their killing put onto an industrial scale and with the bloodshed soaking into the sand, Beau was glad to be out of it. In comparison to that line of work, hunting down bounties was a walk in the park.

But perhaps not this one.

His thoughts went to Adolfo González. On reflection, fifty grand was probably a generous quote for a job that was fixing to be particularly difficult.

He had heard about the six dead Italians on the news this morning. Ambushed in the desert, shot to shit, and left out for the vultures. He had seen the video on YouTube before it had been taken down. He recognised Adolfo's voice. The cartels were all bad news, but La Frontera was the worst. Animals. And Adolfo was the worst of all. Getting him back across the border wasn't going to be easy.

He wondered whether he should have turned the job down.

There were easier ways to make a living.

He edged the Jeep forwards again and braked at the open window of the kiosk.

"Ten dollars," the attendant said.

Beau handed it over.

"Welcome to Mexico."

He drove south.

Chapter Ten

MILTON PAUSED in the restaurant's locker room to grab an apron and a chef's jacket. He sat down on the wooden bench and smoked a cigarette.

He changed and went through into the kitchen.

It was a big space, open to the restaurant on one side. The equipment was a mixture of old and new, but mostly old: four big steam tables; three partially rusted hobs; two old and battered steamers at the far end of the line; three side-by-side, gas-fired charcoal grills with salamander broilers fixed alongside; a flattop griddle. The double-wide fryer was where he would be working. The equipment was unreliable, and the surfaces were nicked and dented from the blows of a hundred frustrated chefs. Most of the heat came from two enormous radiant ovens and two convection units next to the fryer station. A row of long heat lamps swung to and fro from greasy cables over the aluminium pass. It was already hot.

Gomez came in and immediately banged a wooden spoon against the pass. "Pay attention, you sons of bitches. We got a busy night coming up. No one gets paid unless I think they're pulling their weight, and if anyone faints, that's an immediate twenty-percent deduction for every ten minutes they're not on their feet. And on top of all that, we got ourselves a newbie to play with. Hand up, English."

Milton did as he was told. The others looked at him with a mixture of ennui and hostility. A new cook, someone none of them had ever seen working before, no one to vouch for him. What would happen if he wasn't cut out for it, if he passed out in the heat? He would leave them a man down, the rest hopelessly trying to keep pace as the orders piled up on the rail. Milton had already assessed them: a big Mexican, heavily muscled and covered in prison tattoos; a sous chef with an obvious drinking problem who lived in his car; a cook with needle scars on his arm and a T-shirt that read BORN FREE – TAXED TO DEATH; and an American ex-soldier with a blond Vanilla Ice flattop.

"Our man English says he's been working up and down the coast, says he knows what he's doing. That right, English?"

"That's right."

"We'll see about that," Gomez said with a self-satisfied smirk, his crossed arms resting on the wide shelf of his belly.

Milton went back and forth between the storeroom, the cold cupboard and his station, hauling in the ingredients that he knew he would need. He looked around at the others methodically going through the same routine that they would have repeated night after night in a hundred different restaurants: getting their towels ready, stacking their pans right up close so that they could get to them in a hurry, sharpening their knives and slotting them into blocks, drinking as much water as they could manage.

The front-of-house girl who Milton had met earlier put her head through the kitchen's swing door. "Hey, Gomez," Milton heard her call out. "Coach of gringo tourists outside. Driver says can we fit them in? I said we're pretty full, but I'd ask anyway—what you wanna do?"

"Find the space."

The machine began rattling out orders. Milton gritted his teeth, ready to dive into the middle of it all. The first time he had felt the anticipation was in a tiny, understaffed restaurant in Campo Bravo, Brazil. He needed a way to forget himself, that had been the thing that he had returned to over and over as he worked the boat coming over, the desire to erase his memories, even if it was only temporary. After five minutes in that first restaurant he had known that it was as good a way as any. A busy kitchen was the best distraction he had ever found. Somewhere so busy, so hectic, so chaotic, somewhere where there was no time to think about anything other than the job at hand.

The first orders had barely been cleared before the next round had arrived, and they hadn't even started to prepare those before another set spewed out of the ticket machine, and then another, and another. The machine didn't stop. The paper strip grew long, drooping like a tongue, spooling out and down onto the floor. They could easily look out into the restaurant from the kitchen, and they could see that the big room was packed out. It got worse and worse and worse. Milton worked hard, concentrating on the tasks in front of him, trying to adapt to the unpleasant sensation that there suddenly wasn't enough air on the line for all of them to breathe. Within minutes he felt like he was baking, sweat pouring out into his whites, slicking the spaces beneath his arms, the small of his back, his crotch. His boots felt like they were filling with sweat. It ran into his eyes, and he cranked the ventilation hood all the way to its maximum, but with it pumping out the air at full blast, the pilots on his unused burners were quickly blown out. He had to keep relighting them, the gas taps left open as he smacked a pan down on the grate at an angle, hard enough to draw a spark.

The floor was quickly ankle-deep in mess: scraps of food that they swept off the counters, torn packaging, dropped utensils, filthy towels; it was all beneath the sill of the window and invisible from the restaurant, so Gomez didn't care. Still the heat rose higher and higher. Milton stripped out of his chef coat and T-shirt because the water in them had started to boil.

It was hard work, unbelievably hard, but Milton had been doing it for months now, and he quickly fell into the routine. The craziness of it, the random orders that spilled from the machine, the unexpected disasters that had to be negotiated, the blistering heat and the mind-bending adrenaline highs, the tunnel vision, the relentless focus, the crashing din, the screams and curses as cooks forgot saucepan handles were red-hot. The rest of his world fell away and everything that he was running away from became insignificant and, for that small parcel of a few hours at the end of a long day, for those few hours, at least, it was all out of mind and almost forgotten.

Chapter Eleven

CATERINA SAT on the bus and stared through the cracked window as they moved slowly through the city. It was getting late, seven in the evening, yet the sun still baked at ninety, and Juárez quivered under the withering blows of summer, a storm threatening to blow in from the north, tempers running high. A steady hum of traffic rose from the nearby interstate, and the hot air blowing in through the open windows tasted of chemicals, car exhaust, refinery fumes, the gasses from the smelter on the other side of the border, and the raw sewage seeping into what was left of the river. The bus was full as people made their way out for the evening.

Caterina had made an effort as she left the flat, showering and washing her hair and picking out a laundered shirt to go with the jeans and sneakers she always wore.

She was thinking about all the girls that she had been writing about. Delores was different. She had dodged the fate that had befallen the others. She had managed to escape, and she was willing to talk.

And she said she could identify one of them men who had taken her.

The brakes wheezed as the bus pulled over to the kerb and slowed to a halt. Caterina pulled herself upright, and with her laptop and her notes in the rucksack that she carried over her shoulder, she made her way down the gangway, stepping over the outstretched legs of the other passengers, and climbed down to the pavement. The heat washed over her like water, torpid and sluggish, heavy like Jell-O, and it took a moment to adjust. The restaurant was a hundred yards away, an island in the middle of a large parking lot, beneath the twenty-foot pole suspending the neon sign that announced it.

Leon was waiting for her. She stepped around a vendor with a stack of papers on his head and went across to him.

"This better be good," he said, a smile ameliorating the faux sternness of his greeting. "I had tickets for the Indios tonight."

"I would never let you pick football over this."

"It's good?"

"This is it. The story I want us to tell."

She was excited, garbling a little and giddy with enthusiasm. Leon was good for her when it came to that. She needed to be calm, and he was steady and reliable. Sensible. It seemed to come off him in gentle waves. Smiling with a warm-hearted indulgence she had seen many times before, he rested his hands on her shoulders. "Take a deep breath, *mi cielo*, okay? You don't want to frighten the poor girl away."

She allowed herself to relax and smiled into Leon's face. It was a kind face, his dark eyes full of humanity, and there was a wisdom there that made him older than his years. He was the only man she had ever met who could do that to her; he was able to cut through the noise and static of Juárez, her single-minded dedication to the blog and the need to tell the story of the city and its bloodied streets, and remind her that other things were important. They had dated for six months until they had both realised that their relationship would never be the most important thing in her life. They had cooled it before it could develop further, the emotional damage far less than it would have been if it had been allowed to follow its course. There were still nights when, after they had written stories into the small hours, he would stay with her rather than risk the dangerous journey home across the city, and on those nights, they would make love with an appetite that had not been allowed to be blunted by familiarity. Being with Leon was the best way to forget about all the dead bodies in the ground, the dozens of missing women, the forest of shrines that sprouted across the wastelands and parks, the culverts and trash heaps.

"Are you ready?" he asked her.

"Let's go."

DELORES KEPT them waiting for fifteen minutes, and when she eventually made her way across the busy restaurant to them, she did so with a crippling insecurity and a look of the sheerest fright on her face. She was a small, slight girl, surely much younger than the twenty years she had claimed when they were chatting earlier. Caterina would have guessed at fourteen or fifteen, a waif. She was slender and flat chested, florid acne marked her face, and she walked with a slight but discernible limp. She was dressed in a *maquiladora* uniform: cheap, faded jeans that had been patched several times, a plain shirt, a crucifix around her neck. Caterina smiled broadly as she neared, but the girl's face did not break free of its grim cast.

"I'm Caterina," she said, getting up and holding out her hand.

"Delores," she said quietly. Her grip was limp and damp.

"This is my colleague, Leon."

Leon shook her hand, too, then pulled a chair out and pushed it gently back as Delores rather reluctantly sat.

"Can I order you a drink? A glass of water?"

"No, thank you." She looked around the room, nervous, like a rabbit after it has sensed the approach of a hawk. "You weren't followed?"

"No," Caterina said, smiling broadly, trying to reassure the girl. "And we'll be fine here. It's busy. Three friends having a meal and a talk. All right?"

"I'm sorry, but if you think a busy restaurant would stop them if they had a mind to kill you, then you are more naïve than you think."

"I'm sorry," Caterina said. "I didn't mean to be dismissive. You're right."

"Caterina and I have been working to publicise the cartels for two years," Leon said. "We know what they're capable of, but you're safe with us tonight. They don't know our faces."

Delores flinched as the waiter came to take their orders. Caterina asked for two beers, a glass of orange juice and a selection of appetisers—tostadas, cheese-stuffed jalapenos, enchilada meatballs and nachos—and sent him away. She took out her notebook and scrabbled around in her handbag for a Biro. She found one and then her Dictaphone. She took it out and laid it on the table between them.

"Do you mind?" she asked. "It's good to have a record."

Delores shook her head. "But no photographs."

"Of course not. Let's get started."

Chapter Twelve

LIEUTENANT JESUS PLATO decided that the two gringo college boys needed to cool their heels for the night. They were becoming boisterous and disruptive when he brought them back to the station to book them, and so, to make a point, he chose to delay the fine he had decided to give them until tomorrow. They could spend the night in the drunk tank with the junkies, the tweakers and the boozers; he was confident that they would be suitably apologetic when he returned in the morning. And besides, he did not particularly want to go to the effort of writing them up tonight. He was tired, and he had promised Alameda and Sanchez that he would go out with them for something to eat. The meal was a self-justifying camouflage, of course; the real purpose was to go out and get drunk, and he had no doubt that they would end up on the banks of the Rio Bravo, drinking tins of Tecate and throwing the empties into what passed for the river around here. Plato had been on the dusty street all day, more or less; he certainly had a thirst.

His shift had been straightforward after booking the two boys. He had pulled over a rental car driven by a fat American sweating profusely through layers of fat and the synthetic fibres of his Spurs basketball shirt, a pimpled teen beauty in the seat next to him with her slender hand on his flabby knee. A warning from Plato was all it took for him to reach over and open the door, banishing the girl as he cursed the end of the evening that he had planned. The girl swore at Plato, her promised twenty bucks going up in smoke, but she had relented by the time he bought her a Happy Meal at the drive-thru on the way home. He had finished up by writing tickets for the youngsters racing their souped-up Toyota Camrys and VW

Golfs tricked-out with bulbous hubcaps and tweaked engines, low-slung so that the chassis drew sparks from the asphalt. They, too, had cursed him, an obligatory response that he had ignored. They had spun their wheels as he drove off, melting the rubber into the road, and he had ignored that, too.

Captain Alameda waved him across to his office.

"Your last week, *compadre*," he said.

"Tell me about it."

"How was today?"

"Quiet, for a change. Couple of drunk gringo kids. Thought a couple of hundred bucks would persuade me to let them off."

"They picked the wrong man, then. Where are they?"

"In the cells. I'll see if they've found some manners tomorrow."

"You heard about what happened at Samalayuca?"

"Just over the radio. What was it?"

"Six men. They didn't even bother to bury them. Shot them and left them out in the desert for the vultures."

"Six? *Mierda*. We know who they are?"

"American passports. The *federales* will look into it."

Plato slumped into the seat opposite the desk.

"Jesus?"

"I'm fine." He sighed. "Just tired is all. How is it here?"

"Twenty-eight no-shows today. Worst so far."

Plato knew the reason; everyone did. Three weeks ago, a wreath had been left on the memorial outside police headquarters on Valle Del Cedro Avenue. A flap of cardboard, torn from a box, had been fastened around the memorial with chicken wire. It was a notice, and written on it were two lists. The first, headed by FOR THOSE WHO DID NOT BELIEVE, contained the names of the fifteen police officers who had been slain by the cartels since the turn of the year. The second, FOR THOSE WHO CONTINUE WITHOUT BELIEVING, listed another twenty men. That section ended with another message: THANK YOU FOR WAITING. The wreath and the notice had been removed as quickly as they had been found but not before someone had snapped them with their smartphone and posted it on Facebook.

The press got hold of it, and then everyone knew.

It had terrified the men.

"Twenty on long-term sick now. Stress. Another fifteen won't go out on patrol. It's not safe, apparently."

"Ten men for the whole district, then?"

"Nine."

"*Hijo de puta.*"

"Halfway to last year's murders and it's only just turned Easter. You're getting out at the right time, *compadre.*"

"Feels like I'm abandoning you."

Alameda chuckled. "You've done your time, Jesus. If I see you here next week, I'll arrest you myself."

"What about you?"

"If a transfer came up? I'd probably take it."

"If not?"

"What else can I do? Just keep my head down and hope for the best."

Plato nodded. It was depressing. There was a lot of guilt. He couldn't deny that. But, and not for the first time, he was grateful his time was up.

"You ready for that beer?" Alameda asked.

"Let me get changed. Ten minutes?"

"I'll get Sanchez and see you outside."

Plato went into the locker room and took off his uniform, tracing his finger across the stencilled POLICIA MUNICIPAL that denoted him as a member of the *municipio*, the local police force that was—laughably, he thought—charged with preventing crime. There was no time to be doing any of that, not when there was always another murder to attend to, another abduction, and then the flotsam and jetsam like the two drunken college boys from this afternoon. Prevention. That was a fine word, but not one that he recognised any more. He had once, perhaps, but not for many years.

The cartels had seen to that.

He clocked out, collected his leather jacket from the locker room, and followed Alameda and Sanchez to the restaurant.

Chapter Thirteen

THE GIRL talked in a quiet voice, her hands fluttering in her lap, her eyes staring down at the table except when they nervously flicked up to the entrance. Caterina took notes. Leon sat and listened.

"I moved to Juárez from Guadalajara for a job," she said. "It was in one of the *maquiladoras* on the banks of the river. Making electrical components for an American corporation. Fans for computers. Heat sinks and capacitors. I started work there when I was fourteen years old. A year ago. They paid me fifty-five dollars a week, and I sent all of it back to my mother and father. Occasionally, I would keep a dollar or two so that I could go out with my friends—soda, something to eat. It was hard work. Very hard. Long hours, no air-conditioning, so it got hot even by nine or ten in the morning. Complicated pieces to put together. Sometimes the parts would be sharp, and when you got tired—and you *always* got tired—then they would cut your fingers. I worked from seven in the morning until eight at night. Everything was monitored: how fast you were working, the time you spent on your lunch, the time you spent in the bathroom. They would dock your pay if they thought you were taking too long. None of us liked the job, but it was money, better money than I could get anywhere else, so I knew I had to work hard to make sure they didn't replace me.

"It wasn't just the work itself, though. There were problems with the bosses—there are more women than men in the factories, and they think it is all right for them to hit on us and that we should be flattered by it, give them what they want. The bosses have cars, and the women never do. Some girls go with the bosses so that they can get rides to work. It's safer than the busses. I never did that."

"They hit on you?"

"Of course."

"But you were fourteen."

"You think they care about that?" Delores smiled a bitter smile. "I was old enough." She sipped at the glass of orange juice that Caterina had bought for her. "They have those busses, the old American ones, the yellow and black ones they use to take their children to school. They were hot and smelly, and they broke down all the time, but it was better than walking and safer, too, once the girls started to disappear. I had a place in Lomas de Poleo—you know it?"

"I do." It was a shanty of dwellings spread in high desert a few miles west of Juárez. Caterina had been there plenty with the *Voces sin Echo*.

"It was just a bed, sharing with six other girls who worked in the same *maquiladora* as I did. The bus picked us up at six in the morning and took us up to the river; then, when we were finished at eight or nine, then they would take us back again."

Caterina's pen flashed across her pad. She looked at the recorder, checking that it was working properly. "What happened to you?"

"This was a Friday. The other girls were going out, but I was tired and I had no money, so I told them I would go home. The bus usually dropped us off in Anapra. The place I was staying was a mile from there, down an unlit dirt track, and it was dark that night, lots of clouds and no moon, darker than it usually was. I was always nervous, and there were usually six of us, but I was on my own, and it was worse. I got off the bus and watched it drive up the hill and then walked quickly. There was a car on the same side of the street as me. I remember the lights were on and the engine was still running. I crossed to the other side of the street to avoid it, but before I could get there, a man came up from behind me, put his hand over my mouth, and dragged me into the car. He was much stronger than I am. There was nothing I could do."

"Where did they take you?"

"There is a bar in Altavista with a very cheap hotel behind it where the men take the women that they have paid for. They took me there. They put me in a room, tied my hands and my feet, and left me on the bed. There was another girl there, too, on the other bed. She had been taken the night before, I think. She was tied down, like me. There was blood. Her eyes were open, but they did not focus on anything. She just stared at the ceiling. I tried to speak to her, but she did not respond. I tried again, but it was no use—she would not speak, let alone tell me her name or where she was from or what had happened to her. So I screamed and screamed until my throat was dry, but no one came. I could hear the music from the bar, and then, when that was quiet, I could hear noises from the other rooms that made me want to be quiet. There were other girls, I think. I never saw any of them, but I heard them. I must have been there for two or three hours before he came in."

"Just one?"

"Yes. I don't know if it was the same one who took me. I can remember him and yet *not* remember him, if you know what I mean. He was nothing special, by which I mean there was nothing about him that you would find particularly memorable. Neither tall nor short, neither fat nor thin. Normal looking. Normal clothes. He reminded me of the father of a girl I went to school with when I was younger. He was a nice man, the father of my friend. I hoped that maybe this man would be nice, too, or at least not as bad as I expected. But he was not like him at all. He was not nice."

"You don't have to tell me what happened."

But she did. She drew a breath and explained, looking down at the table all the time. She was a little vague, relying on euphemism, but Caterina was able to complete the details that she left out. Delores's bravery filled her with fury. She gripped her pen tighter and tighter until her knuckles were pale against the tanned skin on the back of her right hand. A fourteen-year-old girl. Fourteen. She vowed, for the hundredth time, the thousandth, that she would expose the men who were responsible for this. She did not care about her own safety. The only thing that mattered was that they were shamed and punished. Now that she had her blog and the thousands of readers who came to read about the disintegration of Juárez, now she was not just another protester. She had influence and power. People paid attention when she wrote things. This would be the biggest story yet.

Femicide.

The City of Lost Girls.

She would make them listen, and things would be done.

"How did you get away?"

"He untied my hands while he—you know—and then he did not tie them again when he went to use the bathroom. I suppose he was confident in himself, and he had made it plain that they would kill me if I tried to run. I knew that my prayers had been answered then and that I had been given a chance to escape, but at first, I did not think that my body would allow me to take advantage of it. It was as if all of the strength in my legs had been taken away. I think it was because I was frightened of what they would do to me if they caught me. I know that is not rational, and I know that they would have killed me if I had stayed—I knew about the missing girls, of course, like everyone does—but despite that, it was as much as I could do to take my clothes and get off the bed."

"But you did."

"Eventually, yes. I tried to get the other girl to get up too, but she told me to leave her alone. It was the first thing she had said to me all that time. She looked at me as if I had done something terribly wrong. She was still tied, too, and I am not sure I would have been able to free her, but it would not have mattered—she did not want to leave. I opened the door—he had not locked it—and I ran. I ran as fast as I could. I ran all the way to the Avenue Azucenas, and I found a policeman. I did not know if I could trust him, but I had no other choice. I was lucky. He was a good man. One of the few. He took me to the police station, away from there."

"Do you know his name?"

"The policeman? Yes—it was Plato. I think his first name was Jesus."

"And the man in the hotel?"

"I do not know his real name. But he liked to talk, all the time he would talk to me and the other girl, and this one time, just before I escaped, he told me about the things that he did for the cartels. He said his father was an important man in El Frontera and that he was a killer for them, a *sicario*, but not just any *sicario*—he said that he was the best, the most dangerous man in all of Juárez. He said that he had killed a thousand men and that, because he was so dangerous, the men who worked with him had given him a name. 'Santa Muerte.'"

Caterina wrote that down in her notebook, underlining it six times.

Santa Muerte.

Holy Death.

Saint Death.

Chapter Fourteen

"SO, OLD MAN—you going to stay in Juárez?"

Plato looked at Alameda and then at Sanchez. They had been goofing around all evening—mostly at Plato's expense, about how it felt to be so old—and this felt like the first proper, serious question. "I don't know," he said after a moment. "The girls are settled here, they got their friends, they're in a decent school. The little one's just been born; do I want to put him through the hassle of moving? There's another one on the way. The wife was born here, her old man's in a home half a mile from the house."

"Come on, man," Sanchez said. "Seriously?"

And Plato admitted to himself then that he had already decided. Ciudad Juárez was no place to bring up a family. Forty years ago, when he was coming up, even twenty years ago when he was starting to do well in the police, maybe he could've made a case that things would have been all right. But now? No, he couldn't say that. He'd seen too much. He had investigated eleven killings himself this month: the man in the Ford Galaxy who was gunned down at a stop sign; three beaten and tortured municipal cops found in the park; a man who was executed, shot in the head; and six narcos shot to pieces in the *barrio* by the army. In the early days, at the start, he had kept a list in a book, hidden it in the shed at the bottom of the garden. They called it Murder City for a reason. It took him two months to learn and give up.

"Maybe," he said.

"Maybe?" Alameda tweaked the end of his long moustache. "You ask me, Jesus, you'd be out of your mind if you stay here. Think what it'll be like when your girls are all grown. Or Jesus Jr, you want him hanging out on the corners when he gets a little hair on his chin? I'm telling you, man, as soon as I got my pension I'm getting the family together and we are out of here, as far away as we can."

"Me too," Sanchez said. "I've got family in New Mexico."

"Yeah, I guess we will move," Plato admitted. "I fancy the coast. Down south, maybe."

"Get to use that boat you're wasting all your time on."

"That did cross my mind."

Sanchez got up. "I'm gonna drain the lizard."

Alameda got up, too, indicating the three empty glasses. "Another?"

He watched Alameda and Sanchez as they made their way across the restaurant, Alameda heading to the bar and Sanchez for the restroom. They had chosen La Case del Mole tonight. It was a decent enough joint. The food was a little better than average, the beer was reasonably priced and plenty strong enough, and the owner—a fat little gringo from El Paso—owed the police a favour, so there would always be a hefty markdown on the bill at the end of the night.

He relaxed in his chair, stretching out his legs so that the ache in his muscles might ease a little. He was getting old, no point hiding it. It had been a long day, too, and if those two had their way, it would be a long night. He thought of his wife trying to get the two girls to behave while she struggled to get the baby to settle, and then feeding them, the chaos of bedtime, and then tidying the house, and for a moment, he felt guilty. He should get home; there were chores to be done, there were always chores, and it wasn't fair to live it up here with the boys and leave her to do everything herself. But then he caught himself; there wouldn't be many more chances to do this, to knock off after a shift and have a beer to wind down, maybe stop at a taco stand and shoot the breeze. He would keep in touch with his old colleagues, that was for sure, but it would be different when he was a civilian. He should enjoy himself. Emelia didn't mind. And she'd given him a pass.

It was almost nine, and as he waited for the busboy to clear the plates away so they could get down to the serious drinking, he idly played with his empty glass and looked out into the parking lot outside. Darkness was falling, the sodium oranges and reds slowly darkening, and the big overhead lights were on. A nice new SUV rolled in, an Audi Q5, the same model that he had had his eye on for a while, the one he knew he probably couldn't afford. He took in the details: silver, El Paso plates, premium trim, nearly a hundred grand if you bought it new. The truck stopped, not in a bay but right out in front of the restaurant, and Plato sat up a little in his chair. The engine was still running—he could see the smoke trailing out of the exhaust—and the doors on both sides slid open, four men getting out, too dark and too far away for him to see their faces well enough to remember them. There was something about the way they moved that he had seen before: not running but not walking either, quick, purposeful. He didn't even notice that he had stopped trailing his finger around the rim of the beer glass, that his hand had cautiously gone to his hip, that his thumb and forefinger were fretting with the clip on the holstered Glock.

Plato heard a woman's voice protesting, saying, "No, no," and then the crisp thud of a punch and something falling to the floor. The men were into the restaurant now, all four of them, fanning out around the room, each of them with something metallic in their hands. Plato had seen enough firearms in his time to pick them all out: two of them had machine pistols, Uzis or Mac-10s, another had a semi-automatic Desert Eagle, and the last one, keeping watch at the door, had an AK-47. Plato had unfastened the clip now, his hand settling around the butt of the Glock, the handgun cold and final in the palm of his hot hand. He looked around, knowing that there were fractions of seconds before the shooting started, looking for Alameda or Sanchez or anyone else who might be able to back him up, but Sanchez was still in the john, and Alameda had his back to him, facing the bar. The other diners, those that had seen the newcomers and recognised what was about to go down, were looking away, terrified, frozen to their chairs and praying that it wasn't them.

Twenty feet away to Plato's left, a fifth man rose from his seat. He recognised him: his name was Machichi. He was a mouthy braggart, early twenties, with oily brown shoulder-length hair and a high-cheekboned Apache face. Two yellow, snaggled buck teeth protruded from beneath a scraggly moustache and an equally scrubby goatee. Machichi had a small Saturday night special in his hand, and he pointed to the table a couple away to his left. Plato knew what was playing out: Machichi was the tail-man, his job was to ID the targets so the others could do the shooting. They were *sicarios*: cartel killers, murderers for El Patrón. But their targets didn't look like narcos. It was just a table of three: two young women and a man. One of the women—pretty, with long dark hair—saw Machichi and his revolver, shouted, "No," and dragged the other woman away from the table, away from the *sicarios*.

Plato felt a pang of regret as he pulled the Glock and pushed his chair away. One week to go, less than a week until he could hang it up, and now this? Didn't God just have the wickedest sense of humour? He thought of Emelia and the girls and little Jesus Jr as he stood and aimed the gun.

"Drop your weapons!"

The *sicario* with the AK fired into the restaurant, hardly even aiming, and Plato felt his guts start to go as slugs whistled past his head. A woman at the next table wasn't so lucky: her face blew up as the hollow point mashed into her forehead, blood spraying behind her as her neck cracked backwards and she slid from her chair. Plato hid behind the table, the cold finger of the Glock's barrel pressed up against his cheek. He hadn't even managed to get a shot off, and now he knew he never would. He couldn't move. Emelia's words this morning were in his head, he couldn't get them out, and they had taken the strength from his legs. He knew he was probably being flanked, the man with the rifle opening an angle to put him out of his misery. Plato knew it would be his wife's words that would be repeating in his head when the bullets found their marks.

Be careful, Jesus.

You got a different life from next Monday.

It was crazy: he thought of the lawn and how it would never get cut.

Gunfire.

The *tic-tic-tic* of the machine pistols.

A jagged, ripping volley from the Kalashnikov.

Screams.

The man who was with the two women had been hit. He staggered against his toppled chair, leaning over, his hand pressed to his gut, then wobbled across the room until he was at Plato's table. Blood on his shirt, pumping between his fingers. He reached for the table, his face white and full of fear, and then his hand slipped away from the edge and he was on his knees, and then on his face, his body twitching. Plato could have reached out to touch him.

He was facing at an angle away from the kitchen, but he glimpsed something move in the corner of his eye, cranked his head around in that direction and saw a cook, covered in sweat and shirtless save for a dirty apron, vaulting quickly over the sill of the wide window that opened onto the restaurant. The man moved with nimble agility, landing in a deep crouch and bringing up his right hand in a sudden, fluid motion. Plato saw a pair of angel wings tattooed across his back as his right arm blurred up and then down, something glinting in his hand and, then, leaving his hand. That glint spun through the air as if the man had unleashed a perfect fastball, like Pedro Martinez at the top of the ninth, two men down, the bases loaded. The kitchen knife—for that was what it was—landed in Machichi's throat.

He dropped his revolver and tottered backwards, clawing at the blade that had bisected his gullet.

It was the spur Plato needed: he spun up and around, firing the Glock. The *sicario* with the Kalashnikov took a round in the shoulder and wheeled away, wild return fire going high and wide, stitching a jagged trail into the fishing net that was hanging from the ceiling. Sanchez appeared and fired from the doorway to the restroom; Alameda was nowhere to be seen. All the diners were on the floor now; the cook fast-crawled on his belly between them, a beeline to the man with the Kalashnikov and, with a butterfly knife that had appeared in his hand, he reached down and slit the man's throat from ear to ear. He picked up the AK.

He popped out of cover, the muzzle flashing.

One of the *sicarios* was hit, his head jerking back.

The cook was beneath the line of the tables, firing a quick burst that left most of the top of the man smeared across the carpet and the wall behind him. The gun made a throaty chugging sound. Like someone with a hacking cough.

The remaining pair scrambled back to the door. Plato watched through the restaurant's large picture window as they hurried to the Q5. The cook stepped around to the window. The car was just fifteen feet away outside. The cook raised the Kalashnikov, calm and easy, braced the stock expertly against his shoulder, and fired a concentrated volley straight through the window. The pane shattered in an avalanche of shards, the bullets puncturing the driver-side window, none going astray, all of them within a neat ten-inch circle.

The car swerved out of control and hit another. The

door swung open. The airbags had deployed. The driver fell out, his head a bloody mess. The passenger was hit, too.

Plato brought up his Glock and aimed at the cook.

"Police! Get down, Señor! Down! On the floor!"

The man got to his knees, put the Kalashnikov on the carpet, then lay down.

Chapter Fifteen

MILTON HAD lost track of time. Suddenly, there had been sirens, police, ambulances. Six men and two women were dead. It was obvious who the gunmen had been after: two of the dead were from the same table. The police fussed around the bodies, taking photographs and judging trajectories, and then, when they were done, the paramedics were called over to lift the dead onto gurneys, covering their faces as they hauled them away. Milton was detained by the older, silver-haired municipal cop who had shot the gunman with the Kalashnikov; he was a little plump around the middle, the wrong side of fifty, and he had the smell of alcohol on his breath. The man told him to get a shirt, told him he was going to have to come back to the station with him to give a statement. Milton said that wasn't necessary, he could just do it there and then, but the cop had been insistent. Then, when they had arrived, he had insisted that he be photographed and have his fingerprints taken. Milton said he wasn't a criminal. The cop said maybe, but he just had his word for that. Milton could have overpowered him easily and could have gotten away, sunk under the surface again, but there was something about the cop that said he could trust him and something about the night itself that said he better stick around.

He let them take their photographs, front and profile. He let them take his prints.

The man was sitting in front of him now.

"So—you're Mr."—he looked down at his notes—"Smith. Right?"

"That's right."

"First name John. Correct?"

"Correct."

"John Smith? Really?"

"Yes, really."

"All right then, Señor Smith. Sorry about bringing you down here."

"That's all right. Why don't you tell me what you want?"

"I just wanted to visit with you a little bit. Talk to you about what happened. That was some trick with the knife. What are you, ex-military?"

"I'm just a cook."

"Really? You don't look like a cook."

"So you say. But that's what I am."

"Don't know many cooks who can handle a Kalashnikov like that, either."

"Lucky shot, I guess." The man shrugged. "Who are you?"

"Lieutenant Jesus Plato. Where you from?"

"England."

"Of course you are. That's a fine accent you got there."

"Thank you very much."

"You want to tell me what happened back there, Señor Smith?"

"You saw it just about as well as I did."

"Why don't you tell me—give me your perspective."

"I was in the kitchen, and I heard shooting. No one seemed to be doing anything much about it."

"And so you did."

"That's right."

"Seriously, Señor, please—you must have been a soldier at some point?"

"A long time ago."

"Don't think I'm ungrateful—you saved my life and plenty of others in that room. It's just—"

"It's just that you have to make a report. It's fine, Lieutenant. Ask your questions. I understand."

"You want a drink of water?"

"I'm fine," Milton said.

"Smoke?"

He nodded.

Plato took out a packet of Luckies and tapped out two cigarettes. Milton took one and let the man light it for him.

Plato inhaled deeply. "You know who those men were?"

"Never seen them before."

"Those boys were from the cartel La Frontera. You'll have heard of them, no doubt."

"A little."

"A word of advice, John. Do you mind if I call you John?"

"If you like."

"Keep your eyes open, all right, John? What you did back there, that's like poking a stick in a termites' nest. People round here, they learned a long time ago that it's best not to fight back when the *sicarios* come around. It's better to let them get on with their business and pray to whatever God it is you pray to that it's not your name they got on their list."

"Let them kill?"

"Most people couldn't make the kind of difference you made."

"I couldn't just stand aside and do nothing, Lieutenant."

"I know. I'm just saying—be careful."

"Thanks. I'll bear that in mind." He drew down on the cigarette, the tobacco crackling. "Who were they after?"

"We're not sure yet."

"But you think it was the kids on the table?"

"Most likely. They missed one of them. Probably thanks to you."

"The girl."

"Yes."

"Was she hit?"

"In the shoulder. She'll live."

"But she's not safe, is she?"

"No."

"What's her name?"

"You know I can't tell you that."

"Where is she?"

"I can't tell you that, either. It's confidential. I've already said more than I should've."

He leant forwards. "You won't be able to keep her safe, will you?"

"Probably not."

"I can, Lieutenant."

"I doubt that."

"I can."

"How long have you been in Juárez?"

"Just got into town today."

"You know what it's like here? You know anything about La Frontera?"

"This isn't my first dance." He rested both forearms on the table and looked right into Plato's eyes. "I can help. I know what they've done to the police. I know about the messages they hang off the bridges when they leave their bodies, I know about the threats they make on police radio, and I know they've got a list with your names on it. I saw what that means tonight. There were three of you. Only you and one of your colleagues did anything at all. The other one was hiding behind the bar."

"This might not be your first dance, John, but if you haven't been to Juárez before, I can guarantee you that you haven't seen anything like the cartels." As he spoke, he took out a notebook from his breast pocket and turned to a page near the back. He wrote quickly, then turned it upside down and left it on the table between them. "You sure you don't want that drink of water? I know I do. Dying of thirst here."

"That's not such a bad idea. I would. Thanks."

"All right, then. I'll be right back."

Plato went out. Milton took the notebook and turned it

over.

There were two lines of writing in Plato's untidy scrawl.

Caterina Moreno.

Hospital San José.

Chapter Sixteen

EL PATRÓN made it a habit to dress well, and this morning, his tailor had presented him with a fine new suit. It was cut from the most luxurious fabric—slate grey with the faintest pinstripe running through it—and it had been fitted expertly, measured to fit his barrel-like frame. His snakeskin boots disturbed small clouds of dust as he disembarked from the armour-plated Bentley, nodding to his chauffeur and setting off for the restaurant. Six of his bodyguards had already fanned out around the street, armed with a variety of automatic weapons. They would wait here while he ate. No one else would be allowed to go inside.

The place had been open for six months and was already the finest in Juárez. That was, perhaps, not the most impressive of accolades since local restaurants did not tend to last very long before they were shot up or firebombed or the management was murdered, but that was all beside the point; it had a fine reputation for its cuisine. Felipe considered himself something of a gourmet, and it was his habit to try all of the best new places. Now, with business to attend to in the city, he had the perfect excuse. He did not often venture down from the sixty thousand square miles of land he owned in the Sierra, not least because the vast space, the battery of gunmen and the fealty of the locals made it an almost impregnable redoubt. But this business was important, and it needed his attention.

The other members of his retinue had already been inside to inform the proprietor that El Patrón would be dining with them tonight. They had collected the cell phones of the other customers and staff and told them—politely but firmly—that no one would be allowed to leave until El Patrón had finished his meal. Of course, no one had protested. As compensation for their inconvenience, their meals would all be paid for. A couple celebrating their marriage had reserved the best table in the house, but they had needed little persuasion that it was in their best interests to move. The room was silent save for the muffled noise of the busy kitchen and the crisp retorts of Felipe's raised heels as they struck the polished wooden floorboards. He went from table to table, beaming his high-voltage smile at each of his fellow diners, clasping the hands of the men and kissing the women on both cheeks. He introduced himself to them and apologised for their inconvenience. They looked at him with fear or admiration or both; the power of his reputation gave him enormous pleasure. El Patrón was almost a mythical figure in Mexico, his exploits the subject of countless ballads and stories. He had outlived enemies and accomplices alike, defying the accepted bargain of a life in the drug trade: your career might be glittering, but it would be brief, and it would always end in prison or the grave.

Not for him.

He left the newlyweds until last. He stood beside their table and treated them to a wide, white-toothed smile.

"Do you know who I am?"

"Yes," the man said. His fear was evident, although he was trying to hide it. "You are El Patrón."

"That is right. I am. And I understand that you are celebrating your marriage?"

"Yes."

"Congratulations. May I ask, when was the happy day?"

"Yesterday."

"And you are not on honeymoon?"

"Money is difficult," the woman said.

Felipe took out the bankroll that he kept in the inside pocket. He had heard that one of his lieutenants had joked that the roll was thick enough to choke a pig, and it probably was. He removed the money clip and started to count notes from the roll—each was a $100 bill—got to twenty and then stopped. Smiling widely, knowing that everyone in the restaurant was watching his display of munificence, he put the roll on the table. He did not know precisely how much money there was—ten thousand, at least—but it didn't matter. Felipe González was responsible for over half of the illegal narcotics imported into the United States every year. He had appeared in Forbes' annual billionaires list. Ten thousand dollars was nothing to him. Chump change.

"Congratulations," he said. "You must take a holiday. You are only married one time, after all."

The woman looked ready to refuse his offer. "Thank you," her husband said quickly before she could speak. He did not want to displease him with ingratitude. He glared at her, and his message understood, her frown became an uneasy smile.

"You are very welcome."

His son, Adolfo González, was waiting for him at the table.

He rose. "*Padre.*"

"Adolfo." Felipe hugged him. He was impetuous and prone to dangerous predilections, but he was still his son, and he loved him. There were other children—other brothers, even—but Adolfo was his oldest still alive and the only one who was born of his first wife. The boy reminded him of her often: she had been impetuous and wild, too, a seventeen-year-old beauty from a village near to his in the heart of the Sierra. She had been the most beautiful girl he had ever laid eyes upon, and his wedding day had been the happiest of his life. That it did not last did not sour the affection he felt for her whenever he recalled her memory. She had eventually become a little too wild, a little too free with her affections and too loose with her tongue, and he had been left with no other option than to do away with her. They had dissolved her body in a vat of hydrochloric acid and poured her into the river.

Adolfo and Raymondo had been twins. Raymondo was the oldest, and as such, he had been the real apple of his father's eye. He had arrived ten minutes before his twin, a protracted delivery that was contrasted by the ease with which Adolfo had followed. Felipe often joked to his wives that that had been the first indication of his character; if he could, Adolfo would always let someone else do all the hard work for him. Raymondo had been shot dead by the army two years ago. Felipe knew that the older boy had exercised a degree of control over his brother. Adolfo had reacted badly to his death, and that, combined with the sudden removal of his brother's restraint, had led to all this blessed nonsense with the girls.

"It is good to see you, *Padre.*"

Felipe sat and made busy with the menu. "Have you eaten here before?"

"When it opened."

"What is good?"

"The steak. Excellent. And we should get some wine. They have a very well-stocked cellar."

He summoned the waiter and ordered an especially fine Burgundy. The man offered to pour, but Felipe dismissed him.

"Adolfo," he began, pouring for his son, "there are things we need to discuss."

"Yes, *Padre.*"

"The Italians?"

"*Pendejos!* It was easy. No survivors."

"Good."

"Have they tried to contact you?"

"No," Felipe said. "And they won't."

He looked at the boy. He was wide-eyed and avid, desperate for his approval. He wondered, sometimes, if that need was the reason for the way he was. Amongst other things, the men called him *El Más Loco.*

The Craziest One.

"You did well, Adolfo. I couldn't have asked for more. But tonight?"

He frowned. "Yes. I know."

"What happened?"

"I'm as unhappy as you, *Padre.*"

"That is doubtful."

"I'm still trying to find out."

"Were you there?"

"No."

"She was just a girl. It is a simple thing, is it not?"

"It should have been simple."

"And yet it wasn't."

"She has been difficult to find. Her *culo* boyfriend was less careful. We have been following him, and he led us to her. There was a third person, a girl; they were meeting her there—another of her stories, no doubt. I put five men on the job. Good men. They have always been reliable. As you say, it should have been easy. They went into the restaurant, but as they were carrying out their orders, they were attacked."

"By whom?"

Adolfo could not hide his awkwardness. "One of the cooks."

"A *cook*, Adolfo?"

"At first. And then two policemen."

"This cook—who is he?"

"I'm going to visit the proprietor. I'll know more after I have spoken with him. Whoever this *puto* is, he isn't just a cook. He threw a knife halfway across the room and hit Javier, and then he knew how to use an AK. I'm thinking he was a soldier."

"And the police?"

"They will be easier to find. Don't worry—they will all be punished."

"Make sure that they are. They work *for* us, Adolfo, not *against* us. Remind them. Make an example out of them."

"I will."

"It is important, Adolfo. I'm meeting the gringos tomorrow. They are cautious men. There must not be any doubt that we are in control. This kind of fuck-up makes us look bad. If they think we cannot get rid of a journalist who has been writing about us, how will they trust us to control this *plaza*? Do you understand?"

He looked crestfallen. "Yes."

He steepled his fingers and looked over them at his son, his brows lowering, his Botoxed forehead crinkling a little into what passed for a frown. "This whole mess would have been unnecessary if it wasn't for your"—he searched for the right word, each one more distasteful than the last—"*problem*. I will hear no more excuses about it; it has to stop. I've told you too many times already. Do you understand me?"

"Yes, *Padre*. It will—it has. No more."

"Very good. You have money, connections, power— you don't need to take your women. They will come to you." Felipe looked up; the waiter was at the edge of the room, shuffling nervously from foot to foot. Felipe smiled and beckoned him over. "Now then. Shall we order?"

Chapter Seventeen

LATER THAT NIGHT, smelling like grease and blood and cigarettes, Milton stepped out of the police station and stood with his back to the wall for a quiet smoke. There, away from the noise of the kitchen, the snarled abuse in the holding pens, the smell of gunpowder, away from the familiarity of boiling fat and plates that burned to the touch, away from the sudden shock of violence and death, all of reality came crashing back in on him.

Here was only the night, the dark, the fecund stink of uncollected trash and the distant highway roar, the ticking sound as the earth gave up the stored heat of the day, the wet pressure of breathing in the humid soup and the fat black cockroaches that crawled through the gutters. The night was warm and fuzzy from the refinery stacks on the other side of the border, from street dust and smoke. The low sky glowed orange. Milton knew that he had travelled far from London and what had happened there, far away from his job and the blood that still dripped from his hands. Suddenly, the thought of going back to the squalid dormitory room with the other men, of smoking cigarettes through the window, trying to read his paperbacks in the glow of his torch or watching Mexican football on Telemundo, too exhausted to sleep, was not what he wanted to do at all. Standing rigid, eyes aching, feet throbbing, blood humming in the hollows behind his ears to fill the sudden quiet, he stared up into the night and the stars, and decided. He pushed himself off the wall. He would get as much sleep as he could, and then, first thing tomorrow, he would head for Hospital San José.

That girl, whoever she was, was in trouble.

And he was going to help.

DAY TWO

"Just a Cook"

Chapter Eighteen

"TAKE A SEAT, Miss Thackeray," the man said.

Anna Thackeray did as she was told. The office was impressive, well appointed, spacious and furnished in the tastefully understated fashion that said that money had not constrained the choices that had been made. There was a wide picture window that offered a view of the Thames toiling sluggishly under a gunmetal grey sky. The room was light and airy. Military prints on the walls. Silver trophies and two photographs in luxurious leather frames: one was of the man on the other side of the desk in his younger days, in full battle dress; the other was of a woman and three children. A central table held a bowl of flowers, and there were two comfortable club chairs on either side of an empty fireplace.

The international HQ for Global Logistics was on the same side of the Thames as the more imposing building in Vauxhall where the important decisions were taken, but that was as far as the similarities went. It was built in the sixties, with that decade's preference for function over form, constructed from red brick and concrete, its anonymous five floors all rather squat and dowdy when compared to the Regency splendour of its neighbours or the statement buildings of government that had been constructed more recently. A grand terrace had been smashed down the middle by a three-hundred-pound Luftwaffe bomb, and this unpromising building had eventually sprouted from the weed-strewn bombsite that had been left. The windows were obscured with Venetian blinds that had been allowed to fade in the sunlight; the staircase that ascended the spine of the building was whitewashed concrete and bare light bulbs; the lift—when it worked—was a dusty box with four walls of faux wooden panels and dusty mirror. And yet the drab obscurity of the building was perfect to cloak its real purpose. The government organisation that did its work here lived in the shadows, a collection of operatives that was secret to all but those with the highest security clearances.

Anna had never even heard of it until yesterday, and she prided herself in knowing *everything*.

"You asked to see me, sir?"

His codename was Control. Only a handful of people knew his real name, and even fewer his background. He was a plump, toad-like man, dressed with the immaculate good taste of the best class of public schoolboy. A well-tailored suit, an inch of creamy white cuff, a regimental tie fastened with a brass pin. His hands were fleshy, his glistening nails bearing the unmistakeable signs of a recent manicure. Anna found that, above everything else, rather distasteful. He was oleaginous and slippery, undoubtedly brilliant but as far removed from trustworthiness as it was possible to be. That, of course, made him ideal for his position. Like the building from which he worked, he was perfect for his purpose. Control commanded Group Fifteen, otherwise known as the Section, Pegasus and the Department. He supervised two hundred civil servants, mostly seconded from MI5, MI6 and the Foreign Office, analysts and spooks that were simply the network that facilitated the work of the twelve men and women who carried out the jobs that Group Fifteen was allocated. When the government found itself with a particularly intractable problem and every other route had failed— commercial, diplomatic, political—Group Fifteen would occasionally be put out into the field. And, for them, all solutions were in play.

"Thank you for coming to see me, Miss Thackeray," Control said.

"Not a problem, sir."

She tried to project a feeling of ease, but she did not

find that simple to do. The occasion was not suited to that, for one, and the formality of the place bothered her. She had already made more concessions than she was comfortable with making: she had removed her earrings, scrubbed the black nail varnish from her fingers and borrowed a trouser suit and a shirt. And of course, there was her hair. She had dyed it red over the weekend, and she was damned if she was going to spend the night before this meeting changing it to something more … conservative.

There were limits.

"Everything I tell you this morning is beyond top secret—I'm sure that goes without saying?"

"It does."

"Very good. I'll be as brief as I can be. Six months ago, one of our most valuable agents went AWOL. Have you read the file?"

"Yes—John Milton."

"Indeed. It is our belief that Mr. Milton suffered a mental breakdown following an unsuccessful operation in France. The decision had been taken to bring him in for observation and treatment, but as one of our agents approached him for that purpose, he opened fire on him. A member of the public was killed, and the agent was badly wounded. We suppressed that from the report for obvious reasons."

"Yes."

"Following those events, Milton has dropped off the grid. We tracked him north to Liverpool, and our working assumption is that he either found work on a boat or stowed away on one. The trail went cold from there, and we have seen neither hide nor hair of him since. That is a state of affairs that we cannot allow to stand. Mr. Milton was our most experienced operative. He has intimate, first-hand knowledge of operations that would cause the government enormous embarrassment if their existence was ever to be disclosed, and that's not even considering the operational knowledge that would be of great interest to our enemies—and to our friends."

"You want me to find him."

"We do. We've been working with your department for some time but, so far, with disappointing results. Your predecessor made no headway, so he has been reassigned, and you are replacing him. I understand from your supervisor that you're the best analyst that GCHQ has to offer."

"No question."

"You don't suffer from false modesty, do you?"

"I don't see the point in it."

"You might come to wish you had been more circumspect because now I expect you to meet with more success." He sipped at his cup of tea; Anna found the sight of his pursed, fleshy lips nauseating.

"I have the file. Is there anything else I need to know?"

"You should be under no disillusions here: John Milton has been trained to be totally invisible. His profession for ten years was to be a ghost. He has operated in some of the most inhospitable, dangerous places you can imagine—if he was not as good at this as he is, he would have been captured and killed years ago. He is not married, he has no children, he has no real friends. No ties, not to anyone or anything. It will not be an easy task to find him, but I must re-emphasise: he *must* be found. This could be the making of your career or"— he paused and spread his hands—"not. Do I make myself clear?"

The implication was very clear.

Find him, or else.

"You do," she said.

Chapter Nineteen

IT WAS early the next day when Anna stooped to position her eye over the iris scanner, the laser combing up and down and left to right before her identity was confirmed and the gate opened to allow her inside. The guard, his SA80 machine gun slung loose across his shoulder, smiled a greeting as she passed him. An exhibit in the main entrance hall contained treasures from the history of British code-breaking: the Enigma machine was her favourite, but she passed it without looking and went through the further two checks before she was properly inside. GCHQ had the feel of a bustling modern airport, with open-plan offices leading off a circular thoroughfare that was known as the Street, offering cafés, a bar, a restaurant and a gym. Anna walked to the store and bought a copy of the *Times* and a large skinny latte with an extra shot of espresso.

Most of the staff were dressed conservatively; the squares on their morning commute might have mistaken them for workers on their way in to the office. Suits and blouses, all very proper. But they would not have mistaken Anna like that. She wasn't interested in conformity, and since she was not ambitious and didn't care whether she impressed anyone or not, she wore whatever made her comfortable. She was wearing a grey Ministry T-shirt, a black skirt, a battered black leather jacket, ripped Converse All-Stars and red tights. She cocked an eyebrow at the attendant working at the X-ray portal; the man, beyond the point of being exasperated with her after the last six months, readied his wand and waved her through. She smiled at him, and when he smiled back, she winked. She had a sensuous mouth, a delicate nose, and well-defined cheekbones that would have suited a catwalk model.

She followed the thoroughfare to the junction that, after another five minutes and a flight of stairs, led to the first-floor SigInt Ops Centre where she had her desk. It was a busy, open-plan area, staffed by mathematicians, linguists and analysts scouring the internet for intel on terrorism, nuclear proliferation, energy security, military support, serious organised crime and counter-espionage in different regions. Computer engineers and software developers helped make it possible; the Tempora program alone, responsible for fibre-optic interceptors attached to subsurface internet cabling, siphoned off ten gigabits of information every second. Twenty-one petabytes a day. The Prism and Boundless Informant programmes added petabytes more. That huge, amorphous mass of data needed to be sorted and arranged. GCHQ's gaping larders were stuffed full of data to be harvested by their algorithm profiles against a rainy day.

There were hackers here, too. A small team of them, including Anna.

Most of them had never considered a career in intelligence.

Anna had wanted the job specifically.

They had instructed her to get it.

And as it turned out, it had been easy.

Thackeray was an anglicised name that she had adopted when she had moved to London. She was born Anna Vasilyevna Dubrovsky in Volgograd in 1990. Her father was a middle-ranking diplomat in the Russian diplomatic service, and her mother worked for the party. She was their only child, and her prodigious intelligence— obvious from a very early age—was a source of tremendous pride to them. She had been precocious in school, a genius mathematician, quickly outpacing her peers and then her teachers. There was an annual children's chess competition in the district, and she had won it for two straight years; she had been banned from entering for a third time. She had been inculcated in data and analysis almost before she could read.

The day she had been given her first computer—a brand-new American-built Dell—was the day that the scales had truly fallen from her eyes. She was taught everything there was to know about it, and then, once again, she outpaced her teachers. Volgograd was a dreary backwater, and the internet spread out like a vast, open vista, a frontier of unlimited possibility where you could do anything and be anyone. She was taught how to live online. It became her second life. She became addicted to hacking forums, the bazaars where information was exchanged, complex techniques developed and audacious hacks lauded. It became difficult to distinguish between her real self and "Solo," as she soon preferred to be called.

Her instructors were pleased with her.

The family travelled with Vasily when he was assigned to the Russian embassy in London.

Her hacking continued. Questions of legality were easily ignored. Property was effectively communal; if she wanted something, she took it. She set up dummy accounts and pilfered Amazon for whatever she fancied. A PayPal hack allowed her to transfer money she did not have. She bought and sold credit card information. She joined collectives that vandalised the pages of corporations with whose politics—and often their very existence—she disagreed. After six months, they told her to draw attention to herself. She left bigger and bigger clues, not so big as to have been left obviously—or to have been the mark of an obvious amateur, which would have disqualified her from her designated future just as completely—but obvious enough to be visible to a vigilant watcher. She was just twenty-two when, from the bedroom of her boyfriend's house, she had hacked into ninety-seven military computers in the Pentagon and NASA. She was downloading a grainy black-and-white photograph of what she thought was an alien spacecraft from a NASA server at the John Space Centre in Houston when she was caught. They tracked her down and charged her. Espionage. The Americans threatened extradition. Life imprisonment. The British pretended to co-operate, but then, at the last minute, they countered with a proposal of their own.

Come and work for us.

She appeared to be all out of options.

That was what she wanted them to think.

She had accepted.

Anna sat down at her desk. It was, as usual, a dreadful mess. The cubicle's flimsy walls were covered with geek bric-a-brac: a sign warning DO NOT FEED THE ZOMBIES; a clock designed to look like an oversized wristwatch; replicas of the Enterprise and the TARDIS; a Pacman stress ball, complete with felt ghosts; a Spiderman action figure. A rear-view mirror stuck to the edge of a monitor made sure it was impossible to approach without her knowledge.

She took a good slug of her coffee and fired up both of her computers, high-performance Macs with the large, cinema screens. On the screen to her right, she double-clicked on Milton's file. Her credentials were checked, and the classified file—marked EYES ONLY—was opened. A series of pictures were available, taken at various points throughout his life. There were pictures of him at Cambridge, dressed in cross-country gear and with mud slathered up and down his legs. Long, shaggy hair, lively eyes, a coltish look to him. A handsome boy, she caught herself thinking. Attractive. A picture of him in a tuxedo, some university ball perhaps, a pretty but ditzy-looking redhead hanging off his arm. A series of him taken at the time that he enlisted: a blank, vaguely hostile glare into the camera when he signed his papers; a press shot of him on patrol in Derry, camouflage gear, his rifle pointed down, the stock pressed to his chest; a shot of him in ceremonial dress accepting the Military Medal. Maybe a dozen pictures from that part of his life. There were just two from his time in the SAS: a group shot with his unit hanging out of the side of a UH-60 Blackhawk and another, the most recent, a head and shoulders shot: his face was smothered with camouflage cream, black war paint, his eyes were unsmiling, a comma of dark hair curled over his forehead. The relaxed, fresh-faced youngster was a distant memory; in those pictures he was coldly and efficiently handsome.

Anna turned to the data. There were eight gigabytes of material. She ran another of her homebrew algorithms to disqualify the extraneous material—she would return to review the chaff later, while she was running the first sweep—reducing it to a more manageable three gigs. Now she read carefully, cutting and pasting key information into a document she had opened on the screen to her left. When she had finished, three hours later, she had a comprehensive sketch of Milton's background.

She went through her notes more carefully, highlighting the most useful components. He was an orphan, his parents killed in an Autobahn smash when he was twelve, so there would be no communications to be had with them. There had been a nomadic childhood before that, trailing his father around the Middle East as he followed a career in petrochemicals. There were no siblings, and the aunt and uncle who had raised him had died ten years earlier. He had never been married nor was there any suggestion that he enjoyed meaningful relationships with women. There were no children. It appeared that he had no friends, either, at least none that were obviously apparent. Milton, she thought to herself as she dragged the cursor down two lines, highlighting them in yellow, you must be a very lonely man.

David McClellan, the analyst who worked next to her, kicked away from his desk and rolled his chair in her direction. "What you working on?"

"You know better than that."

McClellan had worked opposite Anna for the last three

months. He'd been square—for a hacker, at least—but he had started to make changes in the last few weeks. He'd stopped wearing a tie. He occasionally came in wearing jeans and a T-shirt (although the T-shirts were so crisp and new that Anna knew he had just bought them, probably on the site that she used, after she had recommended it to him). It was obvious that he had a thing for her. He was a nice guy, brain as big as a planet, a little dull, and he tried too hard.

"Come on—throw me a bone."

"Above your clearance," she said, with an indulgent grin.

McClellan returned her smile, faltered a little when he realised that she wasn't joking, but then looked set to continue the conversation until she took up her noise-cancelling headphones, slipped them over her ears, and tapped them, with a shrug.

Sorry, she mouthed. *Can't hear you.*

She turned back to her screens. Milton's parents had left a considerable amount in trust for him, and his education had been the best that money could buy. He had gone up to Eton for three terms until he was expelled—she could not discover the reason—and then Fettes and Cambridge, where he read law. He passed through the university with barely a ripple left in his wake; Anna started to suspect that someone had been through his file, carefully airbrushing him from history.

She watched in the mirror as McClennan rolled back towards her again.

Coffee? he mouthed.

Anna nodded, if only to get him out of the way.

Milton's army career had been spectacular. Sandhurst for officer training and then the Royal Green Jackets, posted to the Rifle Depot in Winchester, and then Special Forces: Air Troop, B Squadron, 22 SAS. He had served in Gibraltar, Ireland, Kosovo and the Middle East. He was awarded the Distinguished Conduct Medal, and that, added to the Military Medal he had been given for his service in Belfast, briefly made him the army's most decorated serving soldier.

She filleted the names of the soldiers who had served with him. Emails, telephone numbers, everything she could find.

McClennan returned with her coffee. She mouthed thanks, but he did not leave. He said something, but she couldn't hear. With a tight smile, she pushed one of the headphones further up her head. "Thanks," she repeated.

"You having trouble?"

"Why—?"

"You're frowning."

She shrugged. "Seriously, David. Enough. I'm not going to tell you."

He gave up.

She pulled the headphones down again and turned back to her notes.

The next ten years, the time Milton had spent in the Group, were redacted.

Classified!

"Dammit!" she exclaimed under her breath.

She couldn't get into the contemporaneous stuff?

They were tying both hands behind her back.

It was impossible.

She watched McClellan scrubbing a pencil against his scalp, and corrected herself: impossible for most people. Hard for her, not impossible.

Anna picked up the fresh coffee and looked at her précis for clues. Where should she start looking? Nothing stood out. Control had been right about him: there was no one that she could monitor for signs of contact. She clicked over into the data management system and calibrated a new set of "selectors," filters that would be applied to internet traffic and telephony in order to trigger flags.

She started with his name, the nub of information

around which everything else would be woven. She added his age—five years either way—and then the names of his parents, his aunt and uncle. She ran a search on the soldiers who shared record entries with him, applied a simple algorithm to disqualify those who only appeared once or twice, then pasted the names of the rest. She inputted credit card and bank account details, known telephone numbers and email addresses. He hadn't had a registered address since he had left the army, but she posted what she had and all the hotels that he had visited more than once.

His blood group, DNA profile and fingerprints had been taken when he joined the Group, and miraculously, she had those. She dragged each of them across the screen and dropped them in as new selectors.

Distinguishing marks: a tattoo on his back, a large pair of angel wings; a scar down his face, the memento of a knife fight in a Honolulu bar; and a scar from the surgery to put a steel plate in his right leg after it had been crushed in a motorcycle crash.

Each piece of data and metadata narrowed the focus, disambiguating whole exabytes held on the servers in the football-pitch-sized data room in the basement. She spun her web around that central fact of his name, adding and deleting strands until she had a sturdy and reliable net of information with which she could start filtering. Dozens of algorithms would analyse the data that her search pulled back, comparing it against historical patterns and returning probability matches. "John Milton" alone would generate an infinitesimally small likelihood rate, so small as to be eliminated without the need for human qualification. Adding his age might nudge the percentage up a fraction. Nationality another fraction. Adding his blood group might be worth a whole percentage point. The holy grail— a fingerprint, a DNA match—well, that happened with amateurs, but not with a man like this. That wasn't a break she was going to catch.

She filed the selectors for approval, took another slug of coffee, applied for capacity to run a historic search of last month's buffer—she guessed it would take a half day, even with the petaflops of processing power that could be applied to the search—and then leant back in her chair, lacing her fingers behind her head and staring at the screens.

Control was right. Milton was a ghost, and finding him through a digital footprint was going to be a very long shot. GCHQ was collecting a vast haystack of data, and she was looking for the tiniest, most insignificant needle. Control must have known that. If Milton was as good as he seemed to be, he would know how to stay off the grid. The only way that he would surface was if he chose to, or if he slipped up.

She stood, eyes closed, stretched out her arms, and rolled her shoulders.

Anna doubted John Milton was the kind of man who was prone to mistakes.

She started to wonder if this job was a poisoned chalice.

The sort of job that could only ever make her look bad.

Chapter Twenty

FIVE IN the morning. Plato looked at the icon of Jesus Christ that he had fixed to the dashboard of his Dodge. Feeling a little self-conscious, he touched it and closed his eyes. Four days, he prayed. Please God, keep me safe for four days. Plato was not usually a prayerful man, but today he felt that it was worth a try. He had been unable to sleep all night, the worry running around in his mind, lurid dreams of what the cartel would do to him and his family impossible to quash. In the end, with the red digits on the clock radio by his bed showing three, he had risen quietly from bed so as not to disturb Emelia and had gone to check on each of his children. They were all sleeping peacefully. He had paused in each room, just listening to the sound of their breathing. Satisfied that they were safe, he had gone downstairs and sat in the lounge for an hour with a cup of strong black coffee. His loaded service-issue revolver was laid on the table in front of him.

The kitchen light flicked on, and Emelia's worried face appeared at the window. Plato waved at his wife, forcing a broad smile onto his face. She knew something had happened last night, but she had not pressed him on it, and he had not said. He didn't want to cause her any more anxiety than he could avoid. What was the point? She had enough on her plate without worrying about him. He might have been able to unburden himself, but it would have been selfish. Far better to keep his own counsel and focus on the light at the end of the tunnel.

Four days.

He started the engine and flicked on the headlights. He backed the car down the drive, putting it into first and setting off in the direction of Avenue 16 de Septiembre and the Hospital San José. He turned off the road and rolled into the underground car park. As he reversed into a space, he found himself thinking of the Englishman. It was out of character for him to break the rules, and he was quite clear about one thing: giving a man he did not know the details of where the witness in a murder enquiry was being taken was most definitely against the rules. The man wasn't a relation, and he had no obvious connection to her. He was also, very patently, a dangerous man who knew how to kill and had done so before. Plato had wondered about him during his night's vigil. Who was he? What was he? What kind of ex-soldier. Special Forces? Or something else entirely? He had no reason to trust the man apart from a feeling in his gut that they were on the same side. Plato had long since learnt that it was wise to listen to his instincts. They often turned out to be right.

Plato rode the elevator to the sixth floor. The girl was being kept in her own room; they would be better able to guard her that way. Sanchez was outside the door. He had drawn the first watch, and his eyes were red rimmed from lack of sleep.

"About time," he grumbled.

"How is she?"

"Sleeping. The shoulder is nothing to worry about—just a flesh wound. They've cleaned it and tidied it up."

"But?"

"But nothing. They shot her up to help her sleep, and she's been out ever since."

"Has anyone told her about the others?"

"No. I didn't have the chance."

Plato sighed. It would fall to him to do it. He hated it, bringing the worst kind of news, but it was something that he had almost become inured to over the course of the years. How many times had he told relatives that their husband, son, wife or daughter had been murdered over the last decade? Hundreds of times. These two would just be the latest. He hoped, maybe, that they would be the last.

"All right," he said. "I'll take over. Have you spoken to Alameda?"

Sanchez nodded. "He called."

"All right?"

"Seemed to be."

"He's still relieving me? I've got to start looking into what happened, for what it's worth. I can't stay here all day."

"He said he was."

Sanchez clapped him on the shoulder and left him.

The room was at the end of the corridor. There was a chair outside it and, on the floor, a copy of *El Diario* that Sanchez had found from somewhere. The front page had a number as its headline, capitalized and emboldened— SEVEN HUNDRED—and below it was a colour picture of a body laid out in the street, blood pooling around the head. It would be seven hundred and eight once they had processed the victims from last night. Plato tossed the newspaper back down onto the ground, quietly turned the handle to the door, and stepped inside.

The girl was sleeping peacefully. She had been dressed in hospital-issue pyjamas, and her right shoulder was swaddled in bandages. He stepped a little closer. She was pretty, with a delicate face and thick, black hair. The silver crucifix she wore around her neck stood out against her golden-brown skin. He wondered if it had helped her last night. She had been very, very lucky. Lucky that the cook had been there, for a start. And lucky that the *sicarios* had, somehow, failed to complete their orders. That was unusual. The penalty for a *sicario*'s failure would be his own death, often much more protracted and unpleasant than the quick and easy ending that he planned for his victims. It was a useful incentive to get the job done, and it meant that they very rarely made mistakes.

It also meant that they often visited hospitals to finish off the victims that they had only been able to wound the first time around.

Plato was staring at her face when the girl's eyes slid open. It gave him a start. "Hello," he said.

She looked at him, a moment of muddied confusion before alarm washed across her face. Her feet scrambled against the mattress as she pushed herself away, her back up against the headboard.

"It's all right," Plato said, holding his hands up, palms facing her. "I'm a policeman."

"That's supposed to make me feel better?"

"I know I'd say this even if I wasn't, but I'm one of the good ones."

She regarded him warily, but as he took no further step towards her, smiling what he hoped was his most winning and reassuring smile, she gradually relaxed. Her legs slid down the bed a little, and she arranged herself so that she was more comfortable. The movement evidently caused her pain; she winced sharply.

"How's the shoulder?"

"Sore." The pain recalled what had happened last night, and her face fell. "Leon—where is he?"

Plato guessed that she meant the man she was with. "I'm sorry, ma'am," he said.

Her face dissolved, the steeliness subsumed by a sudden wave of grief. Tears rolled down her cheeks, and she closed her eyes, her breathing ragged until, after a moment, she mastered it again. She buried her head in her forearms with her hands clasped against the top of her head, her breathing sighing in and out. Plato stood there helplessly, his fingers looped into his belt to stop them fidgeting. He never knew what to do after he had delivered the news.

"Caterina," he said.

She moved her arms away. Her eyes were wet when she opened them again, and they shined with angry fire. "The girl?"

Plato shook his head.

"Oh God."

"I'm very sorry."

She clenched her teeth so hard that the line of her jaw was strong and firm.

"I'm sorry," he said again, not knowing what else he could say.

"When can I get out of here?"

"The doctors will want to see you. It's early, though. I don't think they'll be here until morning. A few hours."

"What time is it?"

"Half five. Why don't you try to get a little extra sleep?"

She gave him a withering look. "I don't think so."

"One of my colleagues watched over you through the night, and I'm going to stay with you now," he said. "The men who did this might come back when they find out that you're still alive."

"And you can stop them?"

There was the thing; Plato knew he would have no chance at all if they came back, and the girl looked like she was smart enough to know that too. "I'll do my best," he told her.

Chapter Twenty-One

PLATO SPOKE to the girl for an hour. He got more of the story and wrote it all down. Eventually, her eyelids started to fall, and as dawn broke outside, she was asleep again. Plato covered her with the coarse hospital blanket and picked up her chart from the end of the bed. They had given her a mild dose of secobarbital, and he guessed that there was still enough of it in her system to make her drowsy. It was for the best, he thought. She would need all her strength about her when she was discharged. He wasn't sure how best to go about that. There was no question that she was in a perilous situation. The cartels wanted her dead, and his experience suggested that they wouldn't stop until that had happened or until she was put out of reach. There was no easy way for him to help her with that. Once she was out of the hospital, she was on her own.

He looked down at his notebook. Her name was Caterina Moreno. She was twenty-five, and she was a journalist, writing for the Blog del Borderland. He wasn't as savvy with computers as some of the others, but even he had heard of it. It was generating a lot of interest, and the cartels had already murdered several of its contributors. The dead man was another of the blog's writers, and the dead girl was a source who was to be interviewed for a story she was writing.

He sat down on the chair outside the room, his pistol in his lap. He watched as the hospital switched gears from the night to day: nurses were relieved as they went off shift, the doctors began to do their rounds, porters pushed their trolleys with their changes of linen, medicines and breakfasts. Plato watched all of them, looking for signs of incongruity, his mind prickling with the anticipation of sudden violence, his fingers never more than a few inches from the stippled barrel of his Glock. They might come in disguise, or in force, they might come knowing that the power of their reputation was enough to grant them unhindered passage. The girl was helpless. Plato resolved to do his best to slow them down.

His vigil was uninterrupted until Alameda arrived at nine.

"*Capitán*," Plato said.

"How is she?"

"Not so good."

"How much does she know?"

"I told her enough."

Alameda scrubbed his eyes. "Stupid kids."

"That's harsh."

"Pretending to be journalists."

"They'd say they *were* journalists."

"Hardly, Jesus."

"We're out of touch."

"Maybe. But writing about the cartels? *Por dios*, man! How stupid can you get? They got what's coming to them."

Plato did not reply. He stood and stretched out his aching muscles.

"How did she take it?" Alameda asked, looking into Caterina's room.

"She's tough. If I were a betting man, I'd say it's made her more determined."

"To do what?"

"This—it won't shut her up."

"You ask me, she should get over the border as fast as she can. She won't last five minutes if she stays here." Alameda sighed. Plato thought he suddenly looked old, as if he had aged ten years overnight. "*Diablo*, Jesus. What are we going to do?"

Plato holstered his pistol. "We're gonna stand guard here until she's discharged, which I guess will be when the doctor comes to see her this morning. We'll make sure she's safe getting to where she wants to go. And then it's up to her." He put a hand on Alameda's shoulder. "Are you all right?"

"Not really. Couldn't sleep."

"Me neither."

"Go on," he said. "I'm fine. Take a break."

"Won't be long. I want to talk to her again when she wakes up."

He said he would take twenty minutes to get them both some breakfast from the canteen, and when Alameda lowered himself into the chair, his hand on the butt of his pistol, he quickly made for the elevator.

He did not mean to be very long.

Chapter Twenty-Two

MILTON CHANGED INTO his jeans and a reasonably clean shirt and walked to the hospital. He stopped in the coffee shop for an espresso and a copy of the morning paper. He scanned it quickly as he waited in line. There'd be nothing about the shooting at the restaurant yet. Instead, he saw a picture of some sort of memorial, a stone cross with a wreath propped up against it and a notice fixed up with wire. When he got to the checkout he asked the girl what time they got the afternoon edition.

"I don't know," she said. "I don't read it."

"Can't say I blame you."

"Haven't read it for years."

"Is that right?"

"Don't you think it's all too depressing? When was the last time you read anything good in the newspaper?"

Milton shook his head. "I don't know," he said. "Probably quite a long while."

"I'll say," she said. "A long while."

He handed her a ten-dollar bill. "I'm looking for a friend," he said. "Young girl. Brought in last night. Gunshot wound. You know where they would've taken her?"

"Try up on the sixth floor," she advised.

Milton told her to keep the change and followed her directions. There was a triage area and then a corridor with separate rooms running off it. He went down the corridor, looking into each room, looking for the girl. There was an empty chair at the door to the last room from the end. He walked quietly to the door and looked inside: the girl was there, asleep, her chest rising and falling gently beneath a single white bed sheet. A man in a white doctor's coat was leaning over her. A loose pillow was lying across the girl's legs. The man reached out his right hand, the fingers brushing against the pillow, then closing around it.

Milton opened the door all the way. "Excuse me."

The man looked up and around.

"Hello."

"Who are you?"

He had smooth brown skin, black hair, an easy smile. There was nothing remarkable about him. The kind of man you would never see coming. "My name is Martinez," he said. "I'm a doctor here. Who are you?"

Milton ignored the question. "What are you doing?"

"Checking that she is okay." He picked up the pillow and tossed it onto the armchair at the side of the bed. "Just making her comfortable."

Milton tapped a finger to his breast. "You don't have any credentials."

The man looked down at his white medical jacket, shrugging with a self-deprecating smile. "I've just come on shift. Must've left it in my locker. Thanks."

"You're welcome."

"Do you know her?"

"I'm a friend."

The doctor looked over Milton's shoulder, and for a tiny moment, a flicker of something—irritation, perhaps, or frustration—fell across his face. He replaced it with a warm, friendly smile. "Nice to meet you, Señor—?"

"Smith."

"Señor Smith. I'm sure I'll see you again."

The man smiled again, stepped around him, and left the room. Milton turned to watch him go just as the policeman from last night, Lieutenant Plato, came in the other direction. The two met in the corridor, Plato stepping to the side to let the other man pass.

Plato was carrying two wrapped burritos. He didn't look surprised to see him. "Who was that?"

"Said he was a doctor, but there was something about him. Seen him before?"

"No."

Milton started to move.

"Was there anyone else here?" Plato asked. "There should've been—"

"No one else."

Plato's face twisted with anxiety. "Is she all right?"

"You better check."

Milton walked quickly and then broke into a jog, passing through the busying triage area to the lobby beyond. The elevator was on the first floor, so he couldn't have taken that. He pushed the bar to open the door to the stairs and looked up and then down. There was no sign of Martinez anywhere. He quickly climbed to the seventh floor, but as he opened the door onto a paediatrics ward, he couldn't see him. He went back down, then descended further, to the fifth, but there was still no sign of him. The man had disappeared.

Chapter Twenty-Three

PLATO SAT on the chair, and Milton stood with his back to the wall. They ate the breakfast burritos that Plato had purchased in the canteen.

"How many people died last night?"

Plato looked at him evenly. "Two of the three on the table—the girl died at the scene, the guy was DOA by the time they got him here. Apart from them, one woman eating her dinner got shot in the head. Three dead, all told, and that's not even counting the five *sicarios* you took out. *Caramba*, what a world."

"The girl who died?"

"That's the coincidental part. Her name was Delores. Poor little thing. I knew I recognised her when they were wheeling her out. I found her a month ago on Avenue Azucenas. Half undressed and beside herself with panic. She was a worker in the *maquiladoras*. She'd been abducted and raped, but she managed to get away."

"You think that had something to do with it?"

He shrugged. "Looks to me like she was there to talk to Caterina. Tell her story, maybe. I don't know—maybe that's why they got shot."

"Why would Caterina want to talk to her?"

Milton knew that the information was confidential, but after just a moment of reluctance, Plato shrugged and said, "She's a journalist. This isn't a safe place to write about the news. The cartels don't like to read about themselves. The dead guy was another writer."

"Newspaper?"

"No," Plato said, shaking his head. "They're online. They call it Blog del Borderland. It's started to be a pretty big deal, not just here but over the border, too. There was a piece in the El Paso *Times* just last week, all about them, and someone told me they've got a book coming out, too. The cartels are all they write about. The shootings, the abductions. It's like an obsession. Most papers won't touch that stuff, or if they do, they don't write about it truthfully. It's all under control, there's nothing to worry about—you know the sort of thing. These kids are different. They've had writers go missing and get murdered before, but it hasn't stopped them yet. This time, though? I don't know, maybe they'll listen now."

"What would you do—if you were her?"

"I'd try to get over the border. But that won't be easy. As far as I can make out, she doesn't have any family here. No ties. She doesn't have a job. She's not the kind of person who gets a visa. As far as I know, no journalist has ever been given one. And I doubt she'd even get a border crossing card. They'll say the chances of her staying over there illegally are too great."

"So?"

"Join the dots. If she's going to get across, she'll have to do it the other way."

Milton finished the burrito, screwed up the paper, and dropped it into the bin. "That doctor—?"

"Who knows. My guess? He was someone they sent to finish her off, and you got here just in time."

"You didn't recognise him?"

"No. No reason why I would."

"Why was she unguarded?"

He frowned. "You'd have to ask my captain that."

"But you're still here."

"How can I leave her on her own?" he said helplessly. "I've got daughters."

"I'll stay with her."

Plato finished his burrito and wiped his hands with a napkin. "Why would you want to do a thing like that?"

"Like you say—how can we leave her on her own. I'm guessing you boys will have to leave her as soon as they discharge her, right?"

"Right."

"And how long do you reckon she'll last without any protection at all? Christ, they almost got her when she was supposed to be guarded. She won't last five minutes, and you know it."

Plato exhaled wearily. "What's your story?—really?"

"You don't want to know."

"You need to give me a reason to let you stay."

"I can help. Come on—you know I can. You saw what I can do. You know I could be useful. That's why you told me where to find her."

"Maybe it was. And maybe I shouldn't've done that, putting you in harm's way as well as her."

"I can look after myself."

"They'll come back again. What makes you think you can stop them?"

"Because I'm not afraid of them, Lieutenant."

Chapter Twenty-Four

THE GIRL was awake. She had shuffled back in bed so that she was resting against the headboard, her knees bent beneath the sheet. Her black hair fanned out behind her, long strands running across her shoulders and across the pastel blue hospital pyjamas and the white of the bandage on her right shoulder. She was staring at Milton through the window. He got up from the chair, knocked on the door, and went inside.

"Hello," he said.

"Who are you?"

"My name's Smith."

"Have we met?"

"Not really."

She looked at him. "No. I recognise you. You were there last night. You work in the restaurant, don't you?"

"I did. Doubt there's a job for me there any more."

"You helped us."

"I did my best."

The conversation tailed off. She was nervous, and Milton felt awkward about it. He pointed to the armchair next to the bed. "Do you mind?"

She shrugged. Her right hand tensed and gripped the edge of the sheet. He could see the tendons moving in her wrist.

He moved the pillow out of the way and sat down. "How are you feeling?"

"Like I just got shot in the shoulder."

"You were lucky—it could've been much worse."

A bitter laugh. "Lucky? I wouldn't call that luck. And my friends—"

"Yes. They were very unlucky. I'm sorry about them."

Her chin quivered a little. She controlled it, a frown

furrowing her brow. He turned his head and looked at her. She was slender and well put together. He saw that her nails were trimmed and painted. She had an intelligent face, sensitive, but her smoky eyes looked weary.

"Do you have any next of kin I could call?" he said.

"No. My parents are dead. I had a brother, but he's dead, too."

"Husband? Boyfriend?"

Her lip quivered again. "I'm not married. And my boyfriend—my boyfriend got shot last night."

"I'm sorry," he said.

She went quiet again. She stared out into the corridor and blinked, like she was about to cry. Like she was ready for it all to come out. Milton found that he was holding his breath. He didn't know what he would do if she started to cry. He wasn't particularly good with things like that.

"I spoke to Lieutenant Plato," he said.

"Does he think I killed her?"

"Who?"

"Delores—the girl—it's my fault she's dead."

"How could it be your fault?"

"She was safe as long as she kept out of the way."

"Of course it isn't your fault."

"I persuaded her to come and talk to me. I went on and on and on at her. Because of that, now she's dead."

Milton didn't know what to say to that. He started to mumble something that he hoped might be reassuring, but she cut him off.

"Why are you here?"

"Because you're not safe, Caterina."

"I can look after myself," she said, her eyes shining fiercely.

"They came back this morning. A man pretending to be a doctor. I saw him off, but it'll get worse as soon as they discharge you."

"Then I'll hide," she said angrily. "I've managed until now."

"I'm sure you have."

He watched her. She was pretty, and her fieriness made her even more attractive.

"Caterina—I want to help."

"You're wasting your time. I don't have any money, and even if I did, I wouldn't give it to you."

"I don't want money."

"Then what?"

"I help people who need it."

"Like some sort of charity?"

"I wouldn't put it like that."

"And I do? Need help?"

"The odds are against you. I can even the odds. That's what I do."

"You know what the cartel is capable of. You saw it. Last night was just them being playful. If they really want to come after me, there won't be anything that anyone can do about it. I'm sorry, Señor Smith, it's not that I don't appreciate the offer, and I don't want to be rude, but at the end of the day, you work in a kitchen."

He let that settle for a moment. And then he said, staring at her evenly, "I did other things before that."

Chapter Twenty-Five

BEAU'S SNAKESKIN cowboy boots clipped and clopped as he stepped out of the red Jeep Cherokee and walked across the pavement and into the hospital. There was a florist in the reception—a pathetic display of flowers, most of them half-dead and fading away in the broil of the early morning sun—but he found a halfway decent bunch of bougainvillea, then went to the shop and supplemented it with a bag of withered and juiceless grapes. He went to the desk and, putting on his friendliest smile, said he was looking for the girl who had survived the shooting at the restaurant last night, said he was her brother. The nurse looked down to the bouquet, bright colours against the blue of the suit, looked up at the warm smile, bought the story all the way, and told him that he could find her on the sixth floor, towards the back of the building, and that he hoped he had a nice day. Beau thanked her most kindly and made his way to the elevator.

He got in and pressed the button for the second floor. The doors closed and the elevator ascended. He stood with his back to the wall, looked down at the toe of his boot, lifted his leg and rubbed the toe against the back of his jeans to clean it off. The lights for each passing floor glowed on the display until the elevator reached the sixth. The doors opened. He reached inside his jacket, his fingers brushing against the inlaid handle of the revolver that was holstered to his belt, and stepped out.

The place smelt of hospitals: detergent and, beneath that, rot. The girl was in a room at the end of a corridor. Beau walked easily down towards it, his heels striking the floor noisily. As he approached, a man who had been leaning against the door jamb, just out of sight, peeled off the wall and stepped out into the corridor. He took a step forwards and blocked the way.

"Who are you?" the man said.

"Beau Baxter. Who are you?"

"Smith."

Beau grinned. "Mr. Smith—?"

The man smiled, or at least, his taut, thin lips rose a little at the edges. "John Smith. What do you do, Mr. Baxter?"

Beau looked him over. Not much to him, really, at least on the surface: a little taller than average, a little slimmer than average for someone his size, running two hundred, maybe two ten. Caucasian, a nasty scar on his face. Salt-and-pepper hair. Heavy, untidy beard. Around forty, maybe. The kind of man who'd be swallowed up by the crowd. He knew that sort. He was anonymous, at least until you looked a little harder. His eyes were different; they were cold and dark, enough to give a man a moment of reflection, a chance to think about things.

Beau shrugged. "I'm thinking you know what I do. Me and you, I'm guessing we're in the same line of work."

"I doubt that. Let me put it a different way: what are you doing here?"

He held up the wilting bouquet. "I brought the girl some flowers."

"She doesn't want them."

"I want to speak to her."

"I don't think so. Not while I'm here."

They both looked through the dirty window into the room. Caterina was sitting up in bed as a doctor examined the wound on her shoulder.

"You're the cook, right? I heard what you did."

"And how would you know about that?"

"My line of business, it pays me to know people who know things."

"Police?"

"Sure—among others."

"What do you want?"

"She had any visitors? Unexpected ones?"

Milton looked at him. He didn't answer.

"Let me describe him for you, tell me how close I am: he's in his forties, his hair is perfectly black, plain skin, smiles a lot but there's something going on beneath the smile that you don't feel too comfortable about. How am I doing?"

"Close enough."

"Thought so—can we talk about him?"

"Talk, then."

"When was it?"

"Half an hour ago."

"And what happened?"

"I scared him off."

"I doubt that. He's a bad man."

"There are a lot of bad men."

"Not like him. He's one of a kind."

"I wouldn't be so sure about that."

"I can get him out of the way."

"You think I can't do that myself?"

"I doubt it. You don't know what you're up against."

"And you don't know who I am."

"I know you ain't no cook." He smiled at him. "Okay. What do you know about him?"

The man didn't answer.

"You speak Spanish?"

"Enough."

"They call him Santa Muerte. Know what that means?"

"Saint Death."

"That's right: Saint Death. Bit grandiose, I'll give you that, but believe me, this dude, my word, he backs it up. This is not a man you want to know. Those people he takes a personal interest in, they tend not to be around for long after he's introduced himself, you know what I mean?"

"I've met people like that before. I'm still here."

He held Beau's gaze without flinching. It was rare to

meet a man like this. It didn't look as if he had an ounce of fright in him. He was either brave or he had no idea what he was dealing with. "You're a long way from home, bro. That accent—English, right?"

"Yes."

"All right, then, old partner. Let me just lay it out for you. Imagine living in a place where you can kill anyone you want and nothing happens except they drop down dead. You won't get arrested. Your name won't get in the papers. You can just carry on with things like nothing has happened. You can kill again, too, just keep on going, and nothing will be different. Look at your friend in there— you can take a woman, anyone you want, and you can rape her for days and nothing will happen. And, once you're done with her, you can kill her, too. Nothing will happen. That kind of place? You're in it. That's Juárez, through and through."

"Sounds awful."

He stripped the good humour from his voice. "You need to pay attention, Mr. Smith. This man, Santa Muerte, even in a place as fucked up as this, he's the worst of the worst. Top of the food chain. What you'd call the apex predator. And you have his attention now. Undivided. All of it. I know what you did in the restaurant. I know what you did here, too, sending him away. And now he's not going to stop. Men like him, they survive because of their reputations. People start to think he's lost his edge, maybe they start getting brave, maybe someone who bears a grudge decides now's the time to get their revenge and stamp his ticket for him. *Reputation*, man. He has to kill you now. And there's nothing you can do to stop him short of putting a bullet in his head."

"What does this have to do with you?"

"I can help you. My line of work: I find people, I settle accounts, I solve problems. And my employers—this group of Italians, not men you'd want to cross—these men, well, see, they have good reason to speak to him.

They had a business arrangement with the organisation he works for. Didn't go to plan. He sent them a video, one of theirs hung upside down from a tree while he sawed off his head with a machete. They're paying me to bring him back to the States. They'd prefer him alive, but that don't really matter, not really, they'll take him dead if that's the only way I can get him to them. And I will get him eventually. The only question is whether it's after he's killed you and your friend in there or before. I don't have any reason to protect you, but I will if you help me out."

"I'll take my chances."

Beau stood up and straightened out the fall of his trousers. "I don't know why, but he wants the girl. He'll drop out of sight now. You won't be able to find him. He'll bide his time, and then he'll come after her. And that's when you'll need me." He took a pen from his pocket, and tearing off a square of the brown paper sheaf that was wrapped around the flowers, he wrote down a number. He handed it to the man. "This is me. When you're ready to start thinking about how to get her out of the almighty motherfucking mess she's got herself into, you give me a call, all right?"

"What's his name?"

"His real name? I've heard lots of possibilities, but I don't know for sure."

"You're sure I can't find him?"

"Have you been listening to me? You don't find him, man. He finds you."

Chapter Twenty-Six

THEY DISCHARGED Caterina a little before midday. The doctor said that she would be fine; there were no vascular injuries, no bones had been clipped, it was all just flesh. They had performed a quick fasciotomy while she was out cold and had cleared away the fabric from her shirt that had been sucked into the wound, and removed the dead tissue. The doctor checked the sutures were holding, gave her a tetanus shot, told her to take it easy, and sent her on her way. Milton led her to the elevator, shielding her as they stepped out into the lobby downstairs.

Lieutenant Plato was waiting for them.

"How are you feeling?" he asked her.

"Better now. Thank you."

"Do you know where you're going?"

"A hotel."

"I was going to ask you," Milton said to him. "What would be a good hotel?"

Plato chuckled. "You know all the hotels get booked?"

"By who?"

"The narcos own them," Caterina answered. "They book the room, but no one ever stays. Perfect way to launder all their money."

"There is a place," Plato said. "La Playa Consulado, up by the border. You should be able to get in there."

"Thanks."

"And then?"

"New Mexico. Señor Smith says he's going to help me. Doesn't seem I have much choice in the matter."

"All right, then. You keep your head down. If I need to speak to you about what happened—the investigation and what have you—I'll be in touch." He reached out a hand,

and she took it. "Good luck, Caterina."

Milton led Caterina out of the hotel. The midday heat was like a furnace. It was so fierce that it had just about cleared the streets, forcing everyone inside. A siesta sounded pretty good right around now, he thought. Those people who were out looked punch-drunk and listless. He led the way down to the cab stand, opened the door of the cab parked there, and ushered her inside.

The car was air-conditioned.

"You know the La Playa Consulado?" he said.

The driver looked at him in the mirror. "Near the US Consulate?"

"That's the one."

"*Sí*—I know it."

They drove out, Milton checking that they were not being followed. If the narcos were good, there would be no way of knowing, but they would have to be very good, and Milton didn't see anything suspicious.

"What about you?" Caterina asked him suddenly.

"What about me?"

"I told you about me. What about you? You married?"

"I was, once. She left me."

"Oh—I'm sorry."

"Don't be."

"Family?"

"My parents died when I was little. No brothers or sisters."

"Girlfriend?"

"I'm never in the same place long enough to get attached."

"You must have someone?"

"Not really," he said with a wry smile. "This is it."

"I'm sorry about that," she said.

"For what?"

"That you're alone."

"Don't be. I choose to be that way."

"You're not lonely?"

"No. It's the way I like it. To be honest, I'm not the best company. I doubt anyone would put up with me for all that long, not unless they had to."

"And you move around a lot?"

"All the time."

"Why Mexico?"

"Why not? I've been heading north the best part of six months. Mexico was just the next place on the way."

"And Juárez? How long have you been here?"

"I got in on Monday."

She stared out of the window. "Good timing."

"I don't know," he said. "I'm glad I was there. It could've been a lot worse."

"But why here? Most people would go a hundred miles in either direction."

"Then I suppose I'm not most people."

"Why do you move around so much? Are you running from something?"

My history, he thought, but rather than that he said, "Not really. I just needed some time alone. To clear my head."

"From what?"

"That doesn't really matter, Caterina."

She thought about his answer. He saw her tension coming back, and she was quiet again.

La Playa Consulado was on Paseo De La Victoria. A two-storey motor court set around a large parking lot, an ugly sign outside advertising Restaurant Cebollero and its flautas, tacos and *hamburguesas*. Milton got out first, his hand resting on the burning roof of the cab as he checked again that they had not been followed. Satisfied, he stepped aside so that Caterina could get out, paid the driver, and went into the reception. Net curtains, wood panels, décor from deep into the eighties. A woman was sitting watching a chat show on TV. She got up and went around behind the desk.

"We need two rooms, one next to the other."

"I can do that. How many nights?"

"I don't know. Let's say a week."

"Weekly rate's forty-five dollars per night plus two dollars seventy-five tax. Cash or card?"

"Discount for cash?"

She took out a calculator and tapped it out. "No discount, sir. Forty-seven dollars, seventy-five cents per night, times two, times seven. That's six hundred and sixty-eight dollars and fifty cents."

Milton took out a roll of notes from his pocket and peeled off seven hundred-dollar bills. He gave them to the woman. "If anyone asks, we're not here. No visitors. No messages, at any time. No one cleans the rooms." He peeled off another note and laid it on the desk. "Is that going to be all right?"

"Absolutely fine, sir."

Milton took the two keys and led the way outside again, following a scrappy path around the parking lot to the row of rooms. He opened the door to the first room, number eleven, and went inside. He waited until Caterina had followed, shut the door again, and closed the curtains. He checked the room: a queen-sized bed with a heavy wooden headboard and a garish quilt cover; purple carpets, stained in places; an artexed asbestos ceiling; a print of a vase of flowers on the wall; and a bathroom with shower. Light from outside came in through the net curtains. Milton switched on the overhead light.

Caterina sat down heavily on the bed.

Milton stood at the window, parted the curtains a little, and looked out through them at the courtyard outside. A few cars, lots of empty spaces, plastic rubbish and newspaper snagged in the branches of sickly creosote bushes. He ran things over in his mind. He got two glasses of water from the bathroom and came back and went to the window again. He took a sip and set the water on the cheap bedside table. Halfway there, he thought.

Caterina slumped back on the bed. "This is crazy. I

can't hide here forever."

"Just for a few days."

"So you can do what?"

"I know someone who'll be able to help you get across the border."

"In exchange for what? I told you I don't have any money."

"He has a problem I can help him with. And there's no harm in you staying here until I can do that, is there?"

She shook her head and stared straight up at the stippled ceiling. "I don't suppose so. I know I can't go home."

"Is there anything you need?"

"Nothing we can't get in New Mexico."

"Sure?"

"There is something—we've got another couple of writers. I have to get word to them."

"Call them?"

"Their details are on my laptop. I need that; then I can mail them."

"Where is it?"

"In my apartment."

"All right—I'll get it. Write down your address."

She did, writing it on a page that she tore from the Gideon's Bible in the drawer. Milton closed the curtains.

"You're not just a cook, are you?"

"No."

"You were a soldier."

"Yes."

"What kind of soldier?"

He thought about what to say. He had a sudden urge to be completely truthful, but he knew that might not be the best policy with her—good for him, bad for her—so he evaded the question a little. "I was in the special forces for a while. And then I was transferred to work for a special detail. I can't really tell you very much about that."

"You were good at it?"

"Very good," he said.

"Have you've killed people before?"

"I have."

She fell silent.

He found the TV remote and tossed it across to the bed. "Try to get some sleep," he said. "And I know you're not stupid, but lock and chain the door, and don't open it to anybody but me. All right?"

"You're going now?"

"There are some things I need to get, too. I might be back late. Maybe this evening. All right?"

She said that she was.

"Don't open the door."

Chapter Twenty-Seven

MILTON TOOK a taxi to the border and then got out and walked. The Paso del Norte Bridge spanned the Rio Bravo, and he took his place in the queue of people waiting to cross. He paid three pesos at the kiosk and pushed through the turnstile. A couple of hundred strides to reach the middle, where Mexico ended and the United States began. He paused there and looked down. The floodplain stretched beneath him, the Rio Bravo a pathetic trickle slithering between stands of Carrizo cane—a chain-link fence on either side, tall guard-posts with guards toting rifles, spotlights and CCTV.

The American gatepost was worse, bristling with security. He walked towards it and joined the queue. Well-to-do housewives chatted about the shopping they were going to do. Bored children bounced. Kids slung book bags over their shoulders, waiting to pass through to their Methodist schools. Vendors hawked hamburgers, cones of fried nuts and bottles of water. A woman in a white dress with a guitar sang folk songs, a handful of change scattered in the torn-off cardboard box at her feet.

It took an hour for Milton to get to the front.

"Hello, sir," the wary border guard said. "Your passport, please."

Milton took out the fake American passport that he had been using since he arrived in South America. He handed it to her.

"Mr. Smith," she said, comparing him with the photograph. "You've been away for a while, sir."

"Travelling."

She stamped the passport. "Welcome home, sir."

He walked through into America.

Milton had a fifteen-minute cab ride to get to where he

was going. He fished out his phone from his pocket and took the scrap of paper that the man in the hospital had given to him from out of his wallet. He dialled the number and put the phone to his ear.

"Baxter?"

"Who's this?"

"John Smith."

"Mr. Smith. How are you, sir?"

"Our friend—how much is he worth to you?"

"He's worth plenty—why? You ready to help?"

"If you help me—then perhaps."

"How much do you want?"

"Nothing. No money. I need you to do me a favour."

"I'm listening."

"Those Italians you work for—I'm guessing it's a reasonably simple thing for them to bring someone across the border?"

"Sure. I've got to get our mutual friend across, and I'm damn sure I ain't taking him over the bridge. I don't reckon it'd be any great shakes to add another to the trip. Who do you got in mind?"

"The girl."

"Makes sense. Yeah—I reckon I could do that. Anything else?"

"A new life for her on the other side. Legitimate papers in a different name. Away from El Paso. Somewhere where they'll never find her."

"That's a bit more demanding. But maybe."

"What would you have to do?"

"Make a couple of calls. You on this number all day?"

Milton said that he was.

"I'll call you later."

The taxi had arrived. Milton put the telephone away, paid the driver, and got out.

The El Paso gun show was held every Saturday at the El Maida Shrine Centre at 6331 Alabama Street. A sign outside the venue advertised roller derbies, pet adoption fairs and home and garden shows, but it was obvious that guns were the big draw. He paid sixteen bucks at the entrance and went inside.

He had seen the show advertised in *El Diario*, a whole-page advert that promised that every gun that he could imagine would be available to buy. Milton could imagine a lot of guns, but after just five minutes, he saw the claim wasn't fanciful. The place was like a bazaar. Several long aisles had been formed by tables arranged swap-meet style, dozens of vendors on one side of them and several hundred people on the other. Milton recognised the hunters, but there were plenty of people buying for other reasons, too. He watched with a detached sense of professional interest as a rotund and cheerful white-bearded man, easily in his seventies, walked past with an ArmaLite and attached bayonet slung casually over his shoulder. A blue-rinsed lady of similar age negotiated hard for extra ammunition for the Smith & Wesson she was purchasing. Other shoppers were pushing handcarts of ammunition out to their trucks.

Milton sauntered along the aisle, looking for the right kind of seller. It didn't take long to find one: the man had a table covered in blue felt, with a selection of weapons sitting on their carry cases, a handwritten sign on the table reading PRIVATE SELLER/NO PAPER. The slogan on the man's black wifebeater read "When All Else Fails, Vote from the Rooftops!" and revealed sleeves of tattoos up both arms. He wore a baseball cap with a camouflage design.

"Afternoon, sir," he said.

"What do I need to buy from you?"

"Cash and carry. No background check, I don't need no address—don't really need nothing, no sir. This is a private party sale. What are you looking for?"

"What have you got?"

The man cast his hand across the heaving table. "I keep a nice selection. All the way from these little stainless steel Derringers, good for concealment, to the long guns. I got the Ruger .22—extremely popular gun. I got weapons with pink grips, for the ladies, engraved pieces with inlaid handles and decorative stocks. Walthers, Smith & Wessons. A lot of people are shooting .40 calibres. Those are pretty vicious. I got revolvers—"

"No, automatic."

"I have nice automatics. I got modern plastic guns. I got the Glock, I got the Springfield. And then, over here, I got the Mac semi-autos all the way up to the rifles: the .208s, the .223s. I got an AK-47 and an AR-15, a .50 calibre with fluted barrel and sniper green finish."

Milton looked down at the metalware lined up across the table. They were all expertly made, although he found it easier to feel affection and admiration for the collector's items with the wooden butts than for the coldly efficient and inorganic weapons that made sense only in combat. The cold grey foreboding of an AR-15. The leaden heaviness of the Czech MFP, modelled on the Kalashnikov.

He picked up a Springfield Tactical .45 auto.

"How much?"

"$480, cash money, and it's all yours, out the door you go."

"I'll take it."

"You want ammo with that, too?"

The Springfield boxed thirteen rounds per magazine; Milton bought four, mixed factory hardball and jacketed hollow points from Federal and Remington, for a straight hundred.

He paid the man, thanked him and went back outside. It was seven in the evening by now, and the winds had picked up. The faint orange dust that had hung in the windless morning had been whipped up into a storm, and now it was rolling in off the desert. He took a taxi back to the border and was halfway across the span of the bridge when the storm swept over Juárez. Sand and dust stung his face and visibility was immediately reduced: first the mountains disappeared, then the belching smokestacks on the edge of town, and then, as the storm hunkered down properly over the city, details of the immediate landscape began to fade and blur. The streetlights that ran along the centre of the bridge shone as fuzzy penumbras in the sudden darkness.

Milton's phone buzzed in his pocket. He took it out and pressed it to his ear.

"It's Beau Baxter."

"And?"

"Smith, are you outside in *this*?"

Milton ignored the question. "Get to it. Can you help?"

"Yeah, it can be done. You help me with our mutual friend, I'll help get the girl where she wants to get and set her up with a nice new identity. Job, place to live, everything she needs. Want to talk about it?"

"We should."

"All right, buddy—tomorrow evening. There's a joint here, does the best huaraches you've ever tasted, and I'm not kidding. I always visit whenever I'm in Juárez, compensation for having to come to this godforsaken fucking town in the first place. It's at the Plaza Insurgentes, on Avenida de los Insurgentes. Get a taxi, they'll know. Eight o'clock, all right?"

Milton said that he would be there and ended the call.

The lights of Juárez faded in and out through the eddies of dust and grit. The Hotel Coahuila's neon throbbed on and off, a huge sign with a girl wearing *bandolero* belts and brandishing Kalashnikov machine guns. He passed a police recruitment poster with a ninja-cop in a balaclava and the slogan *"Juárez te necesita!"*—Juárez Needs You. There was no one in the gate shack on the Mexican side of the river. No passport control, no customs checks, no one to notice the Springfield that was tucked into the back of his jeans or the clips of ammunition that he had stuffed into the pockets of his jacket. There was no queue, either, and he pushed his way through the creaking turnstile and crossed back into Juárez.

Chapter Twenty-Eight

THE STORM gathered strength. Milton took a taxi to the address that Caterina had given him. He told the driver to stop two blocks earlier and, paying him with a twenty-dollar bill, told him to stay and wait if he wanted another. He got out, the sand and grit swirling around him, lashing into his exposed skin, and walked the rest of the way. It was a cheap, dingy area, rows of houses that had been sliced up to make apartments. He passed one house, the road outside filled with SUVs with tinted windows. The cars were occupied, the open door of one revealing a thickset man in the uniform of the *federales*. The man turned as Milton passed, cupping his hand around a match as he lit a cigarette, the glow of the flame flickering in unfriendly eyes. Milton kept going.

Caterina's apartment was just a few doors down the street. Milton felt eyes on his back and turned; two of the SUVs were parked alongside one another, their headlights burrowing a golden trough through the snarling, swirling dust. He turned back to the house, walking slowly so that he could squint through the sand at the third floor. There was light in one of the windows; a shadow passed across it. A quick, fleeting silhouette, barely visible through the darkness and the grit in the air.

Her window?

He wasn't sure.

A narrow alleyway cut through the terrace between one address and its neighbour, and Milton turned into it, gambling that there was another way inside around the back. The roiling abated as he passed inside the passageway, but it wasn't lit, the darkness deepening until he could barely see the way ahead. He reached around for the Springfield and pulled it out, aiming it down low, his finger resting gently on the trigger.

The passageway opened into a narrow garden, fenced on both sides, most of the wooden panels missing, the ones that were left creaking on rotting staves as the wind piled against them. The ground was scrub, knee-high weeds and grasses, scorched clear in places from where a dog had pissed. There was a back extension attached to the ground-floor property, no lights visible anywhere. He looked up: there was a narrow Juliet balcony on the third floor. There was his way inside. Milton climbed onto a water butt and then boosted himself onto the flat roof, scraping his palms against the rough bitumen. He stuffed the Springfield back into his trousers and shinned up the drainpipe until he was high enough to reach out for the bottom of the balcony, shimmied along a little and then hauled himself up so that he could wedge his feet between the railings.

He leaned across and risked a look inside.

There was no light now.

He took the gun and pushed the barrel gently against the doors. They were unlocked, and they parted with a dry groan. He hauled his legs over the railing, and aware that even in the dim light of the storm he would still be offering an easy target to anyone inside, he crouched low and shuffled forwards.

He heard movement in the adjacent room: feet shuffling across linoleum.

Milton rose and made towards the sound. He edged carefully through the dark room, avoiding the faint outlines of the furniture.

He reached the door. It was open, showing into the kitchen. The digital clock set into the cooker gave out enough dim light to illuminate the room: it was small, with the cooker, a fridge, a narrow work surface on two sides and cupboards above. A man was working his way through the cupboards, opening them one by one and going through them. Looking for something.

Milton took a step towards him, clipping his foot on the waste bin.

The man swivelled, a kitchen knife in his hand. He slashed out with it.

Milton blocked the man's swipe with his right forearm, taking the impact just above his wrist and turning his hand over so that he could grip the edge of the man's jacket. The man grunted, trying to free himself, but Milton plunged in with his left hand, digging the fingers into the fleshy pressure point behind the thumb, pinching so hard that the knife dropped out of his hand. It had taken less than three seconds to disarm him. Maintaining his grip, Milton dragged the man's arm around behind his back and yanked it up towards his shoulders, pushing down at the same time. The man's head slammed against the work surface.

"Who do you work for?" he said.

"Fuck you, gringo."

Milton raised his head a little and slammed it back against the work surface.

"Who do you work for?"

"Fuck you."

Milton reached across and twisted the dial on the hob, the gas hissing out of the burner. He pushed the button to ignite it, the light from the blue flame guttering around the dark kitchen. He guided the man towards the hob, scraping his forehead across the work surface and then the unused burners, raising him a little over the lit one so that he could feel the heat.

His voice remained steady and even, implacable, as if holding a man's face above a lit flame was the most normal thing in the world. "Let's try again. Who do you work for?"

The man whimpered. There was a quiet yet insistent crackle as his whiskers started to singe. "I can't—"

"Who?"

"They'll—they'll kill me."

133

Milton pushed him a little closer to the flame. His eyebrows began to crisp. "You need to prioritise," he suggested. "They're not here. I am. And I will kill you if you don't tell me."

He pushed him nearer to the flame.

"El Patrón," the man said in a panicked garble. "It's El Patrón. Please. My face."

"What are you looking for?"

"The girl—the girl."

"But she's not here. What else?"

"Contacts."

"Why?"

"They've been writing about La Frontera. El Patrón—he wants to make an example of them."

Milton turned the man's head a little so he could see him better. "Where can I find him?"

The man laughed hysterically. "I don't know! Just look around. He's everywhere." He squinted at him. "Why would you even wanna know that?"

"I need to speak to him. He needs to leave the girl alone."

"And you think he'll listen?"

"I think he will."

"Who *are* you, man?"

"Just a cook."

The man laughed again, a desperate sound. "No, I tell you what you are—you're fucked. What you gonna do now? Call the *federales?* How you think that's going to go down, eh? You stupid gringo—El Patrón, he *owns* the cops."

"I won't need the cops."

Milton snaked his right arm around the man's throat and started to squeeze. The man struggled, got his legs up, and kicked off the wall. Milton stumbled backwards, and they went to the floor. The man was trying to get his hands inside Milton's arm, but he could not. Milton squeezed, the man's throat constricted in the nook of his arm. He braced his left arm vertically against his right, his right hand clasped around his left bicep, and he pulled back with that, too, tightening his grip all the time, his face turned away. The man was flailing wildly, his arms windmilling, and he scrabbled sideways over the floor, kicking over the waste bin, treading dusty prints up the kitchen cupboards. His sneakers squeaked against the linoleum floor. He was gurgling, a line of blood trickling from his mouth. He was choking on his own blood. Milton squeezed harder. The man's legs slowed and then stopped. Milton relaxed his grip. The man lay jerking. Then he stopped moving altogether.

Milton got up and flexed his aching arm. He poured himself a glass of water and drank it, studying the dead man gaping up from the floor. Early twenties, a cruel face, even in death. His eyes bulged, and his tongue lolled out of blue-tinged lips. He crouched down next to the body, frisking it quickly: a mobile phone, a wallet with three hundred dollars, a small transparent bag of cocaine. Milton took the money and the phone, discarding the wallet and the cocaine, and then took a dishcloth and a bottle of disinfectant he found under the sink and cleaned down anything that he might have touched. He wiped the glass and put it back in the cupboard. He wiped the tap. He wiped the hob.

Milton took the man's torch and went into the bedroom. The laptop, covered in stickers and decals—WikiLeaks, DuckDuckGo, Megaupload—was under the mattress, where Caterina said it would be. He slipped it into a black rucksack he found in the closet and dropped the Springfield and the ammunition in after it. He climbed down from the balcony and followed the passageway back to the front of the house. The storm had still not passed. Visibility was poor. Milton walked back in the same direction from which he had arrived. He passed the parked SUVs, ignoring the man smoking a cigarette in the open door, his eyes fixed straight ahead. He found the taxi again and got in.

"La Playa Consulado," he said.

He bought cheeseburgers, fries and Big Gulps from the take-out next to the hotel. He could hear the sound of the television as he approached the door to Caterina's room. The curtains were drawn, but light flickered against the edges. Milton stopped in his room first, taking out the revolver and ammunition and the things that he had taken from the dead man, hiding them under the sheet. He locked the door behind him and knocked for Caterina.

"Who is it?"

"It's John."

He heard the bedsprings as she got to her feet and then her footsteps as she crossed the room. The lock turned, and the door opened. Milton went inside.

"You were hours."

"I'm sorry. It took longer than I thought. Was everything all right?"

"The cleaner tried to come in, but I sent her away."

"Nothing else?"

"No. I've been watching TV all day."

She looked tired, and despite the permanent glare of defiance, her red-rimmed eyes said that she had been weeping.

"Here." Milton put the wrapped meals on the bed. Caterina was hungry and so was he; he realised that he hadn't had anything to eat since breakfast this morning. The meat in the cheeseburgers was poor, but they both finished quickly, moving onto the little cardboard sheaths of greasy fries. Milton watched the TV as he put the food away; Caterina had tuned it to a channel from El Paso: news about local Little League sports, a fun run to raise money for cancer research, the pieces linked by glossy presenters with white teeth and bright eyes. It was a different world north of the river, he thought. They had no idea what it was like down here.

Milton put the rucksack on the bed and took out the

laptop. "Is this what you wanted?"

"Perfect, thank you," she said. "Did you—did you have any trouble getting it?"

"No trouble at all."

Chapter Twenty-Nine

THREE MORE DAYS.

Jesus Plato reminded himself, again and again, as he stared up at the bridge.

It was Wednesday today.

Just three more days and then an end to all this.

It was a fresh morning, a cool wind blowing after the fury of the storm last night. Plato was at the concrete overpass known as Switchback Bridge. The bodies had been called in as dawn broke over the endless desert, ropes knotted beneath their armpits, tied to the guard rail, and the dead tossed over the side. They both dangled there, the rope creaking as they swung back and forth in the light breeze, twenty feet above the busy rush of traffic at the intersection. A small crowd of people had gathered to watch as a fire truck was manoeuvred around so that the ladder could get up to them. Former school busses from across the border, now ferrying workers to and from the sweatshops, jammed up against one another, and behind them, a queue of irate drivers leant on their horns. Just another day in Ciudad Juárez. Another morning, another murder. No one was surprised or shocked. It was an inconvenience. This was just how it was, and that, Plato thought, was the worst of it.

He could see that the bodies had both been decapitated. Hands had been tied behind their backs, and their feet flapped in the wind. He hadn't had a proper breakfast yet, just a Pop-Tart as he left the house, and he was glad. The bodies revolved clockwise and then counterclockwise, bumping up against each other, a grotesque and hideous display. They were suspended between advertising hoardings for Frutti Sauce and Comida Express fast food, and the *sicarios* had left their own message alongside their prey. A bed sheet was tied to the guard rail, and painted on it was a warning: "FREEDOM OF THE PRESS" and then "ATENCION—LA FRONTERA." A fireman scaled the ladder, and with help from colleagues on the bridge, the carcasses were untied, lowered to the ground, and wrapped in canvas sacks to be taken to the morgue.

Plato was about to head back to the station when he saw John Milton and Caterina Moreno. The girl was crouched down, leaning her back against the side of his Dodge, hugging her knees tight against her chest. Her face was pale, and on the ground next to her, there was a puddle of drying vomit. Milton was leaning against the bonnet, his face impassive and his arms folded across his chest.

"What are you doing here?" Plato asked him.

"She knows who they are."

"Who?"

"Up there." He pointed. "She knows them."

"Even without their—you know—without their heads?"

"They used to write for her blog."

"Shit."

"I know." Milton pushed himself away from the car and led Plato out of the girl's earshot. "She wanted to see them before I get her over the border. Warn them that they should get out, too. We went to their address, but—well, we were too late, obviously. The place had been turned over. We saw the bodies from the taxi as we were driving back to the hotel. Went right underneath them. They were husband and wife. Daniel and Susanna Ortega."

"This is what happens if you get on the wrong side of the cartels. There's nothing anyone can do about it."

He pointed to the bridge. "That wasn't a five-minute job. There must have been witnesses—passing traffic?"

"They don't care. No one's going to say anything."

Plato nodded to Caterina. "And it'll happen to her, too—they won't stop. When are you taking her across?"

"I'm working on that."

The white morgue van backed up and drove away. The fire truck was lowering its ladder.

"Work faster."

Chapter Thirty

FELIPE WATCHED from the car as the Cessna 210 touched down on the rough gravel runway that had been constructed right down the middle of the arid field. It had big tyres and metal strips under the nose to protect the engine from stones. It was one of several that Felipe owned. He had sent it north this morning, touching down in a similar field in New Mexico to collect its passengers and refuel, and then returned to deliver them to him here. He stepped out of the Jeep. Adolfo had already disembarked and was leaning against the bonnet, watching as the plane taxied across the field, dust kicking up from the oversized tyres. Felipe shielded his eyes against the sun and waited for the plane to come to a halt.

"Wait here," he said to his son.

"*Padre?*"

"Stay here."

He stared at him sourly. "Yes, *Padre.*"

"Pablo."

Felipe and Pablo crossed the desert to the plane. He was not particularly concerned about his guests. They would have been frisked before they got onto the plane, and he knew very well that the fear of his reputation was the most effective guarantee of his own security. That said, you couldn't be too careful, and with that in mind, Adolfo and the men in the second Jeep were all equipped with automatic rifles.

The ramp was lowered, and the three passengers inside descended. Felipe was wearing a Stetson; he removed it, wiped inside the rim with his handkerchief, wiped his forehead, and put the hat back on. He paused and allowed the gringos to come to him.

"El Patrón?" said the man who had stepped to the

front.

"That's right." He smiled at them. "Welcome to Mexico. How was your flight?"

"Was good—thanks for arranging it." He was a thick-limbed Texan, tall, a little colour in his face.

"You are Isaac?"

"I sure am."

"And your friends?"

"Kevin and Alejandro."

"Your business partners?"

"That's right."

Felipe smiled at the other two. His first impression: they were not particularly impressive. Isaac was the owner of the business that they were going to use and was, not surprisingly, the most interesting.

Felipe turned and indicated in the direction of the two Jeeps. Adolfo and the other two men were lounging against the vehicles, the brims of their hats pulled down to shield their eyes from the glare of the sun. "We'll drive back to Juárez and discuss our business."

"Forgive me, El Patrón," Isaac said. "Before we do, there's something I'd like to clear up."

Isaac was standing with the sun behind him, and Felipe couldn't see his face through the glare. Why hadn't he made sure that he had approached the plane from the opposite direction? He clenched his teeth in frustration at his error and Isaac's presumption. "Of course," he said, squinting a little and yet managing to smile.

"Listen, I hope you can forgive me—I don't mean to be blunt, but there's no point in pussyfooting around it, so I'm gonna come right out and get to the point. I'm sure you know all about this, but there's a whole lot of coverage about the girls that are going missing over here. Someone's been writing about it, and now the TV channels and newspapers and suchlike over the border have got hold of it."

"How is this relevant?"

"It's extra heat, right? More attention? Makes things more—what would you say—more *precarious*."

"I would say you shouldn't worry. And that you should trust me."

"I'd like to be able to say that I can, El Patrón, truly I would. I'm sure, in time, we'll come to trust each other like brothers. But now, well, we don't even know each other."

His tone suddenly lost the avuncular tone he had been working hard to maintain. "What does that have to do with us?"

"The word over the border is that your men are behind it. They say they're doing it for sport. Now, I'm sure that ain't true, El Patrón, because if it was, well, yessir, if someone was allowing them to get away with hijinks like that, then we'd have to question whether that someone was the sort of someone we'd want to get into business with. Not morally—I don't care about none of that. It's business—a person who'd allow someone to bring so much attention to his operation, well then, that wouldn't make no sense."

Besa mi culo, puto! Felipe breathed in and out: the sun in his eyes, the *huevos* on this man, coming over to Mexico as his guest and insulting his hospitality like this! It would have taken a moment for him to signal to Adolfo and his goons to bring up their rifles and perforate them, blow them away. All he would have to do would be to click his fingers. It was tempting, but he could not. Since he had ended his business relationship with the Luciano family— and ended it in such a way that a reconciliation was impossible—he needed Isaac and his *pajero* friends to distribute his product in the south-west. He had tonnes to move. Without them he would have to split the product between small-time operators, and that would mean less leverage for him, less profit and much greater risk. It was impossible.

So he forced himself to swallow his anger and cast out

a bright smile. "I know the stories, Isaac, and I can assure you, they are nothing to do with La Frontera. If I found out that my men were responsible, they would be dealt with. But they are not. The police here suspect a group of serial killers. In fact, they have already charged one man—perhaps you have read about that, too?"

Isaac shrugged. "That's what I thought."

"As I say, you needn't worry. Now—shall we go? There is much to discuss."

Chapter Thirty-One

ANNA THACKERAY had almost forgotten about John Milton. The results of the first sweep had come back negative and then the second and then the third. She had tried everything she could think of trying, feeding every combination of selectors through every megabit of data that they had. She ran it again and again and again, working well into the night, but every variation, every clever rephrasing, none of them returned anything that she could use. Since he had disappeared, it appeared that Milton had neither used the internet in any way that could be traced back to him, nor been referred to by anybody else.

No emails.

No social media.

No banking activity.

No credit cards.

No immigration data.

Anna had been warned that he would be good at this, and she had not doubted it. But she had not expected him to be *this* good. Control had been right. It was as if he had sunk beneath the surface of the world, leaving not even a ripple behind him.

"What are you missing?" she said aloud.

"I don't know—what?" David McClellan said.

"Excuse me?"

"Talking to yourself again."

"Sorry," she said, managing a laugh. "Just frustrated."

"Going to tell me what about?"

"Not really, it's—"

"—classified," he finished for her.

"I don't know—all this computing power, all this information, but if you really want to drop out of sight, if you can drop everything and get off the grid, all of this is useless. You can still do it. I keep thinking I'll think of something different—anything—something that'll change the results, but I know that's not going to happen. This guy is either a hermit, living in some jungle somewhere, or he's dead. If I was going to find anything at all, I'd have found it long before now."

But she couldn't give up, so she thought it through again.

Eventually, she knew, they would have to go out into the field. The realistic plan was to confirm her assumption that nothing concerning John Milton existed in any data that GCHQ or the NSA held. After that, she would appeal to Control to broaden the scope of the exercise. Interviews with victims, witnesses, reporting parties, informants. Anything that might buy her more information, more selectors to add to the sweep. She knew from unredacted excerpts from his file that he had been in contact with people in East London before he had disappeared. Elijah and Sharon Warriner. They would be a good place to start.

"Coffee," McClellan said. "Look at you. You need caffeine. Fancy it?"

She stood and stretched, working the kinks out of her stiff muscles. "Sorry, David, I would, but I'm meeting someone tonight."

He looked almost comically crestfallen. "A boyfriend?"

"A friend," she said. She logged off and collected her leather jacket from the back of the chair. "I'll see you tomorrow."

THE RENDEZVOUS had been arranged the day before and was to take place in the Beehive, a pub two miles away in the centre of town. Anna made her way into the car park where she had left her motorbike. It was her one concession to luxury in an otherwise ascetic life: it was a

Triumph Thruxton, built in the style of the '60s, an authentic café racer in Brooklands green, with low-rise bars, eighteen-inch spoked wheels and megaphone-style silencers. It was a beautiful machine, and she loved it. She lowered her helmet over her head, straddled the bike, and gunned the 850cc engine. David was coming down the steps into the car park as she pulled away; he looked flustered, the wind billowing his open coat around him. He started as she twisted the throttle and revved the big engine.

The cloud was low and leaden, and the wind was cold. She was thankful for her leathers as she hurried along the A40. She arrived at the pub ten minutes later, parked the bike, and went inside to her usual table before the fireplace. A man was waiting for her. She didn't recognise him, and that made her nervous.

"Haven't I seen you before," she said as she paused beside him. "Waterloo station?"

He was plain, early middle age, a receding hairline, nondescript, just like they all were.

"I think it was Liverpool Street," he corrected, completing the introduction.

Satisfied, she sat down. "Where is Alexei?" she said curtly.

The man spoke in quiet Russian. "He has gone home. Don't worry about him. You deal with me from now on."

"Fine. But in English, please. You are less likely to draw attention."

"Sorry." The man switched languages. "Yes, of course."

"Have you done this before?"

"No. You are my first."

She sighed. "Wonderful. Why couldn't this wait until Saturday as normal?"

"Your last report has been passed to the highest levels. There are some questions."

"A little more information about you before we can

talk, please."

"Very well. I work in the same department as you, but I work in the consulate. My name is Roman. I know you are going back to Moscow in two weeks, and I know they want to sit down with you and talk officially about your work, your performance, and so on, but before that, we need further details after your last report."

"Okay. What do you want to know?"

"The English spy—are you any nearer to finding his location?"

"Not yet. And I'm not sure that I'll be able to. He's good."

"Too good for you?"

"Probably not. But they are withholding information from me. It makes it very much harder."

"Have you seen Control again?"

"Daily progress reports. It's all one-way, though. I get nothing back."

"Do you know why they're looking for him?"

"He tried to resign. They wouldn't tell me why. But they're not happy."

"The fuss with the other agent—in London?"

"Classified. Like almost everything else. But obviously connected."

"What about him?"

"Milton? He knows how to drop out of sight."

"But they value him?"

"Yes—very much. I get the impression he was one of their best. I'd say this has caused them serious problems. They are very keen to have him back."

"Colonel Shcherbakov is to be kept up to date. You must contact me if you make a breakthrough."

"Why is he so interested?"

"You know better than to ask that."

"Yes. But—?"

"I believe they have something planned for Mr. Milton."

Anna's iPhone bleeped.

Roman cocked an eyebrow.

She took it out of her pocket and checked it. She had set up the system to ping her if any of her selectors were tripped. The message said that that was precisely what had happened.

"What is it?"

"The spy. I might have found him."

SHE GUNNED the Triumph on the way back to headquarters, touching seventy as she weaved through the slow-moving evening traffic. She didn't wait to strip out of her leathers as she hurried through security for the second time.

The report that the system had emailed to her indicated that the selector that had been triggered was for fingerprints.

A fingerprint?

Seriously?

She jogged to her desk and sat down, and there it was: a scanned PDF of a row of fingerprints inked onto a strip of paper with instructions in Spanish printed along the side in green ink. The strip had, at some point, been scanned and dumped into a database. The NSA's XKEYSCORE program had picked it up in transit.

"No fucking way."

She sat down and fumbled for her mouse, scrolling through the metadata.

```
NAME: JOHN SMITH
ALIAS: None
DOB: Unspecified
SEX: M
RACE: White, Caucasian
HEIGHT: 182
WEIGHT: 80
EYE COLOUR: Blue
```

```
HAIR COLOUR: Black
SCARS/TATTOOS:  Scar  on  face  //
Tattoo (angel wings) on back.
RESIDENCE: None
OCCUPATION: Cook
SOC. SEC. NO.: Unspecified
STATE ID NO.: Foreign
LOCATION:      Ciudad      Juárez,
Chihuahua, MEX
ORGINATING  AGENCY:  Juá.  Muncipal
Police, District 12
OFFICIAL  TAKING  PRINTS:  Lt.  Jesus
R Plato
```

"Fuck," she said. The probability matrix was off the charts: the name, personal statistics, identifying features, the metadata all ringing back super-strong hits. But the prints themselves were the thing: the system had matched them with the positive set that she had taken from Milton's SAS file, and they were unquestionably the same.

The loops and ridges, whorls and arches, delta points and type lines.

One set fitted snugly over the other when they were overlaid.

That kind of thing couldn't be a mistake or a coincidence.

It was him. There was no doubt about it.

She moused over to the second data packet that had been marked for her and opened it.

She nearly fell off her chair.

Pictures, too?

There were two: front and profile. In the first, Milton stared out into the camera. His eyes were the iciest blue and his expression implacable. He had a full beard, and his hair was unkempt. The second offered a clear angle of the scar that curled down from his scalp. He was holding a chalkboard with his name and a reference number. Again, the board was written in Spanish. It was marked Ciudad

Juárez.

"Hello, Milton," she said. "I found you, you sneaky *ublyudok*. I *found* you."

DAY THREE

Desperado

"If Juárez is a city of God, it is because the Devil is scared to come here."

Street *dicho*, or *saying*.

Chapter Thirty-Two

ADOLFO GONZÁLEZ slammed the door of the hotel behind him and stalked to his car. He had been furious, and the girls had borne the brunt of his temper. There were two of them this time, just the right age, plucked from outside the car park of the *maquiladora* that made the zips for the clothes that bargain retailers sold over the border and in Europe. His men had called him and told him that the two were waiting for him in the usual place. He had bought the hotel a year ago, just for this purpose, and it had earned back the hundred thousand dollars he had paid for it. Earned it back and then some.

Esmeralda and Ava.

They had struggled a little. More than usual, anyway. He preferred it like that.

He'd leave the cleanup to the others.

He took off his bloodied latex gloves and dropped them into the trash. He opened the door of his car and slipped into the front seat. His ride was a 1968 Impala Caprice, *"Viva La Raza"* written across the bonnet in flaming cursive, the interior featuring puffy cream-coloured cushions and a child's doll on the dash, dressed in a skirt bearing the colours of the Mexican flag. The car seats were upholstered in patriotic green, white and red.

He took off his dirty shirt, took a replacement from the pile on the rear seat, tore off its plastic wrapping, and put it on. He opened the glove compartment, took a packet of baby wipes, and cleaned his face. His movements were neat and precise: the shallow crevices on either side of his nose, the depressions at the edge of his lips, the hollows in the corners of his eyes. He pulled a fresh wipe to mop the moisture from his brow, tossed the shirt and the wipes into the trash, took a bottle of cologne and sprayed it on each side of his throat, then quickly worked a toothpick around his teeth. Better. Once he was finished, he enjoyed his "breakfast"—a generous blast up each nostril from the cocaine-filled bullet that he carried in the right-hand hip pocket of his jeans. The cocaine was unadulterated, fresh from the plane that had brought it up from Colombia. It was excellent, and he had another couple of blasts. He hadn't slept for two straight nights. He needed something to keep him alert. That should do the trick.

Adolfo was always angry, but last night had been unusually intense. His father had been the cause of it. The old man had castigated him as they drove back to Juárez yesterday evening. The gringo *bastardos* had angered him, so he had taken out that anger on his son. He had told him—ordered him—to find the journalist and the cook. They were to be found and killed without delay.

Fine.

With pleasure.

He started the car and crossed town, the traffic slowing him up, cars jamming behind the big busses that took the women to and from the factories. The busses stirred up layers of grey dust that drifted into the sky and rendered the sun hazy, settling back down again on the lanes and the labyrinth of illicit electricity cabling that supplied the *colonia* shacks. When he pulled into the vast car park that surrounded La Case del Mole, he was hot and irritated. He shut off the engine and did another couple of blasts of coke. He got out. He took a pistol from the trunk, slotted home a fresh magazine, pushed it into his waistband, pulled his shirt over it, and walked across the asphalt. There was blood there: a pool of blood so thick that it was still sticky underfoot two days later, the still-congealing red glistening in the sunlight.

He climbed the steps and knocked on the glass door. Nothing. He turned to look out at the city: the belching smokestacks, the traffic spilling by on the freeway on the other side of the border, the heat haze. He turned again and tried the handle. It was locked. He took a step back and kicked the glass; it took another kick to crack it and a third to stave it all the way through. He reached through the broken glass, unlocked the door from the inside, and stepped into the lobby.

He paused, listening. He sniffed the air. He heard someone in the other room, hurrying in his direction.

"What the fuck you doing?"

He was a fat man, his belly straining against a dirty T-shirt.

"You in charge here?"

"What the fuck you doing, man, breaking the fucking door like that?"

"Are you in charge?"

"Who's asking?"

"Better just answer the question, friend."

"All right, yeah, sure—as far as you're concerned, I am in charge. And unless you tell me what the fuck you think you're doing, busting the door like that, I'm going to call the cops."

Adolfo pulled back his jacket to show a holstered Glock. "Wouldn't do that."

"Oh, Jesus, I'm sorry—I didn't mean to cause offence."

"You didn't?"

"No, sir. I'm sorry if I did. I've had a hell of a couple of days."

Adolfo fingered one of the lobster pots that had been fixed to the wall. "What's the point of this? We're nowhere near the sea."

"Just a bit of decoration."

"It's plastic. It's not even real."

"It's just for atmosphere."

Adolfo let the lobster pot fall back again. "What's your name?"

"Gomez."

"Well, then, Gomez. I'm looking for one of your cooks."

Gomez looked at him anxiously. "I don't ever get to know them that good. We get a high turnover here—in and out, all the time. There's always someone new practically every day."

"But you know the one I want to find."

"The Englishman."

"English?"

"Sounded like it. The accent—"

"What else?"

"That's all I got."

"What does he look like?"

Gomez thought. "Six foot tall. Muscular, but not too much. Black hair. Scruffy. Had a beard. And cold eyes— no light in them."

"What else?"

"He just started Monday. He was pretty good on a fryer, but you know, I—"

Adolfo let his jacket swing open again. "Come on, Gomez," he said. "This is poor. Really—very, very poor."

The man turned away and scrubbed his fist against his head. "Oh, shit, wait—there is something. He asked if I could recommend a place to stay, so I told him about that place on Calle Venezuela. Shitty place, bums and drunks— just a flophouse, really—I could give you the address if you want."

"I know where it is."

Gomez spread his flabby arms. "That's it—I ain't got no more."

"That's it?"

"I don't know what else I can tell you."

A toilet flushed somewhere.

"Who's that?"

"Maria. Front of house."

"Tell her to come through."

The man called out.

"Jesus, Gomez, it's dark in here." A woman stood in the doorway. Her hand drifted slowly away from the switch as she saw him. "I knew this wasn't done with."

"He wants to know about the cook. The Englishman. Did you speak to him?"

"Only when he came in. Not really."

Adolfo pulled the pistol from the holster and shot both of them once each through the head, one after the other, and put the gun back in the holster. The woman had just enough time to open her mouth in surprise as she fell. Adolfo walked back out to his car. He got in, started it, and backed around and drove out onto the busy road and back towards the middle of town.

Chapter Thirty-Three

HE WOUND THE window down as he drove through the city, an old Guns and Roses CD playing loud, his arm out of the window, drumming the beat with his fingers. "Welcome to the Jungle." That was just about right. Welcome to the fucking jungle. He turned off the road and onto the forecourt of the hostel and reverse parked. He took out the bullet and did another couple of blasts of cocaine. He went through to the office.

The office was hot. No AC. A television tuned to Telemundo was on in the back, a football match on. The heat made it all woozy. A dazed fly was on its back on the desk, legs twitching. The man behind the desk was dripping with sweat.

"*Hola*, Señor," he said. "Can I help you?"

"You have an Englishman staying here?"

"Who's asking?"

"Yes or no, friend?"

"I can't tell you anything about our guests, Señor."

Adolfo smiled, pulled his shirt aside, and took out the pistol. "Yes or no?"

The man's eyes bulged. "Yes. He ain't here."

"How long has he been staying?"

"Got in the day before yesterday."

"Say much?"

"Just that he wanted a bed."

"That it?"

"Quiet type. Hardly ever here."

"What time do you expect him back?"

"I don't know, Señor. He left pretty early yesterday; don't think he's been back."

"He leave any things?"

"Couple of bags."

"Show me."

The dormitory was empty. Ten beds pushed up close together. Curtains drawn. Sweltering hot. A strong smell of sweat, dirty clothes, and unwashed bodies. The man pointed to a bed in the middle of the room. It had been neatly made, the sheets tucked in snugly. All the others were unmade and messy. Adolfo told the man to leave, and he did. He stood before the bed and sniffed the air. He took the pistol and slid the end inside the tightly folded sheets, prising them up an inch or two. He yanked the sheets all the way off and looked inside them. He prodded the pillows. He looked beneath the bed. There was a bag. He took it and opened it, tipping the contents out onto the bed.

A pair of jeans.

Two T-shirts.

A pair of running shorts.

A pair of running shoes.

Underwear.

Books. English.

The Unbearable Lightness of Being.

Great Expectations.

No money. No passport. No visas.

Adolfo's cellphone vibrated in his pocket. He fished it out and pressed it to his ear.

"Yes?"

"It's Pablo."

"What do you want?"

"You know Beau Baxter?"

"Works for our friends?"

"He's in town. Spotted him an hour ago."

"Where?"

"Plaza Insurgentes. Avenida de los Insurgentes. Driving a red Jeep Cherokee."

Adolfo ended the call and went back to the office. The television was still on, but the man wasn't there. He went outside, got into his car, and left.

Chapter Thirty-Four

ANNA STRAIGHTENED the hem of her skirt and knocked on the door.

"Come in."

There were two men with Control.

"Anna," he said. "Thank you for coming."

"That's all right."

"Do you know the Foreign Secretary?"

"Only from the newspapers," she said. She took the man's outstretched hand.

"Hello, Anna. I'm Gideon Coad."

"Pleased to meet you."

Anna noticed Control was fidgeting with his pen, and as she glanced at him, she heard him sigh. He was uncomfortable introducing her to the politician; that much was obvious. She turned to the older man and gave him a polite smile. She was not nervous at all. She felt comfortable, not least because she had done a little illicit research before leaving the office last night. There had been rumours of Coad's extramarital affair with a male researcher, and true enough, it had been easy enough to find the evidence to demonstrate that those rumours were true. Emails, bank statements, text messages, hotel receipts. Anna would have been fired on the spot for an unauthorised and frivolous deployment of GCHQ's resources for the purposes of muckraking, but if you were good enough—and she most certainly was good enough—there were simple enough ways to hide your footsteps.

There was another reason for her amusement: she was right at the heart of government now.

That was good. It was confirmation that they knew nothing about her at all.

Control turned to the second man. "And this is Captain Pope."

He was tall and grizzled. Slab-like forehead. A nose that had been broken too many times. Cauliflower ears. Anna recognised the type: unmistakeably a soldier.

"Captain Pope is one of our agents," Control explained. "Like Captain Milton was." He cleared his throat. "As you know, the Foreign Secretary has asked for a briefing from you about your findings."

"Fine. Here."

She handed them each a folder labelled JOHN MILTON, CAPTAIN. The name was followed by his government record number neatly typed on the cover. It was a much slimmer volume than the reports she typically provided, but since her predecessor had found nothing at all, she felt that her smirk of pride was justified.

"You wanted everything I could find about him. I've written up his early history, plus sections on his time in the army and the SAS, his friendships—that's a short section—relationships with the opposite sex—even shorter—where he lives, his bank accounts, medical records, the cars he's driven, and so on and so forth. Everything I could get my hands on. I've found a decent amount. There are three hundred pages."

Coad looked at the report with a dismissiveness that Anna found maddening. "The potted version will be fine for now, please."

She mastered the annoyance that threatened to flash in her eyes, nodded with polite servility and, when she began to speak, her voice was clipped and businesslike.

"Milton is a very private man, but even so, I was able to build up a picture of his life in the years before he disappeared. He's forty years old, as you know. Single. He married a Danish national in 1999. Martha Olsen. A librarian. There were no children, and the marriage didn't last. They were divorced two years later. Olsen has remarried and has two children, and save a couple of emails and texts between them, they don't appear to have kept in touch. There have been affairs with other women: a businesswoman in Chelsea, a Swiss lawyer in Basel, a tourist in Mauritius. Nothing serious, though."

"Milton's not marriage material," Pope said.

"My main task was to find Mr. Milton's current location. That was not a simple assignment. He is evidently an expert in going off the grid, and it would appear that he has an unusual dedication to doing that—this is not the sort of man who makes silly mistakes. The task was made considerably more complicated by the fact that all the information after he started to work for you"—she nodded at Control—"remained classified. That was like having one hand tied behind my back."

She didn't try to hide the note of reproach. Control glared at her and then turned to the Foreign Secretary. "Some things about Milton must remain private."

"Quite. Get on with it, Miss Thackeray."

"I ran all of the usual searches, but none of them paid off. I wasn't able to find anything on him at all. No obvious sources of income—"

"Then how is he affording to live?"

"Frugally. There was a withdrawal of £300 in Liverpool before you lost him but nothing since. He has £34,534 left in the account. It's been untouched for six months. He's not stupid—he knows that's the first place a decent analyst would look. There is another savings account with another £20,000, also untouched. No pension."

Pope laughed. "He wouldn't have anticipated retirement. Not that sort of job."

"My guess would be that he has been picking up work on the way. Bar work? Bouncing? Something that attracts migrants. Cash-in-hand, no questions asked. I don't think we'll be able to find anything substantial. How detailed shall I be?"

"Whatever you think is relevant."

"There's been no correspondence with any of the few contacts I was able to find," she continued, casting a reproachful look at Control. "He has no family, and there have been no emails, calls or texts to the friends he does have. He dropped off the face of the earth."

"And yet you found him."

"Mostly down to a stroke of luck. He was fingerprinted in Mexico. Ciudad Juárez. The Mexican police upload all their data to a central database in Mexico City, and we picked it up en route. Pictures, too."

She flicked to the page with the picture of Milton in the police station.

"And there he is," Pope said.

"This was taken on Monday night. Standard procedure. The passport he gave to the local police is a fake."

"He'll have several," Pope observed.

"I'm sure he does."

"What else?"

"Knowing which passport he has been using made it much easier to get more on him—like where he's been for the last six months, for example." She flipped forwards to a double-page map of South America. "The red line marks the route that he's taken. Passport data is collected at most borders these days, and that data is very easy to find. Once I knew the number of the passport he was using, it was quick to find out where he's been. He landed in Santos in Brazil in August. He came ashore from the MSC *Donata*, a cargo ship registered in Panama. It sailed from Liverpool two weeks earlier. From there, he started west. He crossed into Paraguay at Pedro Juan Caballero, then into Bolivia and Peru. Since then, he's always headed north—Ecuador, Colombia, Nicaragua, Guatemala, then Mexico. Most of the time he was photographed at the border, and I have those pictures, too."

She flicked through to a series of photographs. The tall cranes of Santos appeared in one picture and the barren deserts of the Brazilian interior in another. Milton was looking into the camera for some of them, bored and impatient. Others had been taken without him noticing.

She scratched her head. The Foreign Secretary examined her with searching eyes. "So he's been in South America since you lost track of him," she said. "No idea what he's been doing in between his border crossings. But we do know where he is now. He came across the Mexican border at Tapachula four weeks ago, travelling by bus. He's been heading north, and it looks like he got to Juárez earlier this week. We've got the police pictures and the prints, so I tried to find something else. I ran face recognition on everything I could think of and picked up this. They're from CCTV from a restaurant in the city."

She turned to the series of stills she had grabbed. Milton was approaching the camera across a broad parking lot. He had a rucksack slung over his shoulder. Black glasses obscured his eyes. He was tanned and heavily bearded.

"How did you find that?" Coad asked.

"The software's pretty good if you can narrow the search for it a little. There was a disturbance at this restaurant the same day this was taken. A shooting. Seven people were killed. Footage from all of the cameras in the area was uploaded by the police. I was already deep into their data. Made it a lot easier to find."

Control scowled at the pictures. "Was he involved?"

"Don't know."

"Was he arrested?"

"Don't think so."

Coad held up his hand. He paused for a moment, drumming the fingers of his right hand on the armrest of his chair before turning to her again. "Do you know where he is?"

"No," she admitted.

"You've checked hotels?"

"First thing I checked. Nothing obvious. He'll be paying in cash."

"So where do we look first?"

"Lieutenant Jesus Plato—the policeman who fingerprinted him. He's the best place to start."

"And if we should decide to send agents to Mexico to find him … what is your estimate of the odds that we would find him?"

"I can't answer that. I'd be speculating."

"Then speculate," Control said.

"If he's as good as I think he is, he won't stay in one place for more than a week or two, and he's been in Juárez since Monday. Plus there's the danger that what happened at the restaurant might have spooked him. But if you're quick? Like in the next couple of days? Decent odds, I'd say. He won't know you're coming. If he's moved on, he won't be far away. A decent analyst might be able to pick up a trail."

Control looked across at Coad, and at the latter's curt nod, he turned back to Anna. "We've been in contact with the Mexican government. They've given us approval to send a team into Mexico to bring him out. Captain Pope will be in charge. Six agents and you, Ms. Thackeray."

"Oh."

"Are you willing to go?"

"I'll do what I'm told."

Pope nodded at her. "Juárez is not a small place," he said, "and if you've done your research, you'll know it's not the easiest city in the world to find something. It's overrun with the drug cartels. Normal society has broken down completely. We might need help tracking him down. And you know him as well as anybody."

"Well?" Coad said.

"Of course," she said.

Control nodded brusquely. "You'll be flying from Northolt and landing at Fort Bliss in Texas. You'll go over the border from there. Do you have any questions?"

"When?" she said.

"First thing tomorrow."

ANNA RODE home, changed out of her leathers, and went out for a walk. Pittville Park was nearby, and she made her way straight for the Pump Room and the ornamental lakes. The building was a fine example of Regency architecture, and the lakes were beautiful, but Anna was not distracted by them. She slowed as she approached the usual bench. She sat and pretended to watch the dogs bounding across the grass. When she was satisfied that she was not observed, she reached down beneath the bench, probing for the metal bars that held the wooden slats in place. Her fingers brushed against the narrow plastic box with the magnetic strip that held it against the rusted metal. She retrieved the box, opened the end, and slid the memory stick inside. It contained her full report on Milton, plus the regular updates that she provided on the operation and scope of GCHQ's data-gathering activities. She didn't know how long she would be out of the country, and she did not want to be late in filing. She paused again, checked left and right, waited, and then reached back and pressed the case back into its place. As she left for home, she swiped the piece of chalk that she held in her hand against the side of the metal bin next to the chair.

Chapter Thirty-Five

CAPTAIN MICHAEL POPE took off his boots and his jacket and went through into his kitchen. It was late, and his wife was asleep upstairs. He looked in the fridge, but there was nothing that took his fancy. He took a microwave meal from its paper sleeve, pierced the film, and put it in the oven to heat. While he was waiting, he reached the bottle of whisky down from the cupboard, poured himself a double measure, added ice, and sipped it carefully to prolong it. He rested his hands on the work surface and allowed his head to hang down between his shoulders.

Did he know Milton?

He did. He knew him very well indeed.

THEY MET twenty years ago. They had both been in the sandpit for the First Iraq War, young recruits who were too stupid to be scared. They were in the same regiment, the Royal Green Jackets, but in different battalions. Milton had been in the Second and Pope in the First. They hadn't met in the desert, but once that was all over, Pope had transferred into the First Battalion. He was assigned to B Company.

That was the same company, and then the same rifle platoon, as Milton.

They were almost immediately sent to South Armagh.

B Company had been assigned to South Armagh. That was bandit country, and Crossmaglen, the town where they would be based, was as bad as it got. It was right on the border, which meant that the Provos could prepare in the south and then make the quick trip north to shoot at them or leave their bombs or do whatever it was that they

169

had planned to do.

The men had been billeted in the security forces base, and their rifle company lived in "submarines," long corridors with beds built three high on one side. Milton had the top bunk, and Pope was directly beneath him. It was the kind of random introduction that the army was good at, but they quickly discovered that it was propitious; they had plenty in common. Both liked The Smiths and The Stone Roses and the films of Tarantino and de Palma. Both liked a drink. Both had girlfriends back home, but neither was particularly attached to them. Milton's sense of humour was dry, and Pope's was smutty. They were both obsessed with getting fitter and stronger, and both intended to attempt SAS selection when they had a little more experience. The chemistry just worked, and they quickly became close.

POPE WASN'T ONE for mementoes, but he had kept a couple of photographs from that part of his career. He took down an album and flicked through it, finding the photograph that he wanted: seven men arranged around a Saracen. In those days, the vehicles were fitted with two gallon containers at the rear. They called them Norwegians. The drivers filled them with tea before they left the sangar each morning, and although the tea grew lukewarm and soupy before too long, it was a life-saver during cold winter patrols. The photograph was taken in a field somewhere in Armagh. Three of them were kneeling, the other four leaning against the body of the truck, each of them saluting the camera with a plastic cup. Milton was at the back, his cup held beneath the Norwegian's tap, smiling broadly. Pope was kneeling in front of him. Milton was confident and relaxed. Pope remembered how he had felt back then: it had been difficult not to look up to him a little. That respect was something that remained constant, ever since, throughout their time together in the regiment and then the Group.

The microwave beeped. He knocked back the rest of the whisky, collected the meal, and took it into the lounge.

He sat down with the album on his lap.

Memories.

He didn't question his orders, but they were troubling. Control had said that Milton had suffered from some sort of breakdown. That didn't seem very likely to Pope. Milton had always been a quiet man, solid and dependable. Extremely good at his job. Impossible to fluster, even under the most extreme pressure. The idea that he might snap like this was very difficult to square. But there again, there was all the evidence to suggest that something *had* happened to him: the trouble he had caused in East London, shooting Callan, and then, after six months when no one knew where he was, turning up again in Mexico like this.

Something had happened.

He had his orders, and he would obey them as far as he could.

He would go and bring him back. But he wouldn't retire him unless there was nothing else for it. He would do everything he could to bring him back alive.

Chapter Thirty-Six

BEAU BAXTER DIDN'T even see him come in. He was hungry, busy with his plate of quesadillas, slicing them into neat triangles and then mopping the plate with them before slotting them into his mouth. It was a public place, popular and full of customers. He had let his guard down just for a moment, and that was all it took. Adolfo González just slid onto the bench seat opposite him, a little smile on his face. It might have been mistaken for a friendly smile, one that an old friend gives to another, except for the fact that his right hand stayed beneath the table and held, Beau knew, a revolver that was pointed right at his balls.

"Good morning, Señor Baxter."

"Señor González. I suppose you think I'm pretty stupid."

"Negligent, perhaps. I'm surprised. Your reputation is excellent."

"And yours," Beau said, with a bitter laugh.

"You know not to make any sudden moves, yes?" Adolfo's English was heavily accented, slightly lispy.

"No need to remind me."

"Nevertheless—"

"There's no need for this to end badly."

"It won't, Señor Baxter, at least not for me."

Beau tried to maintain his composure. He laid the knife and fork on the plate, nudging them so that they rested neatly alongside each other. "Let me go back to New Jersey. I'll tell them to lay off."

"I could let you do that."

"They'll listen to me. I'll explain."

"But they won't, Beau—do you mind if I call you Beau? You know they won't. I killed your employer's brother. I removed his head with a machete. I killed five more of their men. They want that debt repaid. I'd be the same if the roles were reversed, although I would do the business myself rather than hide behind a *panocha's* skirts."

"I've got money in the car. Twenty-five grand. I'll give it to you."

"That's the price they put on me?"

"Half. You're worth fifty."

"Fifty." He laughed gently. "Really? Beau, I'm disappointed in you. You think I need money?"

He realised how stupid that sounded. "I suppose not."

He indicated the half-finished quesadilla. "How is the food here?"

"It's all right."

"Do you mind?" González picked up Beau's knife, used it to slice off a triangle, then stabbed it and put it in his mouth. He chewed reflectively. "Mmmm," he said after a long moment. "That *is* good. You like Oaxaca?"

"I like it all right."

"It is a little too Mexican for most *Americanos*."

"I'm a little too Mexican for most Americans."

González took a napkin from the dispenser, folded it, and carefully applied it to the corners of his mouth. Beau watched Adolfo all the time. He looked straight back at him. Beau assessed, but there was nothing that he could do. The table was pressed up against his legs, preventing him from moving easily, and besides, he did not doubt that Adolfo had him covered. A revolver under the table, it didn't matter what calibre it was, he couldn't possibly miss. No, he thought. Nothing he could do except bide his time and hope he made a mistake.

"We're alike, you and I," he said.

González did not immediately answer. "Let me tell you something, Beau. I want to impart the gravity of your"— he fished for the correct word—"your predicament. Do you know what I did last night? I went out. Our business has a house in a nice neighbourhood. Lots of houses, actually, but this one has a big garden in back. Not far from here. We had two men staying there. *Hijos de mil cojeros.* They used to be colleagues, but then they got greedy. They thought they could take my father's money from him. Do you know what I did to them?"

"I can guess."

"Indeed, and discussing the precise details would be barbaric, yes? I'm sure a man such as yourself must have an excellent imagination. We had some enjoyment, but then, eventually, after several hours, I shot them both. And then, this morning, I visited the restaurant where a journalist and her friends were eating on Monday night. The owner and the *cuero* he was with, they didn't give me the information that I wanted. So I shot them, too. Just like that."

"I don't doubt it."

"Another question: do you know what a *pozole* is?"

"I'm pretty sure you're fixing to tell me."

He smiled, his small teeth showing white through his thin, red lips. "A *pozole* is a Mexican stew. Traditional. Hominy, pork, chillies. It's important to keep stirring the soup while it is on the stove so that the flavours blend properly. One of my men has acquired a nickname: he is known as *El Pozolera*. The Stewmaker. It is because he is an expert in dissolving bodies. He fills a plastic drum with two hundred litres of water, puts in two sacks of caustic soda, boils it over a fire, and then adds the body. You boil them for eight hours until the only things left are teeth and nails, and then you take the remains—the soup—to an empty lot and burn it up with gasoline. It is disgusting for those without the constitution necessary to watch. A very particular smell."

"Why are you telling me this?"

"Because, Beau, I need you to understand that, even though we might be in the same business, you are mistaken: we are *not* alike. You deliver your quarry alive. You even allow them to bargain with you. To negotiate, to offer you a better deal. Mine cannot. I do not make bargains, and I do not negotiate. I'm not open to persuasion, and I can't be dissuaded with whatever you have in your car, by the money in your bank account or by any other favour you might offer me. Once I have decided a man must die, that is it—they will die. A final question before we leave. You have killed people. Not many people, I know, but some. Tell me: what does it feel like for you?"

"Feels like business."

"Again, a point of difference. For me, it is *everything*. It is the sensation of having someone's life in the palm of your hand and then making your hand into a fist, tightening it, squeezing tighter and tighter until the life is crushed. That is power, Beau. The power of life and death."

"You're crazy."

"By your standards, perhaps, but it hardly matters, does it?" The man leaned back. He studied Beau. "I'll be honest. You will die today. It will not be quick or painless, and I will enjoy it. We will record it and send it to your employer as a warning: anyone else you send to Mexico will end up the same way. The only question is where, when and how. I will give you a measure of control over the first two of those. The how?— that you must leave to me."

Beau looked out of the restaurant's window. "I know where the girl is."

"Good for you."

"The Englishman—I know where he's taken her."

"Ah, yes, the Englishman. *Caro de culo.* An interesting character. I can find out nothing about him. What can you tell me?"

"I could give you him, too."

"You're not listening, Beau. I don't barter. You'll tell me everything I want in the end, anyway."

"I could deliver him to you in five minutes."

He smiled again, humouring him. "You said you know where the girl is?"

"Yeah."

"You know, Beau. It still doesn't matter."

"And why is that?"

"Because there is nowhere in Juárez where the Englishman could hide her from me. This city is mine, Beau. Every hovel in every *barrio*. Every street corner, every alleyway. Every hotel, every mansion, every last square inch. How do you think I found you? All I have to do is wait. She will be delivered to me eventually. They always are."

Chapter Thirty-Seven

MILTON WATCHED the conversation through the windows of the diner. The place was on Avenida de los Insurgentes in a strip mall with a large plastic sign in the shape of a lozenge that said Plaza Insurgentes. Milton's taxi had pulled over on the other side of the road, behind a 1968 Impala Caprice with *"Viva La Raza"* written across the bonnet. The passenger-side window was down, classic rock playing loudly.

He recognised the driver as the doctor from the hospital.

Milton stood quietly and watched.

The diner was busy. Beau Baxter was alone in a booth, and González made his way straight to him, slipping down opposite and beginning to talk. Beau's body language was stiff and stilted, and his face was pale; this was not a meeting that he had requested. Curious, Milton crossed the street to get a little closer, watching through an angled window so that neither man could see him. He looked closer and saw that González had not moved his right hand above the table. He was armed, or he wanted Baxter to think that he was.

Milton moved away from the window and leant against a telephone kiosk. He looked up and down the street and across the strip mall, but if González had other men here, they were good. Milton could see nothing that made him think that there was any sort of backup. González was on his own. He could feel the reassuring coldness of the Springfield's barrel pressed against his spine. Thirteen shots in the clip, one in the chamber. He hoped they would be enough.

Beau and González got up.

Milton moved to the entrance. There was a bench next

to the door, an advertisement for a law firm on the backrest. He sat down behind a newspaper he found on the ground, the Springfield hidden in his lap. Beau came out first, González behind him. Milton let them pass, folded the newspaper over the arm of the bench, and picked up the gun. He followed. When they reached González's car, Milton pressed the barrel against González's coccyx.

"Nice and easy," he said.

González turned his head a little, looking back from the corner of his eyes.

"You again."

"That's right."

"I still don't know your name."

"I know."

"English, then. Why are you always involved in my business, English?"

Milton glanced at Baxter. "You all right?"

"Feel a bit stupid."

"Get his gun."

Baxter frisked him quickly, finding a gold-plated Colt .45 in a holster clipped to his belt. He unfastened the holster and removed it.

"Look at this. Gold? You might have money, but you can't buy class."

González said nothing. He just smiled.

"Beau," Milton said. "What are you driving?"

"The Jeep," he said, nodding to the red Cherokee with tinted windows.

"Get it started."

"You have already taken too long, English," González said. "My family has eyes everywhere. They are our falcons—waiters, barmen, newspaper vendors, taxi drivers, even the *cholos* on the street corners. A hundred dollars a week so that we may know everything about the comings and goings of our city. My *padre* will know what you are doing before he sits down to dinner. And then he will find you."

"You'll be halfway back to New Mexico by then, partner," Beau said.

Milton prodded González in the back and propelled him towards the Jeep. When they reached the car, the Mexican finally turned around to face him. "Every moment in your life is a choice, English. Every moment is a chance to go this way or that. You are making a choice now. You have picked an unwise course, and you will have to face the consequences of your decision."

Milton watched him carefully, a practiced assessment that was so automatic that he rarely realised he was making it. He watched the dilation in his eyes and the pulse in the artery in his neck. He saw the rate of his breathing. The man was as relaxed as if they were old friends, meeting up by coincidence and engaging in banal small talk about their families. Milton had seen plenty of disconcerting people before, but this man—Santa Muerta—this man was something else. A real piece of work.

"The way I'm coming at it," Beau said, "you ain't in a position to lecture anyone."

González kept his eyes on Milton. "Not everyone is suited to this line of work, English. Having a gun pointed at someone can sometimes lead people to exaggerate their own abilities. They tell themselves that they are in control of events where perhaps they are not."

"Don't worry yourself on my account," Milton said. "I'm as used to this as you are. Get in the car."

Baxter opened the door, and smiling serenely and without another word, González got in.

Chapter Thirty-Eight

EL PATRÓN had a small mansion on the outskirts of Juárez. He had dozens, all around Mexico. This was in the best part of the city, St. Mark's Close, a gated community approached through a series of arches and set around a pleasant green. It was a quiet retreat of mansions, each more garish than the next. Outside some were vehicles marked with the corporate logos of the owners of the *maquiladoras*. In other forecourts were SUVs with blacked-out windows and bulletproof panels; those belonged to the drug barons. The community had a private security detail that Felipe bolstered whenever he was in residence. His men were posted at the gates now, in the grounds of the mansion and in the watchtower that he had constructed at the end of the drive. Twenty of his very best men, most related to him by blood or marriage, vigilant and disposed towards violence. His doctor had advised him that sleep was important for a man of his age, and he made sure that he always slept well.

He had bought the place a year ago, persuading the prominent lawyer who had owned it that it was in his best interests to sell. He hadn't stiffed him on the price—he felt no need to drive a hard bargain—and he had sent three bags with a million dollars in each as a mark of his gratitude. He had visited the house before the lawyer had owned it, and he had always been fond of it. It was surrounded on all sides by tall brick walls. It had been built with a small cupola, an architectural shorthand for extravagance in Juárez. Inside, there were baroque tables mixed with minimalist leather couches, red velvet curtains and a disco ball, Oriental rugs and, on the wall above the fireplace, a knockoff of Picasso's "Guernica." The décor was not systematic thanks to the fact that it had been purchased, at various times, by several of Felipe's wives. There was a glass-enclosed pool. A room in the basement held a large pile of stacked banknotes—four feet cubed— a little over twenty million, all told. Another held his armoury, some of the guns plated in gold. There were just a few street-facing windows and, at his insistence, the best security system that money could buy.

Marilyn Monroe had owned the house at one time; the rumour was that the purchase was a drunken extravagance after a night in the Kentucky Bar following her divorce from that American writer. It reminded him of another time in Juárez, so different from how things were today that it was almost another place. Salaciousness and audacity, everything for sale, most of it carnal.

Not an innocent time, because Juárez could never be innocent, but innocent compared to what had followed in the wake of the narco wars. He was old enough to remember all of it, the town's history as evident to him as the rings on a split tree trunk.

The house was busy tonight. He was hosting a party for the gringos. Plenty of his lieutenants were present, together with a significant delegation from the city. The deputy mayor, representatives from the *federales*, senior officers from the army. They had erected a wrestling ring in the garden, and a tag team of *luchadores* were putting on an athletic display: wiry, masked wrestlers who grappled and fought, climbing the turnbuckles to perform ever more impressive dives and twists. The best *cueros* from the brothels that Felipe owned had been brought to the house to provide their own kind of entertainment. Drink and drugs were unlimited.

He and Isaac were enjoying a bottle of very expensive wine. Isaac's colleagues were partying with the women. They were gross *Americanos*. Both were drunk. No style or class. *Que te den por el culo*, he thought. He had no respect for them, none at all, but he put on a wide smile and played the generous host. Business was business, after all, and they stood to make him a lot of money.

"Are you happy, Isaac?" Felipe asked.

"Yes, El Patrón."

"Our arrangement is satisfactory to you?"

"Are you kidding? It's perfect."

They had discussed the arrangement for a couple of hours. Felipe would deliver his product across the border in a number of different ways: by truck and car through Juárez, by ultralight into the fields of New Mexico and Texas, and through the tunnel that he was in the process of building. Isaac owned several commercial ranches across the south-west and had a fleet of trucks to deliver the slaughtered cows and sheep to market. The product would be hidden inside the carcasses of the animals and distributed to a network of dealers that the two would arrange together.

Yes, he thought. It was satisfactory. Business came first, but there would come a time when another means of distribution was available to him, and when that happened, he would not forget the way that Isaac had spoken to him in the desert. The impudence. The unspoken threat: we will return north without speaking to you if you do not give us the reassurances that we want. Felipe had a long memory, and he bore a grudge. There would be an accounting.

"I'm looking forward to seeing your new facility," Isaac said.

"Ah, yes. The lab. It is nearly finished."

"When will it be ready?"

"By the end of the week. Twenty pounds of meth every day. Excellent quality, too. I will show you."

"Who is your cook?"

"An American. He used to work for a pharmaceutical company. Blue chip."

"How'd you find him?"

"I keep my eyes open, Isaac."

The man grinned at him. "When can we go see it?"

"Tomorrow. We will fly."

He was interrupted by Pablo. The man was scared. "El

Patrón," he said, his face bleached of colour. "Please—may I have a word with you?"

"What is it?" he said mildly.

The man looked agonised. "In private, El Patrón, *por favor.*"

"Excuse me," he said with an easy smile even as his temper was bubbling. He moved to the side, out of earshot, and glared at Pablo. "What *is* it?"

"Your son. It is Adolfo. He has been abducted."

"What on earth do you mean?"

"There is a gringo bounty hunter in town."

"Working for who?"

"The Lucianos. There is a price on your son's head—the killings in the desert."

"And this man—he has him?"

"Yes—him and another. Adolfo had surprised the bounty hunter. We were going to take him out into the desert and kill him, but as they left the place where they had met, he was stopped by a second man. We think he was the man at the restaurant on Monday night."

"And who is he?"

"We don't know, El Patrón."

His temper flared. "Do we know *anything*?"

"He's been protecting the journalist from the restaurant. Adolfo visited her this morning to finish her off, and this man was there. He is English. There is some connection between them."

"Then if we cannot find him, we must find her, and then he will come to us." He put down his glass of wine. Isaac was looking at him quizzically; he replaced the angry mask that had fallen across his face with a warm and reassuring smile. "Call the police," he said quietly to Pablo. "They are to put roadblocks on every road out of Juárez. No one leaves without the car being checked. And put the word out: a million dollars to whoever can bring me her. A million dollars if anyone can bring me him. Tell all our falcons. I want them found."

Chapter Thirty-Nine

ANNA HAD been picked up from her two-bedroom flat in Cheltenham High Street at four in the morning. The car was a black BMW with tinted windows and a uniformed driver. She wasn't used to being chauffeured, and she felt a little out of place, her grubby Doc Martens against the spotless cream carpet inside the car. The man said very little as they headed west, following the A40 until it became the M40. That suited her well. She slept for the first half hour, and then, roused as the sun rose into a sky of wispy low clouds, she took out her laptop and reviewed—for the hundredth time—the report she had made on John Milton.

She was excited. It wasn't unheard of for an analyst to be sent out into the field, but it was the first time that it had happened to her. The rationale was obvious and made sense: if Milton slipped beneath the surface again, it was best to have an expert in situ to help track him down again.

And they were right: she knew him as well as anyone.

The trip also promised to furnish her with a much better idea of how Group 15 worked. They had always been unable to find out much about them, save the rumour and gossip that occasionally reached the ears of the Federal Security Service; they had certainly never been on actual operations with them. That, she knew, would stand her in excellent stead with Colonel Shcherbakov.

The driver turned into Ickenham and then, after a further few minutes, turned and slowed to a stop outside the armed guards stationed at the entrance of RAF Northolt. He showed his credentials and drove onto the base, following a route that brought him straight onto the main runway. A Gulfstream G280 was being readied for flight. It was painted gleaming white, the sunlight sparking off the fuselage. The driver took her luggage from the boot and added it to the pile of gear that two technicians were loading into the hold. Anna got out and stared at them. A large black fabric bag was open, the contents being checked. Anna saw automatic rifles, the metal glinting black and icy in the early light.

She paused at the steps to the cabin.

The pilot, performing a final external check, smiled at her. "Miss Thackeray?"

"Yes."

"Good morning, ma'am. Up you go. They're waiting inside."

Anna climbed the steps and entered the jet. The cabin was plush. Decadent. Eight handcrafted leather seats, a workstation and a three-person sofa. Large porthole windows. Proper cutlery on the tables. Pewter crockery. Crystal glasses. One of the portholes faced the door, and she glimpsed her reflection: the boots, the ripped jeans and the faded and frayed T-shirt looked completely out of place. She swallowed, daunted, her usual confidence knocked just a little. She almost wished that she had worn something more—well, something more *appropriate*.

Five men and a woman were arranging themselves around the cabin.

She felt self-conscious. "Hello," she said.

Captain Pope turned to her. "Good morning, Miss Thackeray."

"Morning."

He looked at her and frowned. It was quizzical—perhaps even amused—and not disapproving. "Get yourself settled. We'll be taking off soon."

"Introductions first?"

He smiled patiently. "You know who I am. Lance Corporal Hammond's over there with the headphones. That's Lance Corporal Callan. Corporal Spenser and Corporal Blake are playing cards. And Sergeant

Underwood is sleeping."

Anna looked the others over.

The woman, Hammond, looked to be in her early thirties. Five eight, black hair cut severely. Compact and powerful. Callan was tall and slender. Strikingly handsome. Hair in tight curls, so blond as to almost be white. Skin was white, too, like alabaster. A cruelty to his thin lips and unfeeling eyes that Anna found unsettling. Alien. Spenser was shorter, bald and heavily muscled. Blake was darker skinned. Something about him was a little exotic. Foreign, perhaps. Underwood had a sleeping mask over his face, obscuring his features.

They looked up at her, but no one spoke.

Pope smiled at her. "Take your seat," he said. "Wheels up in five minutes."

Chapter Forty

THERE WAS a sign on the wall of the room that said that the motel had Wi-Fi. Caterina booted up her laptop, located the network, and joined it. She had installed police scanner software, and it was then, listening to those disinterested voices bracketed by static, that she heard about the body of the missing girl who had been found.

The police said that the girl had been identified as Guillermina Marquez.

The body had turned up on scrubland near to the Estadio Olímpico Benito Juárez. The Indios played there; Leon had taken her to see them once. It was close to the motel. A twenty-minute walk, maximum. Fifteen if she ran. She thrust her camera and her notepad into her rucksack, scribbled a quick note to Milton explaining where she was going, locked the door behind her, and set off towards the river.

It was growing late, and the light was leaving the city. Caterina crested a shallow hill and looked out across the border to El Paso, the lights twinkling against the spectrum of greys across the desert and the mountains beyond. She wondered what it was like over the border. She had never been. She had an idea, of course, on a superficial level—she was in contact with journalists on the other side of the line, there was television and the movies—but it was more than the superficial things that she wondered about. She wondered what it would be like to live in a city that was safe. Where you were not woken with yet another report of dead bodies dropped on your doorstep. Where the army and the police were not as bad as the criminals. Where children were not abducted, were not tortured, mutilated, bruised, fractured or strangled or violated.

The stadium was across a bleak expanse of scrub. Other girls had been found here: she thought of the map in her room, with the pins that studded this part of town, a bristling little forest of murders. She remembered two of them left in the dust with their arms arranged so that they formed crucifixes; she remembered those two particularly well.

She walked faster.

Dusk was turning into night. Two police cruisers were parked on the scrub next to a thicket of trees and creosote bushes. Blue and white crime scene tape had been strung around the trunks of three of the trees, fluttering and snapping in the breeze, forming a broad triangular enclosure. Uniformed officers were inside, gathered around a shapeless thing on the floor. Caterina ducked down, pulled the tape over her head, and went forwards. She could see the body covered with a blanket, the naked feet visible where the blanket was too short. She took out her camera, shoved in the flash, and started taking pictures.

One of the policemen turned. "Excuse me."

She moved away from him, circling the body, continuing to take pictures.

"Excuse me, Señorita. No pictures, please."

"What was her name?" she asked, the camera still pressed to her face.

"I recognise you," the policeman said.

She lowered the camera. "Do I know you?"

"I'm *Capitán* Alameda. You don't remember?"

"No, I—"

"It's Caterina, isn't it?"

"Yes—how do you know my name?"

"I was at the restaurant on Monday night. I was with you in the hospital."

"Oh."

He put a hand on Caterina's shoulder. "You shouldn't be here."

"Who was she?"

"We don't know yet."

"When was she found?"

"A couple of hours ago." He guided her back and away from the covered body. "Come on. It's not safe. I thought you were going over the border."

"Soon. Tomorrow, I think."

"You need to keep off the street until then. If they find out where you are— look, where are you staying?"

She paused.

"Don't worry—I know the cook is looking after you. My colleague—*Teniente* Plato—he's been speaking with him. I'll take you back there. We can talk about what happened here in the car. I'll answer all your questions."

She paused.

"Caterina—I'm the captain of the police. Come on. You can trust me."

She relented.

Chapter Forty-One

FELIPE EXCUSED HIMSELF from the party. It would continue in the grounds of the mansion, but out of sight, the garages were busy with activity. He had called in his best men. His best *sicarios*. Their cars were parked in the wide bay before the triple garage, and they were milling there, waiting for his instructions. Pablo had opened the arms cache and was in the process of distributing the heavy artillery. The way Felipe was thinking, if Adolfo wasn't returned to him soon, he would have to do something to focus the attention of the authorities. Firing a few AR-15s in the marketplace, tossing in a few grenades, that ought to do the trick. They knew, but perhaps they needed to be reminded: there were some things that could not be allowed to stand.

An unmarked police car rolled up the slope that curved around the mansion and parked next to the garages. Two of the men broke away from the rest, their hands reaching for their pistols. Felipe watched as the door opened and a man he recognised stepped out.

The municipal cop. *Capitán* Alameda.

The two men recognised him, too, and stepped aside.

"El Patrón."

"Not now, *Capitán*. I'm busy."

"I know about Adolfo."

"Then you'll understand why this is not a good time."

"No—I know who has him. And how you can get him back."

Felipe turned to Pablo. "You go in five minutes," he called.

"Yes, El Patrón."

"Be quick, Alameda. And don't waste my time."

"The girl from the restaurant. The one you didn't get.

The Englishman is trying to keep her safe."

"And?"

"I have her. There was a body in the park next to the stadium. She was there. Taking pictures."

"Where is she?"

He nodded in the direction of his car. "In back."

"Get her."

Alameda went back to the car and brought the girl out. She was cuffed, her wrists fastened behind her back.

"Do you know who I am?" Felipe asked.

She spat at his feet.

"She's feisty," Alameda suggested. "Took a good swing at me before I got the bracelets on."

"Where is the Englishman?"

"*Come mierda y muerte.*"

"If you help me get my son back, I'll let you go. You have my word."

"Your word's no good."

Felipe shifted his weight. "Look around—you're on your own. The Englishman can't help you now. You don't have any other choice."

Chapter Forty-Two

BEAU PULLED the Jeep into the motel parking lot. Milton opened the rear door, stepped outside, and pulled Adolfo out with him. Beau followed close behind, the barrel of his pistol pushed tight into the small of the Mexican's back. Milton unlocked the door and opened it.

The room was empty.

"Caterina?"

The bathroom door was open. Milton checked. It was empty, too.

"Where is she?" Beau said anxiously.

"I don't know."

Her laptop was on. Milton checked it: a police scanner application was open, the crackle of static interrupted by occasional comments from the dispatcher. A scrap of paper was on the desk next to the computer. A note had been written down.

"There's been another murder. She's gone to cover it."

"We don't wanna be hanging around, partner. The sooner we get them both over the border, the better."

"Not without her."

"I know, but we're not on home turf here."

"It's not open to debate. You can go whenever you want, but he stays until I have her back."

Milton's phone started to ring.

He looked at the display: an unknown number.

"*Hola.*"

He didn't recognise the voice. "I think you have the wrong number," he replied in Spanish.

The caller spoke in accented English. "No, I have the right number."

"Who is this?"

"I am Felipe."

A pause.

"You know me now?"

"I've heard of you. Where's the girl?"

"In a minute. I don't know your name. What shall I call you?"

"John."

"Hello, John. You are the Englishman from the restaurant?"

"That's right."

"You have caused me some—awkwardness."

"I'm just getting started. Where's the girl?"

"She's here. Safe and sound. Where is my son?"

"With me."

"He is—?"

"He's fine."

"We seem to be at an impasse."

"Seems so. What do you want to do about that?"

Felipe paused. Milton knew he was trying to sweat him. Pointless. "I'm waiting," he said. There was not even the faintest trace of emotion in his voice.

Felipe was brusque. "We each have something the other wants. I don't know why you have involved yourself in my business, but I am going to propose a short truce. An exchange: the girl for my son."

"Where?"

"There is a village south of Juárez. Samalayuca. Turn right off the 45 and drive into the desert. We can meet there. Tomorrow morning. Nine."

"You wouldn't be thinking about trying to ambush me, would you, Felipe?"

"A truce is a truce."

"I know you don't know who I am."

"So why not tell me, John?"

"All you need to know is that you don't want to know me. Don't do anything stupid. You might think you're a frightening man, and people around here would say that you are, but you don't frighten me. There's nothing here I haven't seen before. If you try anything, if the girl is hurt—if anything happens at all that I don't like—I give you my word that I will find you and I will kill you. Do you understand me?"

When he replied, the man's voice was tight, with fury behind it. Milton knew why: he was not used to being threatened. "I believe I do," he said. "Let's make this exchange. After that—well then, *John*—after that, well, you know how this is going to turn out, don't you?"

"No. Do you?"

"Yes, I do. And so do you."

The line went dead.

"They have her?" Beau said.

Milton nodded.

"Ignorant dogs!" Adolfo gloated. "You—"

Milton did not even look at him; he just backhanded him with a sudden, brutal clip that snapped his head around and sent him toppling backwards onto the bed. When Adolfo sat back up, his lip was dripping with blood.

Milton wiped the blood from his knuckles. "Put him in the bath. If he tries to come out, shoot him."

Beau did as he was told. Milton took his phone and found the number he had been given at the police station three days earlier. He entered the number and pressed CALL.

It connected. "Plato."

"It's John Smith."

"John—what can I do for you?"

"I need to talk to you. It's the girl."

"What about her?"

"She's been taken."

An audible sigh. "When?"

"A couple of hours ago."

"You said you were going to the hotel."

"I'm here now. I went out, and she's gone.

"You left her?"

"Temporarily. She left on her own."

"You know that for sure?"

"She left a note."

"How do you know she—"

"I just had a call from Adolfo's father."

"*Cojer!*" Plato cursed.

"I'm guessing he's in charge around here?"

"Felipe González. El Patrón. He *is* La Frontera. What did he say?"

"I'd rather not talk on the phone. Can we meet?"

Milton heard the long sigh. "You better come over here. Do you have a pen and paper?"

"Yes."

Milton took down the address that Plato dictated.

Chapter Forty-Three

JESUS PLATO SLID underneath the hull of the boat, hooked the pot with his hand, and dragged it toward him. He dipped his brush into the paint and started to apply it. He had been looking forward to this part of the project for weeks. There were few things that made an old boat look better than repainting it. The *Emelia* had a tatty, ancient gel-coat finish, and Plato was going to replace it with two new coats of urethane paint. The paint wasn't cheap, but he figured it'd be worth it for the difference it would make. It was calming work, too—meditative—and something where the gratification from the job would be quick.

A taxi turned into the road. He looked up as it slowed to a halt. Milton got out, paid the driver, and walked up the driveway. Plato slid out from beneath the boat and then stood, pouring a handful of white spirit into his palms and wiping away the stained paint. "In here," he said, leading the way through the open garage door. He hadn't told Emelia that Milton would be coming over, and he didn't want her to worry.

The boat's gas engine was in pieces on his work desk. He had a small beer fridge in the corner, and he opened it, taking out a couple of cans.

"Thanks—but I don't drink."

"Suit yourself." Plato put one back, tugged the ring pull on the other, and drank off the first quarter. It was a hot day, and he had been working hard; the beer tasted especially good. "You better tell me what's happened."

"I met a man at the hospital. He's a bounty hunter. He's here for Adolfo González."

"Good luck with that."

"He says he can help get the girl over the border and

set up on the other side."

"He's doing that out of the goodness of his heart?"

"Of course not. I said I'd help him find González."

Plato sighed.

"I was going to meet him to talk about it. A restaurant. González was there. We've got him."

Plato watched him carefully over the rim of his can. "You've got him?"

"Baxter does. The bounty hunter."

"Beau Baxter?"

"You know him?"

"I've heard of him. He used to work on the line before he got into what he does now. Border Patrol."

"And?"

"Back then he was old school. A hard man. But I don't know about now. You don't normally get much integrity out of men in his line of business. You saying he's got Adolfo now?"

Milton nodded.

"And you don't think he'll just up and leave? Get him over the border and get paid?"

His icy blue eyes burned with cold. "I saved his life. And he's not that stupid."

"All right."

Milton clenched and unclenched his fists. "When I got back to the hotel, the girl was gone. It didn't happen there. No sign of a struggle. Nothing disturbed. I looked through her stuff. She'd written this down."

Milton handed him a piece of paper. Plato recognised the address. The note said that she had gone to investigate a murder.

"There was a body found here earlier," Milton said. "Another of the dead girls."

"That's right. It was on the radio. She must have gone to cover it."

"I'll ask around. Maybe whoever was there might've seen her."

"Thank you."

"This phone call you had with Felipe—what did he say?"

"He knows we've got his son. He wants to exchange. Her for him."

"You do know you can't trust anything he says?"

"Of course. I've dealt with men like him before, Plato."

"I doubt it," he said, shaking his head. "Not like him. Where does he want to meet?"

"A village south of Juárez. Samalayuca."

"I know it. It's off the 45. Not a good place for you."

"Why?"

"Open ground. No one else around for miles. And he'll know it well. I've been out there more than a few times over the years. One of their favourite places for dumping bodies."

"That's one of the reasons I'm here. I'm going to need some help."

Plato shook his head.

"There's me and Baxter, but I don't think that's going to be enough."

"I'm sorry."

"I need someone who's good with a rifle."

"No, Smith, I'm sorry—I just can't."

"Don't think about me, Lieutenant. Don't think about Baxter. It's the girl. You know if we don't do something they'll kill her."

"I know that, and it's awful, but she knew the risks, and it doesn't make any difference. I still can't. Look—let me tell you a story. I've been dealing with the cartel about as long as they've been around, least in the form they're in at the moment. Before El Patrón, there was another boss. They called him *El Señor de Los Cielos*. Lord of the Skies, on account of the jumbo jets they said he had, packed full of cocaine up from Colombia. He was Mr. Juárez for years. And then La Frontera came over from Sinaloa, trying to muscle in on his turf. There was a war, a proper one, a shooting war."

He took another long pull on his beer.

"Bad things happened. Over the years, I got to see some pretty awful shit. The line of work I think you're in, I'm guessing you've seen those things, too. And I've met bad men. But recently, things have gotten worse. The men have gotten worse—younger—and the old rules don't apply. The one I remember more than all the others, he was just a kid. Fourteen years old from out of the *barrio*. This kid had been given a gun and told to shoot two dealers for the Juárez cartel. They were trying to sell on a corner that La Frontera was claiming for itself. And he did it. Point blank, one shot each in the back of the head and then another while they were on the ground. We picked him up. He didn't try to run. I interviewed him. Looked like he wanted to talk about it. Like he was proud. He told me that he'd been wanting to kill someone since he was a little boy. Said that if he got out, he'd do it again, and I believed him. There are others like him. Dozens of them. What does that say for the future, John? What chance have we got?"

Milton looked at him. Had his face softened a little?

"Look around, man—I've got a family. Wife and kids. And look at me. I'm fifty-five years old. I retire on Friday. I'm going to fix up this boat, drink beer, and go fishing. There's no place for a man like me in a world like that. You always had to go to work knowing that there's a good chance you might get shot today. I could live with that. But now it's worse—now, they'll go after your family, too, and I won't do that. I've done my time. I'm out. You understand?"

Milton did not answer.

There was no disapproval, just a quick recalibration of circumstances.

"I understand. This place—Samalayuca. Can you give me directions?"

DAY FOUR

"One More Day"

Chapter Forty-Four

BEAU BAXTER had his face in the dust. The toes of his boots were against the gravel of the ridge, his pelvis pressed tight against it, his elbows prised up against rough stones. His Jeep was back up the ridge; his jacket was hanging from a Joshua tree. He pushed his Stetson back a little, loosening the hand-braided horsehair stampede string that was tight up against his neck. The rifle on the ground next to him was a Weatherby Mark V Deluxe with the claro walnut stock and highly polished blued barrelled action, chambered for the .257 Wetherby Magnum cartridge. He had been here since dawn, and it had been so quiet, he thought, that you could damn near hear your own hair grow. He had a pair of twenty-power Japanese binoculars he had bought in Tijuana. He swept the scrubland below with them. The valley floor was made up of a reddish-brown lava rock that, depending on the angle of the sun, could turn a blackish lavender. There were tracks of wiry javelina pigs and mule deer but nothing human. Beau stuffed his mouth with chewing tobacco and waited like a grizzled old buzzard guarding his roadkill.

He saw the dust cloud. It blurred in the shimmer and drifted north, the faint desert breeze catching it and pushing it back towards the city. It grew into a long yellow slash of dust, gradually rising, eventually growing to a mile long before he could make out the hire car Smith was driving at its head. It bumped off the asphalt and onto the rough track, greasewood bushes and pear cactus on either side, slowing to negotiate the deeper potholes. He put the glasses to his eyes and focussed. Eventually it was close enough for Beau to see Smith at the wheel and, in the back, Adolfo González. The cloud of dust kept drifting north.

Beau still wasn't sure that he was doing the right thing. He had Adolfo. All he had to do was cuff him, wrists and ankles, put him in the back of the Jeep, cross the border, pick up his money. Smith would have let him do it, too, if it hadn't been for the girl. Beau had watched as Smith spoke to El Patrón, and although he had kept his voice calm, he had seen the flashes of anger in his eyes. He would never agree to let him have Adolfo now, not until they had gotten Caterina back again. Beau wondered for a moment about drawing down on him, just taking the greaser and bugging out for the border, but there was something about the Englishman that told him that that would be a very bad idea. He didn't want a mean dude like that on his tail. That, and the fact that he had just saved his life.

They had agreed to meet El Patrón out here in the desert and get the girl but try and get away with Adolfo, too. Beau was taking the risk with the bounty, so Smith had agreed that he should be the one with the rifle. Much less dangerous away from the action. Smith would make the exchange, and Beau would provide cover, should Smith need it.

Beau knew that he would.

As a kid in the woods of southeast Texas, Beau had never really been good at much in particular with the exception of hunting. This talent was honed in Vietnam, where he was trained as a sniper by the 101st Airborne in Phu Bai. He did his stint on a hunt-and-kill team with the Fifth Infantry Division out of Quang Tri Province.

He learned plenty, like how to shoot.

The sun behind him was a good thing: there would be no reflection off his glasses or the scope. It was climbing into a perfect blue sky, already blazing hot. There was no wind. No cloud cover. No shelter. The air shimmered in the heat. The deep shadow of the ridge and the Joshua tree were cast out across the floodplain below him. A little vegetation: candelilla and catclaw and mesquite thickets.

He put the binoculars down and mopped at his forehead with a handkerchief. He gazed out over the land. To the west and east were the mountains. To the south, the arid scrub of the *barrial* that ran out into the deeper desert. He saw another cloud of dust on the 45. He picked up the glasses again and found the road. It was another car, an SUV, with tinted windows. A narco car. It turned off the road and followed Smith down the same long track. He replaced the glasses, took a slug of water from the canteen shaded by his hat, and picked up the rifle. His vantage point was nicely elevated, not too much, well within the range of the Weatherby. He nudged the forestock around until he had the car in his sights. He slipped his finger through the trigger guard.

The narco who had climbed the mesa behind him had followed him all the way from Juárez. The man was a tracker, a coyote with experience of smuggling people over the border. He knew how to move quietly, how to avoid detection.

Beau never even saw him.

The first thing he knew about it was the click as the man cocked his revolver.

Chapter Forty-Five

MILTON GOT out of the hire car. The air was arid and clear all the way to both horizons, where it broke up into morning haze. The heat was already unbelievable. The sun was ferocious. He could feel the skin on his face beginning to burn. It seemed to coat him from the top of his head to the tips of his toes, and he broke out into a sweat almost immediately. He felt the moisture seeping into his shirt, sticking the fabric against his stomach.

The Mercedes Viano rumbled down the bare track towards him, a cone of dust pluming in its wake. The sun reflected off the windscreen with a dazzling glare. Milton took off his jacket, folding it neatly and laying it on the driver's seat. He opened the rear door, took Adolfo by the crook of the elbow, and dragged him out of the car. He shoved him forwards so that he fell forwards onto his knees, took the Springfield, and aimed at his back.

"Nice and easy," he said.

The Viano slowed and swung around, coming to rest opposite the hire car. Milton leant against the bonnet. The metal was already searing hot.

The passenger-side door of the SUV slid open. Milton looked inside. Too dark to make much out.

"Where's the girl?" he called.

Two men stepped down. One had a short-barrelled H&K machine pistol with a black leather shoulder strap. The other had a twelve-gauge Remington automatic shotgun with a walnut stock and a twenty-round drum magazine.

"She ain't here, *ese.*"

Milton racked the slide of the Springfield. "Where is she?"

"Don't worry. You'll see her."

He took a step forward and jabbed the muzzle into the nape of Adolfo's neck.

"Are you calling my bluff?"

Milton tightened his grip on the pistol.

"Shoot him!" Adolfo screamed at the men.

Milton glanced around. The sun dazzled him. What was Beau waiting for?

A plume of dust kicked up a foot to his left; the cracking report of the rifle echoed across the desert.

"Your friend can't help you. Drop the gun."

A second shot rang out, this one a foot to his right. The bullet caromed off the rocks and ricocheted away into the scrub.

Milton tightened his grip and half-squeezed the trigger. Another ounce or two of pressure and González's brains would be splashed across the sand. But what then? The two *sicarios* looked like they knew how to use their weapons, and the man with Beau's Weatherby was a decent shot, too. He could shoot González, but then Caterina would be killed. He didn't know what the right play was, apart from the certainty that it wasn't shooting the man. Not yet.

He stepped back, released his grip, and let the pistol drop to the scrub.

Adolfo's cuffs were unlocked. He sneered at Milton. He took the shotgun and flipped it around. "Fuck you, English," he said. He swung the shotgun. The stock caught him on the chin and staggered him. The blazing bright day dimmed, just for a moment, but he did not go down. Adolfo flexed his shoulders, as if he was straightening out a kink, then swung again.

This time, the light dimmed for longer, and he went down. He dropped to the hard-packed dirt and sat there, the taste of his blood like copper pennies in his mouth. His instinct was to get up, so he did. He rose and stood, swaying. A wave of blackness came over him. He took an uncertain step forwards. Blood ran out of his mouth freely now. Adolfo stepped back for extra space and jabbed the stock into his unguarded chin as hard as he could. The black curtain fell and did not rise again. Milton fell face first into the dust.

Chapter Forty-Six

PLATO LEFT his cruiser at home and took the Accord. He was dressed in jeans and a white shirt and a trucker's cap. He had his shotgun in the footwell next to him, and there was a box of shells on the seat. He reversed out of his driveway and set off to the south. He didn't look back; he didn't want to see Emelia's face in the window. He wondered sometimes that the woman was practically psychic. She always knew when he had something on his mind. He had managed to avoid her this morning, creeping out of bed and leaving the house as quietly as he could. Even then, he had heard the floorboard in the bedroom creaking as she got out of bed. He'd nearly stayed, then, the reality of just how stupid this was slapping him right in the face. But then he thought of his old man, and his badge, and what that all meant, and he opened the door and set off.

The lights out of the city were all on green for him. One after the next, the whole sequence, all of them green. He wouldn't have minded if they were all red this morning. He couldn't help the feeling that they were hastening him towards something terrible.

Plato escaped the ring of *maquiladoras* arranged in parks on the outskirts and accelerated away. He knew Samalayuca. It was hardly a village, just a collection of abandoned huts. The road, the 45, cut right through the desert. The *barrial* was a prime cartel dumping spot. He had lost count of the number of early morning calls that had summoned him to Samalayuca, Ranchería or Villa Ahumada.

A trucker had seen a body on the side of the road.

A pack of coyotes observed tugging on fresh meat.

Vultures wheeling over carrion.

And those were just the bodies that La Frontera wanted them to find.

How many more hundreds—thousands—were buried out here?

The right-hand turn approached. The junction had no stop sign, just thick white lines that had melted into the blacktop. To the right, the road became a dirt track, cutting across the desert like a scar across sun-cooked skin. He slowed the car and pulled to the side of the road. He wound down the window, and hot air rushed inside. He glanced left and right, south and north, and saw nothing at all except heat shimmer and distant silver mirages. He left the engine running, reached across to the passenger seat, took his binoculars, and scanned the country, looking across the caldera towards a low ridge of rock. A mile away on the floodplain were two vehicles parked forty or fifty feet apart. A late-model Ford sedan and an SUV. He lowered the binoculars and looked over the country at large. It was already hot. Stifling. He pushed back his cap and wiped his forehead with his bandana and put the bandana back in the hip pocket of his jeans.

He raised the glasses again. There were men in between the cars. Two of them were armed. One was motionless on the ground. A fourth man was above him, kicking and stamping at him.

Was he too late?

He watched. The man on the ground was hauled to his feet. It was Smith. He was unconscious. They dragged him through the dirt to the SUV. They tossed him inside, and then the other men got inside, too.

The SUV reversed.

Plato dropped the glasses on the seat, pulled out on to the highway, and continued south. After half a mile he swung around on the margin, rattled over the bars of a cattle guard, and stopped. He fetched the glasses. The SUV was on the road and heading back towards the city. There was little he could do: confronting them would be suicide, and he did not have a death wish. He was frightened, for himself and his family. His instinct told him to switch off the engine and let them drive away. But he couldn't do that. Finding out where they were going would have to be enough. He put the car into gear, pulled onto the blacktop again, and keeping a safe distance behind them, he followed.

Chapter Forty-Seven

CATERINA MORENO had tried everything. The door was locked and the window, too. She had wondered whether she might be able to take a chair and smash it, but it was toughened glass, and anyway, it looked down onto a sheer thirty-foot drop. Then her thoughts had turned to weapons. Could she arm herself? The only cup in the room was plastic and too strong for her to break. There was the chair, again, but it was too well put together to be broken apart and too unwieldy as it was. There was a mirror in the bathroom, and eventually, her hopes focussed on that. She unplugged a table lamp and used the base to smash the glass. A jagged piece fell free, and she picked it up, wrapping the thicker end in a towel. It wouldn't be easy to use, but it was sharp, and perhaps, if she was careful, she might be able to maintain an element of surprise. She took it to the bed and hid it beneath the pillow.

She returned to the window. It was in the side of the house, looking out onto a stand of pecan trees. She heard the thump of bass from a powerful sound system. If she pressed her face against the glass, she could see a sliver of the rear garden, and occasionally, guests from the party would pass into and out of view. Servants ferried crates of beer and trays of food from a catering tent. They passed directly below her; she banged her fists against the window, but they either could not hear her or paid her no heed.

She went back to the bed but was unable to settle. She got up and started to pace. She returned to the window. The drive to the house snaked through the trees beneath her, and as she watched, a Mercedes SUV approached and stopped. The branches obscured her view a little, but she saw a door opening and then two men hauled John Smith out. It didn't look as if he was conscious: he was a deadweight, the two men dragging him across the driveway, his toes scraping against the asphalt. A second man followed. Caterina recognised him from the cowboy hat he was wearing: the man from the hospital who had wanted to speak to her, the man Smith had sent away.

She went back to the bed and sat.

Five minutes later, the door was unlocked and opened.

A man came into the room and locked the door behind him.

He was bland. Average. Nothing out of the ordinary about him at all.

"Hello, Caterina."

She backed away.

"You've caused us quite a lot of trouble."

She sat on the edge of the bed.

"This business of ours—we don't welcome publicity."

She shuffled backwards, her hand reaching beneath the pillow.

He tutted and waggled a finger at her. "Don't," he said, nodding towards the bed. He took out a pistol and pointed the barrel up to a tiny camera on the wall that Caterina had not seen.

"Who are you?"

"You can call me Adolfo." He stepped further into the room. "Let's have a talk."

"What do you want to talk about?"

"Why have you been writing about me?"

"What?"

"The girls."

She thought of what Delores had told them.

He was nothing special, by which I mean there was nothing about him that you would find particularly memorable. Neither tall nor short, neither fat nor thin. Normal looking. Normal clothes.

"It's you?"

"I can't take the whole credit. Me and a few friends."

She tore the pillow off the bed, grasped the shank, and rushed him. He pulled the gun quickly, expertly, and held it steady, right at her face. She stopped. She thought about it, calling his bluff, but her legs wouldn't move.

He nodded to the shank.

She dropped it.

"Your hand."

She had taken the glass too hastily and had cut her index finger.

"I'll send someone in to wrap that for you," he said.

"Don't bother. I don't need your favours."

"We'll see. I am going to speak with your friend, the Englishman, and then we have some business that needs to be seen to. Once I am finished, I will be back. We have lots to talk about."

Chapter Forty-Eight

ANNA STRAPPED herself into her seat as the captain of the Gulfstream announced that they were on their final descent into Fort Bliss. She had been working for most of the flight, ostensibly refining her report on John Milton but, in reality, observing everything she could about the six agents. There was very little conversation between them: some slept, others listened to music.

She pulled up the blind and looked out onto the New Mexico landscape five thousand feet below. It was desert for the most part, with nearly two thousand square miles of terrain within its boundaries and adjacent to the White Sands missile range. The populated area was set on a mesa, was six miles by six miles and housed several thousand soldiers and civilian personnel. It was practically a small city, and the biggest US Army base in the world. She watched as the plane arced away to port and then dropped into its glide path. Details in the desert became clearer, the mountains and the blue sliver of the Rio Bravo, and then the asphalt strip of the runway at Biggs Army Airfield. The pilot cut the speed, raised the nose, and executed a perfect landing, taxiing across to the parking area.

Anna disembarked, following Pope down onto the runway. It was unbearably hot. The heat wrapped around her like a blanket, and she quickly felt stunned by it. There was pressure in the air. A hundred miles away to the south-west she could see lightning flickering. Faint sheets and bolts of dry electricity discharging in a random display.

A soldier with colonel's pips was waiting for them. "Welcome to the United States," he said.

"Thank you."

"I'm Stark."

"Captain Pope."

"Good flight?"

"Straightforward, Colonel."

"Glad to hear it. I'll be your liaison here. Anything you need, you just holler. Can I do anything for you now?"

"Not really. We'd just like to get started."

"No sense in delaying."

"That's right."

"Thought you'd say that. We've got you a couple vehicles ready to go. We'll get your gear unloaded and repacked, and then you can be on your way."

"The border?"

"That's all arranged. The Mexicans know you're coming. We'll get you straight across."

"That's very helpful. Thank you, Colonel."

"My pleasure." He took off his cap and squinted against the sun. "Don't suppose you can tell me what you folks have come all this way to do?"

"Afraid not," he said.

He laughed. "Didn't think so. Completely understand."

Two identical SUVs were standing at the edge of the taxiway. Pope led Anna to the nearest.

"You'll be with me," he said. "We'll speak to the police. I'll send the others to the restaurant; see if they can find anything out there."

"Fine."

Anna turned to watch as the army technicians started to unload the cargo from the Gulfstream. The weapons were ferried to a cart and then wheeled across to the SUVs.

They had a lot of firepower.

She wondered whether they would need to use it.

Chapter Forty-Nine

MILTON CAME around. He was groggy, and as awareness returned, so did the pain. He assessed the damage. Red hot spears lanced up from his face. His head throbbed. His arm was difficult to move. A couple of ribs broken? He tried to open his eyes. His left was crusted with dried blood, and his right was badly swollen; he could only just open the first, and he could see nothing through the second. There were bones broken there: the orbital, perhaps, and something in the bridge of his nose. He felt a stubborn ache from his shoulders and realised that his hands were cuffed behind his back.

"You all right?"

He looked to his left. It was Beau.

"I'll live."

"You don't look so good. They worked you over some. I saw when they marched me down the mountain. They pretty much had to pull Adolfo off you."

"I've had worse."

"Really? Doubt that, partner."

Milton winced; his lips were cracked and bloodied.

He looked over at Beau. His shirt was ripped to the navel, revealing a tiger's tooth that he wore on a chain around his neck. He was sitting down, leaning back against the wall. His arms were shackled with FlexiCuffs behind his back.

"You got any bright ideas?" Beau asked.

"Not right at this moment. Has anyone been in to see us?"

"Not yet."

"Where are we?"

"Back in the city. South side. Looked like a pretty swanky neighbourhood, at least by standards around here.

My guess is we're in one of El Patrón's houses."

"And this room?"

"First floor. End of a corridor. I didn't get the chance to see all that much."

"Anything else?"

"Only that I'm not sure why they didn't just cap us out in the desert."

"He strikes me as the kind who'd want to make a point."

"I reckon that's right. The way I'm thinking, that roughing up they gave you out there ain't going to be a pimple on a fat man's ass compared to what they're going to do to us next. It ain't going to be pretty for us."

"Or them."

Beau laughed bitterly. "Jesus, man. Has anyone ever told you you're full of it? Look around, will you? We're cuffed, in a locked room, waiting for a psychopathic motherfucker to come and do whatever the fuck he wants to us. This ain't the time for bravado."

"It's not bravado, Beau. They should have killed me when they had the chance. They won't get another."

Beau was quiet for a minute. Milton assessed himself again: save his face and some bruising down his arms and trunk, there were no major breaks or internal injuries. He flexed his muscles against the cuffs. The sharp edges bit into the skin on his wrists.

"You think the girl's still alive?" Beau asked him.

"I don't know."

"If she is, she probably don't want to be."

THEY DIDN'T have to wait long. The door was unlocked, and Adolfo and another man stepped inside. He was older and bore a passing resemblance to Adolfo. His skin was unnaturally smooth; Milton guessed there had been a lot of plastic surgery involved.

"Hey, Adolfo," Beau said.

"*Hola,* Beau."

"I'm guessing this is your old man?"

"I am Felipe," the man said calmly. "You are Señor Baxter, and you are Señor Smith?"

"That's right. I don't suppose you want to get these cuffs off me?"

The man smiled broadly. "I don't think so."

"I was saying to Adolfo earlier, things don't have to be unfriendly between us."

"It's a little late for that, isn't it? You came here to murder my son."

"Come on, man. Who said I was gonna murder him? I was paid to deliver him."

Another indulgent smile. "We both know that would have been the same thing."

Milton tensed against the FlexiCuffs again. The two men were close enough to him—if he could free his hands, he knew he could take them both—but the plastic was too strong. He tried again. There was no give at all. Dammit.

Felipe noticed him. "Señor Smith. Unlike Señor Baxter, I know very little about you."

"Not much to know."

"I doubt that. You are mysterious—hiding something, I think. You will tell me what it is."

"You think?"

"They always do."

"They're not like me."

"You talk a good game."

"Where's the girl?"

"She's here."

Milton sat forwards and then got onto his knees. "I'm going to give you one chance. Give her to me, give us a car, and let us leave."

"And if I don't?" Felipe asked.

"Then it won't go well for you."

Adolfo stepped over and backhanded him across the

face. Fragments of broken bone in his nose ground against each other and his nerve endings.

Milton looked up at Adolfo and smiled. "Or you."

Adolfo drew back his foot and kicked him in the ribs. Pain flared, and Milton gasped.

Felipe put a restraining hand on his son's shoulder. "Enough. You will both stay here for now. We have business to attend to. We'll send for you when we are ready."

They stepped outside. The door was locked behind them.

"Come on, man," Beau said. "What was that about? You got a death wish?"

"Something like that."

Chapter Fifty

"LET ME do the talking," Pope told her. "All right?"

"All right."

"If there's anything I need to know, I'll ask you."

"Fine."

Anna, Captain Pope, Lance Corporal Hammond and Lance Corporal Callan had been the first across the border. The SUV was plenty big enough for the four of them and the extensive amount of weapons and other equipment that had been unloaded from the hold of the Gulfstream. The second SUV had followed behind. They had dispensation to cross the border, passing swiftly through a filter lane reserved for the army, border patrol and government agents. Anna had never been to Mexico before, and the sudden, abrupt change from the affluence of El Paso to the poverty of its twin was shocking. The buildings south of the border were dilapidated and scarred, and the people bore the fatigued look of the perpetually defeated. It was all a stark contrast to the optimistic, banal chatter of the hosts on Sunny 99.9FM, still within range as they drove south.

They had been busy. The second van had peeled off for the restaurant, but their first stop was to the headquarters of the municipal police for details on Lieutenant Jesus Plato. After being made to wait for an hour, they had finally been directed to a block station in the west of the city. It was a small, boxy building, cut off from the rest of the neighbourhood by a tall wire-mesh fence. There was a second line of concertina wire, the windows had bars, and they had to wait for the door to be unlocked.

"Pleasant neighbourhood," Pope said.

He led the way inside.

The receptionist regarded them with wary eyes.

"*Teniente* Plato, please."

"Take a seat."

Anna sat down. Pope did not. She watched him from behind a magazine as they waited. He stood, arms folded, impassive. There was no expression on his face. He made no effort to engage with her. The woman behind the desk tried to get on with her work, but she didn't find it easy; there was a restive presence about Pope that was impossible to ignore.

The officer who came out to see them was old. Anna would have guessed mid-fifties. His hair and moustache were greying, and he was a little overweight.

"I'm *Teniente* Plato. Who are you?"

"Pope. Is there somewhere we can talk?"

"I'm just going to smoke a cigarette. We can talk outside."

They went back out into the humid morning.

"We're here on behalf of the British government," Pope began.

"That right?"

Pope took out a passport.

Plato glanced at it. "Captain?"

"That's right."

"Army?"

He nodded.

"That's a coincidence."

"How's that?"

"Had an Englishman in here three days ago."

"The man you arrested?"

"Didn't arrest him."

"But you fingerprinted him?"

"Standard procedure."

"Name of John Smith?"

"That's right. How'd you know all that?"

"We need to see him."

"I need some reciprocation here, okay, Señor?"

"What did Mr. Smith tell you—about himself?"

"Next to nothing."

"That's not surprising.

"But there's more to him than he's letting on—right?"

"We're here to help him. We work together."

"Doing what?"

Pope made a show of reluctance. "Let's call it intelligence and leave it at that."

"You know he said he was a cook? What's he done?"

"*Lieutenant*, please—we need to speak to him. Please."

"You're going to have to move fast. He's in a whole heap of trouble." Plato dragged down on his cigarette. "Someone he's been helping out has got herself mixed up with the cartels. A journalist, writes about them, not a good idea. They abducted her yesterday night. This morning, your friend went out to the desert to try to negotiate with them to get her back. Didn't go so well— the cartels, they're not big on negotiating. Him and another man who went with him were taken away."

"How do you know that?"

"I was watching," he said. The answer seemed to embarrass him.

"Where?"

"Place out of town."

"Got any idea where they'd take him?"

"Better than that—I know. I followed. Place not too far from here."

"You'll take us?"

Plato shook his head. "That's not a place for a policeman like me." Again, Anna saw shame wash across his face. "I'm done with getting myself into scrapes like that. But no one's stopping you. You want, I'll give you directions."

Chapter Fifty-One

DUSK FELL as they travelled across the city. Anna sat at the back of the SUV and said nothing. No one spoke. There was a sense of anticipation among the three agents. Determination. Callan had disassembled his handgun and was cleaning the mechanism with a bottle of oil and a small wire brush, as ritualistic as a junkie with his works. Hammond was listening to music again, her eyes closed and her head occasionally dipping in time with the beat. Pope was driving, his eyes cold and resolute, fixed on the road ahead. Their equipment was laid out on the floor in the back of the van: MP-5 SD3 suppressed machine guns equipped with holographic sights and infrared lasers, a large M249 Squad Automatic Weapon, H&K machine pistols, a Mossberg 500 shotgun, three 9mm M9 Beretta pistols, M67 grenades and a Milkor Mk14 Launcher, M84 flashbangs, and night-vision goggles. The agents were each wearing jeans, T-shirts and desert boots with khaki load-carrying systems strapped on over the top. Each gilet was equipped with pouches for ammunition, hooks and eyelets for grenades and flashbangs, and each was reinforced with Kevlar plates.

The second SUV was directly behind them. They had visited the restaurant and found it closed down, boarding fixed across the front door. They had asked around at the other businesses nearby and discovered that there had been a second shooting, two days after the first. The owner and the woman who ran the front of house had both been shot dead. No clues as to who did it. It was them who they needed to talk to. Since they couldn't, that trail had run cold.

But it looked like they didn't need that trail after all.

Anna was nervous. She would have preferred to stay

behind, but Pope had insisted that she come. If the operation proceeded as he hoped, they would not delay in getting out of the city and back across the border again. There would be no opportunity to detour and pick her up. Pope had explained what she would have to do calmly and without inflection: stay in the van, don't get out of the van, leave it all to us.

And Pope needed her help, too.

He parked a hundred yards away from the gated entrance to the compound. Anna saw a guard shack and two men, both of whom were armed with rifles.

"All right, Anna," Pope said. "There's the house. See it?"

"I'm not blind."

"Do your thing."

She opened her laptop and connected with the internet. Her slender fingers fluttered across the keyboard as she navigated to the website for the *Comisión Federal de Electricidad* and, after correctly guessing the URL for the firm's intranet, forced her way inside.

"I can't be surgical about this," she said. "It'll be the whole block."

"Doesn't matter. Can you do it?"

"Just say when."

"Ready?" Pope asked the others.

Hammond said, "Check."

"Check," said Callan.

"All right then. Here we go."

They quickly smeared camouflage paint across their faces. Pope put the van into gear again and slowly pulled forwards. When they were twenty feet away from the gatepost, the guards came to attention, one holding up his hand for them to stop. The van had tinted windows, and the two of them were unable to see inside. The men made no effort to hide the automatic rifles they were carrying. Pope pulled a little to the left, opening up an angle between the driver's side of the van and the gatepost. One of the man spat out a mouthful of tobacco juice and stepped into the road. Hammond brought her MP-5 up above the line of the window, aimed quickly, and put three rounds into each guard. Anna was shocked: the gun was quiet, the suppressor so efficient that all you could really hear was the bolt racking back. The men fell, both of them dead before they hit the ground.

Anna's heart caught. She had never seen a man shot before.

Suddenly, it all seemed brutally, dangerously real.

Pope calmly put the van into gear again and edged forwards through the gate.

Anna compared what she could see in the gloom with the map she had examined earlier. It was a crescent-shaped street that curved around a central garden. Mansions were set back behind tall fences. It was nothing like the rest of the city; it was as if all the money had fled here, running from the squalor and danger outside and cowering behind the gates. One of the gardens was lit up more brightly than the others: strings of colourful lights had been hung from the branches of pecan and oak trees, and strobes flashed. The sound of loud *norteño* music was audible. Pope pulled over outside the driveway of the mansion. They pulled down full-face respirators and added night-vision goggles.

They collected their weapons.

The time on the dashboard display said 21:59.

"Now, Anna."

She hit return.

Her logic bomb deployed.

The time clicked to 22.00, and all the lights went out.

The streetlights.

The lights in the mansion, the colourful lights in the grounds.

The music stopped.

"Go, go, go," Pope said.

Chapter Fifty-Two

PLATO AND SANCHEZ ended up on their usual jetty, looking out onto the sluggish Rio Bravo. The brown-green waters reached the city as a pathetic reminder of what it must have been, once, before the factories and industrial farmers choked it upstream for their own needs. They were beneath the span of the bridge, sitting on the bonnet of Plato's Dodge. The headlights were on, casting out enough light so that they could read the graffiti on the pillars. Several of the concrete stilts had been decorated with paintings of the pyramids at Teotihuacán. He could see the fence and the border control on the other side. The low black hills beyond El Paso. America looked pleasant, like it always did. The day was ending with the usual thickening soup of smog muffling the quickly dying light.

Sanchez pulled another two cans of Negra Modelo from the wire mesh.

Plato took a long draught of his beer. He sighed. His heart wasn't in the banter like he hoped it would be.

"What's on your mind, man?" Sanchez asked. "You've been quiet all night."

"Been coming here for years, haven't we?"

"At least ten."

"But not for much longer. All done and finished soon."

"What? You saying you won't still come down?"

"Think Emelia will let me?"

"You wait. She'll want you out of the house. You'll drive her crazy."

"Maybe." Plato tossed his empty can into the flow. It moved beneath him, slow and dark. Sanchez handed him another.

"What am I doing?"

"What?"

Plato looked at the can, felt it cold in his palm. He popped the top and took a long sip. "I can't stop thinking about that girl."

"From the restaurant?"

"And the Englishman. Going after her like that. Going after the cartels, Sanchez, on his own, going right at them. Makes me ashamed to think about it. That's what we're supposed to do—the police—but we don't, do we? We just stand by and let them get on with their murdering and raping and their drugs. We swore the same oath. Doesn't it make you ashamed?"

He looked away. "I try not to think about it."

"Not me. All the time. I can't help it. All that bravery or stupidity, whatever you want to call it, how do I reward him?—by sending him on his way to a death sentence and not doing anything to help him. And then three of his colleagues turn up, and I won't even take them to where he is. Didn't even try to help them. I just tell them where to find him. They go there, that'll be another three deaths that keep me up at night. All I can think about, all day, is what am I doing? I've just been trying to keep my head down. Get my pension and get out."

"You've done your years."

"Not yet. I've still got one more day."

"So keep that in mind. One more day, then all you need to worry about is your family and that stupid boat."

"No, Sanchez. I don't agree. I've been doing that for months, and it's selfish. I'm police for one more day. My oath should still mean something."

They heard a dog somewhere. An anguished, hungry howl.

The receiver crackled inside the car. "We got a 246 at St. Mark's Close. Repeat, a 246 at St. Mark's Close. Possible 187."

"That's the narco mansions, right?"

"Yep," Plato said.

"González's mansion?"

Plato nodded. He pushed himself off the bonnet. His bones ached.

"No one's answering *that* call."

"I will," Plato said.

"You're joking—right?"

"No. You coming?"

He gaped at him. "Someone's shooting up González's mansion, and you want to respond? It can only be another cartel. You want to get in the middle of *that?* Are you crazy?"

"That's what we're supposed to do."

"You promised Emelia—don't get shot. One more day, amigo. You stay away from shit like that. How stupid would it be to get yourself shot now?"

"I've been making the wrong decisions all week. And now I'm thinking what am I going to do to set them right?"

Chapter Fifty-Three

THE LIGHTS went first. The live music, which had been playing loud all evening, petered out and then stopped. Milton winced as he pushed himself upright against the wall. Small-arms fire rattled from the grounds outside the house. Beau got up, went to the window, and put his eye to the crack between the shutters.

"Can you see anything?"

"Not really."

"Yes or no?"

"It's too dark."

The door opened, and a guard came into the room. "*Bajar*," he told Beau, waving his ArmaLite at him. *Get down.* He unlatched the shutters, threw them aside, switched the rifle, and used the stock to smash out the glass. He swept away the shards still stuck to the frame and then put the stock to his shoulder, glancing down the sight and opening fire.

All right, then. Milton winced as he moved forwards onto his knees, sliding his hands all the way down his back, his shoulders throbbing with pain as he passed them over his backside and then down into the hollow behind his knees. He rolled his weight forwards until the momentum brought him to his feet, stepping over the loop of his closed hands, raising himself up. Milton dropped his cuffed hands around the man's throat, and with his left shoulder pressed as near to perpendicular to the man's head as he could manage, he yanked quickly to the right and snapped his neck.

"You've done that before."

Milton frisked the dead guard, found a butterfly knife in his pocket, shook it open, and sliced through the plastic shackles. He did the same for Beau. He stooped to collect the ArmaLite, checked the magazine, added a second from the guard's pocket, and went out into the corridor.

"We're getting out, right?"

"Not without the girl."

"Come on, man, we're fucked as it is. You want to waste time looking for her? Forget what they said—they were pulling your chain. That psychopath probably did her yesterday. She's already dead, man. Dead."

"We get her first."

"She's dead, and you know it. And we got to get out. I don't know who that is outside, but I'm willing to bet they ain't gonna be too friendly with us. Another cartel. Military. Anyone in here's gonna be fair game."

"We get her; then we get González. How much if you bring him back?"

"Twenty-five large."

"So why do you want to leave?"

"Can't spend it when you're dead."

"If you want to go, there's the door. Go. I'm not stopping you."

Beau sighed helplessly. "I'm gonna regret this."

"Stay behind me."

"You're as crazy as they are." He settled in behind him. "I need a gun."

Milton brought the ArmaLite up and tracked down the corridor. As he passed a window, all the glass fell out of it. He hadn't even heard the shot. He looked out of the next window: a pandemonium of gunfire had broken out. Muzzle flashes spat out, three of them, shots aimed by the guards, and as Milton watched, all three were taken out by a single frag grenade. That portion of the garden was subdued; Milton saw a flash of khaki as a figure in night-vision goggles crab-walked to a forward position, an MP-5 cradled easily between practiced hands.

"It's not a cartel," he muttered.

The next room to the one in which they had been held was occupied by two men. They were pressed against the wall on either side of an open window. One had a shotgun; the other had an M-15. Shots from outside passed through the window and jagged across the ceiling. Milton turned into the doorway and raked both men with a quick burst of fire.

"Smith! Look out!"

A third Mexican was coming up the stairs, reaching for a small machine gun he carried on a strap. Milton turned and fired, the ArmaLite cracking three times, blowing the top of his head against the wall and sending his body spinning back down the stairs.

"There's your gun," he said. "Help yourself."

Beau took the shotgun.

There was a window at the end of the corridor. It smashed loudly, a six-inch canister crashing through it and then bouncing once, twice, before it came to rest against the wall.

Gas started to gush from both ends.

Milton's mouth was filled with the impossibly acrid taste of tear gas before he covered his face with his sleeve. Whoever was attacking the mansion was professional. They'd cut the power, and now they were going to disable everyone inside. Too organised and too well equipped for a cartel. There was precision here. A plan.

If he didn't know better, he would have said it was Special Forces.

Chapter Fifty-Four

FELIPE GONZÁLEZ watched as the grenade looped in a graceful arc over the swimming pool, bounced against the tiled floor, and collected against the cushion of one of the loungers. It immediately started to unspool a cloud of brown-tinged smoke, and within moments, the guests on that side of the garden started to choke. Women screamed. One of the guests—it was the mayor, for fuck's sake—stumbled and fell into the water. Felipe turned back to the mansion—the lights had all been extinguished there, too—and then he heard the first rattle of automatic weaponry.

What?

Que Madres?

More screams.

What the fuck was going on?

"El Patrón?" Isaac said.

"Come with me—all of you."

He hurried around the pool, away from the spreading cloud of gas. The gringos stumbled after him, drunk.

"Sir," Pablo said. "Come."

"Who is it? Army?"

"I do not know. But whoever they are, they are very good."

"Los Zetas?"

"We need to get you away from here."

"Where is Adolfo?"

"Inside—with the girl."

Felipe cursed. "Get him."

"Javier has gone for him. Come, please, El Patrón."

"Bring the gringos," he said, pointing back to the three Americans.

"We will. But we must leave—now."

There was a garage at the end of the garden. Pablo hurried him down the path towards it. A BMW was waiting, the engine running. An Audi waited behind that. The automatic gates did not function without power, so they were being dragged open by hand. Two other men were waiting with AKs, aiming back towards the house. Felipe allowed himself to be jostled into the back of the car. The gringos were loaded into the Audi. He turned and looked back towards the mansion, his fists clenched in impotent rage. There was an explosion from the first floor. Debris plumed upwards and out, falling down onto the patio below: bricks, bits of window frame, shards of glass.

He thought of his son.

The driver stamped on the gas, the wheels spinning until the rubber bit, the car lurching for the gate and the road beyond.

Chapter Fifty-Five

MILTON STOOD listening at the door. He took a step back and kicked it open. A bedroom, plush, thick carpets, art on the walls. Caterina was on the bed. A Mexican stood at an open door across the room. Milton dropped him where he stood. He stepped out of the doorway and stood with his back to the wall. He ducked his head around to look in again. Now the second door was shut. He locked eyes with Caterina. She looked at the door and nodded. Milton pressed in the second magazine and fired a steady burst through the door. A jagged hole was torn from the middle of the panel. He looked through it and saw a spray of pink blood across a white-tiled wall.

"Beau," he said, indicating the bathroom. "Check it."

"Right you are."

He went forwards and fired three more rounds through the door, then kicked it open and went in, the shotgun held out.

Milton went to the girl. "Are you all right?"

She nodded.

"They didn't—?"

She shook her head.

"What happened?"

"The police captain—Alameda—he is working for them."

"Well, lookit here," Beau called out. He stepped back, the shotgun still aimed into the bathroom. "Out you come."

Adolfo González came into the bedroom. His hands were above his head. "Don't," he said, staring at the business end of the Remington.

"Hiding in the bath," Beau said. "On your knees, boy. Hands behind your back."

235

There was a nest of FlexiCuffs on the dresser. Beau looped one around Adolfo's right wrist, then his left, and yanked them tight. He kicked the man behind the knees, forcing him to the floor, and went to the wide window that looked down onto the gardens outside. Beau edged carefully alongside it and looked down below.

"Hey, Smith," he called. "You want to see this."

"What is it?"

"The firefight outside? Them fellas ain't Mexican."

Milton counted six attackers, each of them wearing load-carrying systems and night-vision goggles. Five moved with easy confidence, passing from cover to cover, popping out to fire tight and controlled rounds that were unerringly accurate. The sixth looked to be limping. Even from this distance, and despite the goggles and the darkness, he recognised them. Five because he had fought alongside them before. The other because he had looked into the barrel of the man's pistol six months ago, in an East End London gymnasium with Dennis Rutherford's body laid out in a bloody mess behind him.

Pope, Hammond, Spenser, Blake, Underwood and Callan.

Oh, shit.

"It's not the cartels," he said. "I know them. It's much worse."

"Wanna tell me what's going on, partner?"

"We don't have enough time."

He was in the window for too long, and Callan saw him. For a moment, their eyes locked, but then the man brought up his M-15. The red laser dazzled his eyes. Milton swung around just in time: the fusillade of bullets shredded the blind and chewed gouts of dusty plaster from the ceiling.

"When you say you know them—?"

"Not in a good way. Look, Beau—you have to listen to me. Get her out of here. Stay away from them. They're coming from the south. I doubt they'll be any more of them—they won't think it's necessary. Get her back to where they had us—there's a fire escape there, end of the corridor, go down and then out the back. I'll hold them off as long as I can."

"There's only the six of them. They'll never take the house."

"They count double. At least. Please, Beau, go—get her over the border."

"All right, all right."

"And fast. They know I'm here. They'll be coming up now."

"All right."

"Caterina—you have to go with him."

"What about you?"

"I'm going to buy you a little time and then make a run for it. I'll see you in America."

Beau hauled Adolfo to his feet and shoved him towards the door. He looped an arm around his throat and held the shotgun, one-handed, to the side. Using him as a shield, Beau edged out into the corridor.

Another barrage peppered the ceiling.

"Get going," Milton implored her, and after a moment, she did.

Chapter Fifty-Six

MILTON KNEW there was no sense in running. The only chance Beau and Caterina had was if he gave the agents what they wanted; if he didn't, they would chew through the house, room by room, taking out anyone and everyone they found until they had who they were there for.

Him.

He thought about it: six months.

It had been a good run, but it was always going to end, eventually.

He wondered, vaguely, how they had found him.

He started downstairs to meet them.

The first-floor half-landing gave him a good view into the darkened gardens. The cartel members were either dead or gone. A few people from the party that he had heard from earlier were scattering. One man—older, portly—was pulling himself out of the swimming pool. A lost hairpiece floated towards the filter. Pope and Callan were working through the gardens and poolside area, the flash of their laser sights raking ahead of them. Emptying canisters leaked gas into the night. A dead narco was draped over a piece of topiary pruned into the shape of a machine gun. Another was laid out in an elaborate swing set as if he was gently reclining, everything normal apart from the smoking hole in his guts.

The patio doors had been blown in.

Hammond was crouched in the empty doorway.

Milton propped the ArmaLite against the balustrade, raised his hands, and came down the rest of the stairs. "Here I am."

She brought her MP-5 to bear. The red laser sight blinded him as she brought it to rest on his forehead, right between the eyes.

"Knees," she said, nodding her head downwards.

Milton did as he was told.

She tapped a throat mic to open the channel. "Got him."

THEY TOOK him outside, to the front of the house. There was an SUV parked in the road with a young woman inside. Milton did not recognise her. They took off their goggles and scrubbed their faces, puckered red outlines around their eyes. Pope, who had swapped his MP-5 for a pistol, took him by the arm, and led him towards the van.

"John."

"Mike."

"You've led us on a merry dance."

"Sorry about that."

"You didn't think it could last forever, did you?" he said quietly.

"I don't know. It was going pretty well."

"What the fuck's been going on?"

"What did he tell you?"

"That you're a couple of sandwiches short of a picnic."

He shrugged. "Well, you know—"

"Fine," Pope qualified. "Even more than usual. Control's been crucified about this. He's made you his personal project."

"Trying to make me feel special?"

"And Callan—"

"Probably best not to get me started on him."

"Callan was all for putting a bullet in your brain right now. You really fucked up his knee."

"He's lucky that's all I did."

"Well, that's as may be, but you're not on his Christmas card list. I don't have the same predisposition, and luckily for you, I'm the ranking officer. So that's not going to happen."

"And what is?"

"I have to take you back, John. Back over the border to Fort Bliss. We've got a jet there. Back to the UK. I'll help as best as I can, but whatever comes next is between you and Control."

"Do whatever you have to do."

Pope paused and looked at him with sudden concern. "What's this all about, John? Really? What's going on?"

"It got to the stage where I'd just had enough. I'm not interested in doing it anymore."

"So what have you been doing instead?"

Milton paused.

"Something useful."

He could hear sirens.

"Come on," Pope said.

The sirens grew louder. Milton turned to the development's ostentatious gate as a police car rushed through, past the two dead bodies on the pavement and towards them.

Chapter Fifty-Seven

JESUS PLATO got out of his car. There were six soldiers. The oldest of the three, the one who had spoken to him at the station, was with Smith. Plato could see dead bodies in the gardens behind him. He saw three, at least, maybe four. A massacre. His stomach turned over. Whoever these six were, they were armed to the teeth and ruthless as hell, and they had just subdued El Patrón's mansion and all of the *sicarios* that he had at his disposal.

And now Captain Pope had a gun pointed at Smith's chest.

"Someone going to tell me what's happening here?"

"This is the man we're here for. We're taking him back over the border."

"You told me he was a colleague."

"He is a colleague."

"And you were going to help him."

"That's true."

"This is helping him?"

"He's also a wanted man."

"For what?"

"That's classified."

"Not good enough."

"I'm afraid it's going to have to do."

Plato shook his head. He drew his Glock and aimed at Pope.

"What are you doing, Lieutenant?"

"Let's just keep it nice and easy."

"Put that down, please."

"I'm going to need you to explain to me why you think you can take him. You got a warrant?"

"We don't need one."

"Afraid you do. Can't let you do anything without

241

one."

"Don't be an idiot," the woman said. "Step aside."

"Wish I could, Señorita, but I'm afraid I just can't. This man is wanted for further questioning—that ruckus at the restaurant on Monday, seems there's a bit more to that than we thought there was. And unless I'm mistaken, this is Mexico, and I'm an officer of the law. The way I see it, that gives me jurisdiction."

Pope spoke calmly. "Think about this for a moment, *Teniente*. We are here with the approval of your government and with the co-operation of the American military. This man is a fugitive. There'll be serious consequences if you interfere."

"Maybe so."

"Your job, for one."

He laughed. "What are they going to do? Fire me? I retire tomorrow. That's what you call an empty threat. Drop your weapons."

They did no such thing.

Plato tightened his grip on his pistol.

A stand-off.

There were six of them and one of him.

He had no second move.

He heard a siren; another cruiser hurried through the gates and pulled over next to his car.

Sanchez got out. He was toting his shotgun. "All right, Jesus?"

"You sure about this, buddy?"

Sanchez nodded. "You were right."

Pope turned to Sanchez. "You too?"

"Let him go."

The shotgun was quivering a little, but he didn't lower it.

"Now, then," Plato said, stepping forward. "I'm going to have to insist that you drop those weapons, turn around, and put your hands on the car."

The younger man fixed him with a chilling gaze.

"Don't be a fool. We're on the same side."

"I think in all this noise and commotion it's all gotten to be a little confusing. I think the best thing to do is, we all go back to the station and work out who's who in this whole sorry mess."

"If we don't want to do that?"

"I suppose you'd have to shoot us. But do you want to do that? British soldiers in a foreign country, murdering the local police? Imagine the reaction to that. International outrage, I'd guess. Not what you want, is it?"

"All right," Pope said. "Do as he says."

He took a step backwards.

Sanchez raised the shotgun and indicated the car with it. "Now, then, please—the guns on the floor, please."

They finally did as they were told.

"Señor Smith," Plato said. "You're riding with me. Señor Pope—you and your friends stay with *Teniente* Sanchez, please."

Sanchez said that he had called for backup and that it was on its way. Plato turned to Smith and took him by the arm. As he moved him towards the waiting cruiser, he squeezed him two times on the bicep.

Chapter Fifty-Eight

MILTON SAT AND watched the streets of Ciudad Juárez as they rushed past the windows of the Dodge.

Plato looked across the car at him for a moment. "You all right?"

"Fine."

"You don't look fine."

Milton saw his reflection in the darkened window of the car: his right eye was swollen shut, lurid purples and blues in the ugly bruise; there was dried blood around his nose and from the cuts on his face. He probed his ribs gently; they were tender. "Looks worse that it is."

"Want to tell me who they are?"

"Ex-colleagues."

"They seem pretty keen to meet with you."

"They've been looking for me for six months."

"You think it was my fault they found you?"

"Those fingerprints you took get emailed anywhere?"

"Mexico City."

"Probably was you, then. Doesn't matter."

"What do they want?"

He sighed. "I used to do the same kind of job that they do. Then I didn't want to do it anymore."

"I know the feeling."

"But the problem is, mine's not the kind of job you can just walk away from."

"And they want you to go back to it again?"

He chuckled quietly. "We're well beyond that."

Plato mused on that. "Where's the girl?"

"With Baxter."

"He got her out?"

"As far as I know."

"Did you speak to her?"

"Briefly."

"And?"

"I don't think they touched her. But you've got a problem."

"I know," he said grimly.

Milton nodded. "Alameda."

"I think I've known for a while. He ducked out when they attacked the restaurant, and if you asked me to bet, I'd say it was him who called González from the hospital, then disappeared so he could do what he came there to do. I checked who responded to that murder, too, when she was taken. It was him."

"She said he took her."

Plato sighed.

"What are you going to do?"

"Haven't worked that out yet."

"What's the plan now?" Milton said.

"You don't wanna see them again, right?"

"Not if I can help it."

"Thought so. Sanchez will keep them busy for an hour or so. Papers to fill out and suchlike. Give you a bit of a head start. The only thing to decide is where do you want to go?"

"North, eventually."

"My opinion? El Paso's too obvious. I'm guessing your passport is shot now, and even if you could bluff your way across, it'd be easy to find you again from here."

"I think so."

"So, if it was me, I'd go east and then go over. You can walk across, somewhere like Big Bend. It's not easy—it's a long walk—but the coyotes take people over there all the time. I've been hunting there, too. I can show you the best place. You'll need some gear. A tent, for one. A sleeping bag. A rifle."

"I'm not going yet."

Plato glanced across at him. "Why not?"

"There's something I need to do first. But I'm going to

need your help."

"Am I going to regret that?"

"Probably. Can we go to your house?"

"That's where we're headed. I was going to kit you out."

He slowed, turned left across the flow of traffic, and headed into a pleasant residential estate. Milton recognised it from before. Oaks and pecan trees lined the broad avenue. After five minutes they pulled into the driveway of the house and parked behind the boat. A light flicked on in a downstairs window, and a woman's face appeared there. Plato waved up at the window and made his way to the garage at the side of the house.

Plato led the way inside, switched on the overhead strip light, and started to arrange things: he took out a one-man tent, a rucksack, and a canteen that he filled with water.

"What are you going to do?" Milton asked him.

"About what?"

"Juárez."

"Stick it out like I've always done."

"And El Patrón?"

"Nothing's changed there."

"But if he finds out you were involved with me? And the girl?"

"Look, man, if he wanted to take me out, he could've done it a long time ago. There's nothing I could do about it if he has it in his mind to make an example out of me. You get used to the thought of it. That's just Juárez."

"And your family?"

Plato looked away. "I'm thinking about that."

"Where do you think he's gone?"

"Don't know for sure—he has a lot of places—but I could hazard a pretty good guess. I reckon, given that you and your friends back there just gave him a bloody nose, he'll go back to where he feels most secure. The Sierra Madre. That's where he's from originally. The whole place out there, it's all La Frontera: hundreds of cartel men, even the locals are on his side. The mountains, too. Inhospitable. You'd need an army to get him out again if that's where he's gone. And I'm not exaggerating."

There was a gun cabinet on the wall. Milton pointed at it. "What have you got in there?"

Plato took a key from his belt and opened the cabinet. There was a rifle, a revolver and several boxes of ammunition.

"The rifle," Milton said.

"I'm guessing you know plenty about guns?"

A small smile. "A little."

"You'll like this, then." Plato took it down and handed it across. "That's the Winchester Model 54. They started making those babies in 1925. Chambered for the .30-06 Springfield. They've developed it some over the years, and some people will tell you the Model 70 is the better of the two, but I don't have any truck with that."

Milton ran his fingers across the walnut stock and the hand chequering. The gun had good rifling and a strong muzzle. The bolt throw still had a good, crisp action. It had been oiled regularly and kept in pristine condition.

"You ever shot with it?" Plato asked.

"Now and again."

"Most accurate gun I ever used. Belonged to my father originally—he took it to war with him. I killed my first deer with it. Must've been no more than ten years old. Had it ever since."

"Do you think I could borrow it?"

"Don't suppose there's any point me asking you what for?"

"You don't need to ask, do you?"

"No. I don't suppose I do."

Milton put the rifle next to the tent and the rest of the equipment that Plato had assembled. He added a box of bullets.

"Your car, too, if that's all right?"

Plato chuckled. "Why not? Lending my rifle and my car to someone I don't know wouldn't be the stupidest thing I've done this week."

"Don't worry, Plato. I won't be long. And I'll bring it all back."

Chapter Fifty-Nine

BEAU HAD STOLEN a Pontiac Firebird from the street near the mansion. Caterina was in the front with him, and González was in back. He was cuffed, his arms behind his back. They had cuffed his ankles together, too. Beau had a pistol laid out on the dash in front of him, and he had threatened González that he would gag him with the duct tape he had found in the glovebox if he made a nuisance of himself. So far, Caterina thought, he had not. She guessed that he was facing something very unpleasant on the other side of the border, and his compliance—up until now, at least—made her nervous. He did not strike her as the kind of man who would just go quietly.

Beau had not explained their route to them, but it was easy enough to guess. They were going to head south and then west, probably to Ojinaga, and then cross into Presidio and Texas. They were close enough to the border for the car radio to pick up the channels on the other side of the Rio Bravo, and as the miles passed beneath their wheels, the channels blurred from stoner rock to throbbing *norteño* and then to the apocalyptic soothsaying of fire and brimstone preachers.

They cut through the savannah and scrub on the 45, the distant buttes of the mountains visible as darker shadows on the horizon. The road was quiet, shared only with trucks, each cab decorated with the coloured lights that the teamster used to distinguish his from the next. A freight train rattled along the tracks to their right, the huge half-mile-long monster matching their pace for a minute or two before splitting off to disappear deeper into the desert. Caterina watched it and then stared out into the night until the swipes of its lights faded from her retinas and she could see the darkness properly again, the quick flashes that were the eyes of the rabbits and prairie dogs watching them from the side of the road as they passed.

They reached the edge of Chihuahua, found the 16, and headed back to the north-east.

"Do you really think this is going to work?"

Beau stiffened a little next to her. She glanced into the rear-view mirror and straight into González's face. He was calm and placid; there was even the beginning of a playful smile on his thin lips.

"Don't reckon you need worry yourself on account of that," Beau said.

"You won't even get across the border. My father owns the border. What is it? Where will you try? Ojinaga? Ciudad Acuña? Piedras Negras?"

"Thought I'd just take a little drive, see which one caught my fancy."

"Fifty thousand is very little to be forever watching your back, Beau."

"It'll do for now."

"I could give you five hundred thousand."

"Haven't we been here before? Shoe was on the other foot, then, as I recall. Answer's still the same."

"The offer stands until the border."

"You know something, Adolfo? You're a piece of work. You might be a scary fucker when it's on your own terms, but when it gets to the nut-cutting, like now, the moment of true balls, all you've got is talk."

The dawn's first light fell upon them as they turned off the highway and headed directly north. The landscape changed suddenly, the flat scrubland replaced by ridges and plateaus, the mountains filling the distance all the way to the horizon. The rock turned from black to blue and then to green as the sun climbed in the sky. Dust devils skittered across the road. The next twin towns on the line east from Juárez and El Paso, Ojinaga and Presidio clung together against the awesomeness of the mountains. It was the most isolated of the crossings. Here, the Rio Bravo was supplemented by the waters from the Conchos, and rather than the insipid trickle that apologetically ran between Juárez and El Paso, it was a surging, throbbing current that was full of life.

Beau stepped on the gas.

"Caterina," González said.

Beau turned to her. "Don't."

"I'm not frightened of him."

"Long as he's trussed up like that, there ain't no need to be. But a feller like him, the only thing he wants to do is put things in your head, thoughts you'll worry about, cause problems down the line."

Caterina set her face and turned a little. "What do you want?" she said into the back of the car.

"Those girls—you want to know what it was like?"

"Shut your trap," Beau ordered.

"Come on, Caterina. You're a writer. You're curious, I know you are. This is your big story. What about that girl you were with in the restaurant? You want to know how it was for her?"

"No, she don't."

"Delores. That was her name. I remember—she told me. I don't normally remember the names—there've been so many—but she stood out. She kept asking for her mother."

"I won't tell you again. Any more out of you and you're getting gagged."

"She's the proof, though, isn't she? Look at what happened to her. You can't escape from us. It doesn't matter where you are. It doesn't matter who is protecting you. Eventually, one way or another, you'll be found and brought back to me."

Beau slammed on the brakes. "All right, you son of a bitch," he said, reaching for the roll of duct tape. "Have it your way."

THEY FOUND a motel on the outskirts of Presidio. The place was a mongrel town, full of trailer parks and strip malls. They had crossed the border an hour ago. Beau had pulled the Firebird to the side of the road as the steep fence and the squat immigration and customs buildings appeared ahead of them. He had taken out his cellphone and made a quick call. A few shops had collected next to the crossing: Del Puente Boots, a Pemex gas station, an Oxxo convenience store, a dental clinic. An all-night shack with flashing lights advertised "Sodas, Aguas, Gatorades." It was practically empty, and only one of the northbound gates was open. Beau slotted the car into it, wound down the window, and reached out to hand over his passport. The customs agent, a nervous-looking forty-something man who reminded Caterina of a rabbit, made a show of inspecting the documents as he removed the five hundred-dollar bills from within their pages. He handed the passport back. "Welcome to America," he had said, opening the gate. Beau had thanked him, put the car into gear, and driven them across the bridge and into the United States.

It was as simple as that: they were on the 67 and across. A neat line of palm trees on either side of the road. A smooth ribbon of asphalt. A large sign that welcomed them to America and invited them to "Drive Friendly – The Texas Way."

The Riata Inn Motel was a low, long line of rooms on the edge of the desert, set alongside a parking lot. They had taken a single room, and now the dawn's light was glowing through the net curtains. They had cuffed González to the towel rack in the bathroom.

"Is this it?" Caterina asked him.

"It is for him. My employer will be here in a couple of hours."

"And then?"

"Not our problem any more. He'll take him off our hands, and then he'll sort you out with what you need:

papers, money, someplace to live."

Beau sat and tugged off his boots. He unbuckled his holster and tossed it onto the bed.

"What do you think happened to Smith?"

"I don't know. That boy's as tough as old leather, though. I wouldn't count him out."

Beau looked at her. She was tired, but there was a granite strength behind it. After all she had been through, well, Beau thought, if it had've been him? He might've been ready to pack it all in.

"Long night," she said.

"Tell me about it."

"I'd kill for a cold drink."

"There's an ice machine outside. I'll get some. Thirty seconds?" He pointed at the door to the bathroom. "Don't—well, you know, don't talk to him."

Her smile said that she understood.

The machine was close, but even though the door to the motel room was going to be visible the whole time, he didn't want to tarry. González was resourceful and smart—thirty or forty or however the hell old he was, practically ancient in narco-years—and although Caterina was smart, too, he didn't want to leave him alone with her for any longer than he had to. He went outside in his stockinged feet and walked across to the machine. He filled the bucket with crushed ice, took a handful and scrubbed it on the back of his neck and then across his forehead and his face.

He was getting too old for this shit.

When he got back to the room, Caterina had taken his Magnum .357 out of the holster. The bathroom door was open. González was on his knees, his hands in front of his face. She was pointing the gun at his head.

"How do you get paid?" she asked him.

"Cash on delivery."

"So, what?—he's got to be alive?"

"He don't got to be. More for me if he is, though."

"Ah," she said. "Sorry about that."

The gunshot was audible all the way across the scrubby desert.

Chapter Sixty

CAPITÁN VICENTE ALAMEDA lived with his wife and three children in the upscale neighbourhood of Campestre. The district rubbed against Highway 45, just before the crossroads with Highway 2, and massive *maquiladoras* were gathered on one edge of the neighbourhood. Plato continued along an avenue that could have been in any city north of the border: a Starbucks, Chili's, Applebee's and strip malls. He turned into Alameda's street and parked. Razor wire lined the top of brick and stucco walls. Uniformed guards stood watch at gated entryways. Gold doors on one home reflected the lamplight. Parked in the driveways were BMWs and Lexuses, many with Texas license plates. Alameda's house had an Audi in the driveway. There was a large garden. A pool. Four or five bedrooms judging from the windows on the second floor. A set of gates, although they hadn't been closed.

It wasn't a policeman's house.

Plato got out of the car and looked up. The sky was full of stars, a rind of moon hanging over the silhouette of the factories on the edge of the neighbourhood. He made his way up the street to a small *zócalo* where the grackles in the eucalyptus trees called out in drowsy alarm.

He pressed the intercom.

"Yes?"

"*Capitán*—it's Jesus Plato."

"Plato? It's late. Do you know what time it is?"

"I know. But I need to talk to you."

"Tomorrow, Jesus, all right?"

"No, sir. It has to be now."

The intercom cut out. Plato stood at the gate, staring through the bars at the home beyond. The curtains in one of the large windows on the first floor twitched aside, and Plato saw Alameda's face.

He held his finger on the intercom for ten seconds.

He would wait as long as it took.

After a minute, the front door opened, and Alameda came outside. He was wearing slippers and a dressing gown.

Plato slipped between the gates and met him in the garden.

"What the fuck are you doing?" Alameda hissed. "You've woken the children!"

"I must be some kind of idiot. How long have we known each other?"

"Ten years."

"Exactly. Ten years and you've never invited me here. We've had barbeques at my place and at Sanchez's, but you never did the same. Don't know why that never struck me as odd. Now I can see why."

"What are you talking about?"

"The first thing I would've asked is where you could possibly be getting the money to afford a place like this. It's not on a captain's salary, I know that much. Not wondering about that could all have been stupidity on my part, I'm capable of that, but I don't think so, not this time. I think it was wilful blindness. I didn't want to look at what was staring me in the face."

"I had an inheritance. My father-in-law."

"No, you didn't. Drug money bought all this."

"Come on, Jesus. That's crazy."

"I don't think so. I'm sorry it's come to this, sir, but you're under arrest."

"You want to do this now? *Now?* You're retiring."

"I've been thinking about that. I'd have to talk to Emelia, of course, but I'm thinking maybe I can stay on another six months. There's a lot of cancer that needs to be cut out. Now's a good a time as any. Maybe I can do something about that."

"You know what that'll mean for you and your family?"

"I know I swore an oath. When I retire, I aim to have done what I promised to do."

"You've lost your mind, Jesus."

"That's as may be, *Capitán*. But you're still under arrest."

Plato took out his cuffs, and with Alameda's wife and children watching open-mouthed from the windows, he fastened them and led him back out and onto the street.

Chapter Sixty-One

"AND THERE YOU HAVE IT," Felipe said with a grand gesture. "The best equipped methamphetamine lab in Mexico."

Isaac and his two colleagues looked suitably impressed. That was good. Felipe had been struggling to maintain their confidence after what had gone down at the mansion. He had struggled a little during the flight south to maintain his mood. The day since the attack had been an ordeal. There was nothing from Adolfo. One of the men thought that he had seen the foolish boy led out of the house at gunpoint, but he couldn't be sure. There had been no word from him. No ransom. No gloating message. Nothing.

Felipe had very little idea of who had been responsible. He only knew who it was not. It wasn't the cartels. Only Los Zetas had the kind of military training to do what had been done, and even then, it would have taken more of them than the six that had been counted. But if not them, then who? The army? Special Forces? The Americans? His sources said not. The Luciano family seeking revenge? Hired mercenaries? Again, there was no suggestion that it was them.

Who, then?

The Englishman?

He was at a loss.

Isaac was admiring the thorium oxide furnace. The gleaming new laboratory had restored his faith.

Felipe knew why: greed.

The promise of great wealth had a way of doing that.

The American Drug Enforcement Agency classified a lab as a "superlab" if it could produce more than ten pounds of meth every week.

The one that Felipe had built could produce twenty pounds *a day*.

Wholesale, a pound of methamphetamine was worth $17,000.

The lab could produce one hundred forty pounds a week.

One hundred forty pounds had a value of over two million dollars.

The lab stood to make him over one hundred million dollars a year.

Isaac wandered further down the line: the hydrofluoric acid solution vat, the aluminium strip and sodium hydroxide mixing tank, the huge reaction vessel, the filtration system, the finishing tanks. The first cook had been completed overnight, and the meth had been broken down and packed in plastic bags, ready to be moved. "May I?" he asked, looking down at the bags.

"Please," Felipe replied.

The gringo opened the bag and took out a larger-than-usual crystal. He held it up to the light and gazed into it.

Felipe knew it was pure.

$C_{10}H_{15}N$.

Eight-tenths carbon.

One-tenth nitrogen.

One-tenth hydrogen.

The formula didn't mean much to him apart from this: it would make him a whole lot of money.

"I knew it was good," Isaac said, "but this is remarkable. How pure is this?"

"Ninety-eight per cent," the chemist said. He looked up and down the line like a proud father.

"Very good," Isaac said. "Very good indeed."

"Have you seen enough, my friend?"

"I think so."

"We should get you back to the plane. You have a long flight ahead of you."

Felipe stepped out of the laboratory and into the

baking heat. The land dropped down on all sides, covered with scrubby brush. The horizon shimmered as if there was another mountain range opposite this one, a thousand miles away. A trick of the heat. His cellphone rang. He fished it out of his pocket and looked at the display. He hoped it might be Adolfo. It was not a number he recognised.

"Hello, Felipe."

"Who is this?"

"You know who I am."

He frowned. "The Englishman?"

"That's right."

"Then I am talking to a dead man."

"Eventually. But not today."

"What do you want?"

"I told you."

"You told me what?"

"That I'd find you."

There was a loud *crack*, and one of Felipe's guards fell to the ground. He looked over at the man; the initial response was one of puzzlement, but as he noticed the man's brains scattered all across the dusty track, the feeling became one of panic. Isaac screamed out. Felipe spun around, staring into the mountains for something that would tell him where the Englishman was—a puff of smoke from his rifle, a glint against a telescopic sight, anything—but there was nothing, just the harsh glare of the sun, a hateful kaleidoscope of refulgent brilliance that lanced into his eyes and obscured everything.

"Felipe."

He still had the phone pressed to his ear.

"Listen to me, Felipe."

"What?"

"I wanted you to know—your son is in America now. He's been delivered. The Mafia, isn't it? How will that go for him?"

Felipe pulled his gold-plated revolver from its holster

and shot wildly into the near distance. "Where are you, you bastard?"

He started in the opposite direction, towards his second guard. The man was on one knee, his AK-47 raised, scanning the landscape. A second *crack* echoed in the valley, and a plume of blood fountained out of the guard's neck, bursting between his fingers as he tried to close the six-inch rent that had suddenly been opened there.

"Felipe."

"Show yourself!"

Isaac and his men ducked down behind the car.

"I should thank you, really," the Englishman said.

He crept backwards towards the entrance to the lab. "For what?"

"I thought I was bad. Irredeemable. And maybe I am."

He backed up more quickly.

A bullet whined through the air, slamming into the metal door and caroming away.

"Stay there, please."

He wailed at the rocks, "What do you want from me?"

"You reminded me—there are plenty worse than me. I'd forgotten that."

The rifle shot was just a muffled pop, flat and small in the lonely quiet of the mountain. He turned in time to see the muzzle flash, fifty feet to his left and twenty feet above him. A stinging pain in his leg and then the delayed starburst that crashed through his head. His knee collapsed. Blood started to run down his leg, soaking his pants. He dropped forwards, flat onto his face, eating the dust. He managed to get his arm beneath him and raised his head. Through the sweat that was pouring into his eyes and the heat haze that quivered up off the rocks, he could see a man approaching him. The details were fuzzy and unclear. He had black camouflage paint smeared across his face, the sort that gringo football players wore. He had a thick, ragged beard. He was filthy with dust and muck. He had a long rifle at his side, barrel down.

Felipe tried to scrabble away, his good leg slipping against the scree.

"Isaac!" Felipe yelled. "Help me!"

There was no sign of him.

The hazy figure came closer.

"Please," Felipe begged.

The man lowered himself to a crouch and blocked the way forwards.

"I'll give you anything."

Felipe raised his head again. The sun smothered him. The pain from his leg made him retch. The barrel of the rifle swung away, up and out of his field of vision. The Englishman straightened up. Felipe saw a pair of desert boots and the dusty cuffs of a pair of jeans. He scrabbled towards them.

The muzzle of the rifle was rested against the top of his skull.

He heard the thunk of a bolt-action rifle, a bullet pressed into the chamber.

The click-click of a double-pulled trigger, and then nothing.

Chapter Sixty-Two

LIEUTENANT SANCHEZ had delayed them for an hour. Captain Pope had made an angry phone call, and eventually, Sanchez had been contacted by someone from the Ministry of Justice in Mexico City and had been ordered to stand down. The six agents had dispersed into the streets to take up the search. Anna had taken a room in a hotel with a decent internet connection, hooked into GCHQ's servers, and spent hours running search after search. She was tired, but she did not sleep. She stayed awake with pots of strong coffee and nervous tension.

She hacked into the municipal police database and withdrew everything she could find about Jesus Plato. She started with his address, plotting alternative routes to his house from the mansion and then looking for CCTV cameras that might have recorded his Dodge as it passed along its route. There were half a dozen hits—the best was a blurred shot from the security camera at a Pemex gas station showing Milton sitting in the front seat of the car while Plato filled the tank—but nothing that was particularly useful.

She extracted the details of Plato's private car and ran that through the number plate recognition system that had recently been installed on the Mexican highway system. That was more successful. The Honda Accord was recorded heading south: first on the 45, then past Chihuahua and onto the 16. It was picked up again on the outskirts of Parral, leaving the city on the 24 and heading south-west.

Towards the Sierra Madre.

Fourteen hours of driving.

She told Pope. He left with two of the others.

It was a long shot. They were hours behind him.

Then she skimmed intelligence from the army that said that Felipe González, the boss of La Frontera cartel, had been shot to death in the mountains.

It was all across the mainstream news hours later.

It started to make more sense.

The Accord was recorded heading north again, on highway 15 this time, heading up the coast. The camera had taken a usable picture, too. Milton was driving. He turned west at Magdalena, back towards Juárez.

She warned Pope that Milton might be meeting with Plato.

They put his house under surveillance.

They watched the police station.

No sign of Milton.

Plato went out in a taxi the next day. They followed him. He picked up the empty Accord in the car park of a *maquiladora* on the edge of town. He drove it back home. They saw him take a rifle from the back of the car and lock it in a gun cabinet in his garage.

The gun that killed González?

It didn't matter.

They had struck out.

Milton was a ghost.

Gone.

ANNA EXCUSED HERSELF for half an hour and found a payphone in a grocery store. The phone was in the back, inside a half booth that was fitted to the wall. It looked private enough. She dialled the number she had been given several years before. She had never had the need to dial it before, and she was anxious as she waited for it to connect.

It did.

"My garden is full of weeds this year, the herbicide isn't working."

"Perhaps you should use a shear to clip the weeds."

"Shears are too indiscriminate; besides, weeds must be pulled out by the roots."

"Thank you," the operator said. "Please wait."

After a moment, the call was transferred.

"Anna Vasilyevna Dubrovsky."

She held the mouthpiece close to her mouth. "Hello, Roman."

"How is Mexico?"

"Hot."

"Did you find the man?"

"We did, but then we lost him again."

"And now?"

"He is still lost. They are looking for him."

"Are you still working on the case?"

"I believe so."

"And do you think you can find him again?"

"It depends on him doing anything foolish like allowing himself to be fingerprinted."

"And if he doesn't?"

"Maybe. I have a better idea where he is headed now. And I know where he has been in the last couple of weeks. There might be something there that I can use. So maybe."

"Shcherbakov wants to talk to you about him."

"The colonel?"

"Your trip to Moscow is postponed. He is coming to speak to you instead."

"In London?"

"Next Monday. Be at the usual place at eight. You will be collected."

Now she really was nervous. The colonel was coming to London? "Fine."

"The man—you saw him?"

"Very briefly."

"What did you make of him?"

"He had been beaten. But there is something about him. He is not the sort of man you would want to have as your enemy. Why is he suddenly so important?"

"The colonel will explain. But an opportunity has arisen that requires a special kind of operative. Someone just like him."

"You know he won't work for us?"

"We think he will. We have something—someone—that he wants."

EPILOGUE

The Coyote

Chapter Sixty-Three

MILTON LOOKED up into the sky. It was midnight, and the stars, spread out across the obsidian canvas like discarded fistfuls of diamonds, burned with a fierceness that was more vivid than usual. He thought of those stars, dead for millions of years, their light only just now reaching the Earth. He paused for a moment to straighten out a kink in his boot and, realising that he was tiring, dropped his pack and allowed himself to sink back down into the sand. He sat and gazed up, lost in the glorious celestial display. The black blended away into infinity and unbeing, and he felt utterly and completely alone, as if he was the only man in the universe. It was a sensation that he recognised, one that had been with him for most of his adult life, and certainly for the last ten years.

He was comfortable with that.

Part of his solitary journey through South America had been to give himself time to come to terms with what, he knew, was the only possible way that he could live out the rest of his life. He had done too many bad things to deserve happiness, and even if he could have accepted that he did deserve it, he was too dangerous to allow anyone else to drift into his orbit. That had been demonstrated to him in spades in London, with what had happened to Sharon and Rutherford. Burned half to death and shot in the head, all because they had allowed him to cross their paths. Death followed him, always close at heel, always avid, always hungry. And now Control had found him again and flung his agents at him from half a world away. What if he had allowed himself to draw closer to someone, perhaps one of the women whose bed he had shared over the last six months? What if he had allowed himself a wife? Children? The thought was preposterous.

The Group would offer him no quarter, and anyone who was found with him would be executed. It would have to be that way. What might he have told them? What secrets divulged? The shoe had been on the other foot before, and he knew what the orders would be. No loose ends.

No.

There had already been too much innocent blood spilt.

He could only ever be alone.

He took off his boot and massaged his heel. He had been travelling for thirty-eight hours straight. He had taken a couple of naps in the car, parked on the side of the road, but that was it. He was as tired as a dog. It was absolutely still, the quiet so deep that it was all-consuming, enough to make you wonder if you had gone deaf. As he listened to his own heartbeat keeping him company, he wondered whether death could possibly be more serene.

He had returned Plato's car, left it in the car park of a *maquiladora* at one in the morning. The rifle was in the back, hidden beneath a travelling blanket. He exchanged it for a stolen Volkswagen and crossed the city. He drove carefully for fear of attracting attention, only accelerating properly once he was among the scrubland and the start of the desert. He had followed the highway for two hundred miles, and then he had pulled over to the side of the road, soaking siphoned diesel into the upholstery and tossing in a match. With the heat of the burning car braising his cheeks, he turned to the north and set his face to America.

He walked.

Big Bend National Park was ahead, the Chisos Mountain range welcoming him to the border. Milton picked the distinctive shape of Emory Peak at the end of a deep valley as his waypoint. He walked. It hardly seemed to draw closer at all, but distance was almost impossible to judge, that was the way of it in the desert, and especially so at night. Milton was not concerned. He had navigated through bleaker landscapes than this.

He was close.

He walked.

He came across an abandoned railway track, an idle row of orphaned boxcars daubed with graffiti across the rust. The dawn was coming up now. The darkness was weakening, lilac blooming at the edges of the horizon, the light fading the constellations, the herald of the glorious golden desert sunrise that would be on him all too quickly. Somewhere on the mesa, a coyote howled. The long, mournful wail was followed by a yipping chuckle until it almost sounded as if the dog was laughing.

He kept walking.

John Milton trudged across the border as the light turned from black to mauve, the sun coming around again.

GET TWO BEST-SELLERS, TWO NOVELLAS AND EXCLUSIVE JOHN MILTON MATERIAL

Building a relationship with my readers is the very best thing about writing. I occasionally send newsletters with details on new releases, special offers and other bits of news relating to the John Milton, Beatrix Rose and Soho Noir series.

And if you sign up to the mailing list I'll send you all this free stuff:

1. A copy of my best-seller, The Cleaner (178 five star reviews and RRP of $5.99).

2. A copy of the John Milton introductory novella, 1000 Yards.

3. A copy of the introductory Soho Noir novella, Gaslight.

4. A free copy of my best-seller, The Black Mile (averages 4.4 out of 5 stars and RRP of $ 5.99).

5. A copy of the highly classified background check on John Milton before he was admitted to Group 15. Exclusive to my mailing list – you can't get this anywhere else.

6. A copy of Tarantula, an exciting John Milton short story.

You can get the novel, the novellas, the background check

and the short story, **for free**, by signing up at http://eepurl.com/Cai5X

Enjoy this book?
You can make a big difference

Reviews are the most powerful tools in my arsenal when it comes getting attention for my books. Much as I'd like to, I don't have the financial muscle of a New York publisher. I can't take out full page ads in the newspaper or put posters on the subway.

(Not yet, anyway).

But I do have something much more powerful and effective than that, and it's something that those publishers would kill to get their hands on.

A committed and loyal bunch of readers.

Honest reviews of my books help bring them to the attention of other readers.

If you've enjoyed this book I would be very grateful if you could spend just five minutes leaving a review (it can be as short as you like).

Thank you very much.

ABOUT THE AUTHOR

Mark Dawson is the author of the breakout John Milton, Beatrix Rose and Soho Noir series. He makes his online home at www.markjdawson.com. You can connect with Mark on Twitter at @pbackwriter, on Facebook at www.facebook.com/markdawsonauthor and you should send him an email at markjdawson@me.com if the mood strikes you.

ALSO BY MARK DAWSON

Have you read them all?

<u>In the Soho Noir Series</u>

Gaslight

When Harry and his brother Frank are blackmailed into paying off a local hood they decide to take care of the problem themselves. But when all of London's underworld is in thrall to the man's boss, was their plan audacious or the most foolish thing that they could possibly have done?

The Black Mile

London, 1940: the Luftwaffe blitzes London every night for fifty-seven nights. Houses, shops and entire streets are wiped from the map. The underworld is in flux: the Italian criminals who dominated the West End have been interned and now their rivals are fighting to replace them. Meanwhile, hidden in the shadows, the Black-Out Ripper sharpens his knife and sets to his grisly work.

The Imposter

War hero Edward Fabian finds himself drawn into a criminal family's web of vice and soon he is an accomplice to their scheming. But he's not the man they think he is - he's far more dangerous than they could possibly imagine.

In the John Milton Series

One Thousand Yards

In this dip into his case files, John Milton is sent into North Korea. With nothing but a sniper rifle, bad intentions and a very particular target, will Milton be able to take on the secret police of the most dangerous failed state on the planet?

Tarantula

In this further dip into his files, Milton is sent to Italy. A colleague who was investigating a particularly violent Mafiosi has disappeared. Will Milton be able to get to the bottom of the mystery, or will he be the next to fall victim to Tarantula?

The Cleaner

Sharon Warriner is a single mother in the East End of London, fearful that she's lost her young son to a life in the gangs. After John Milton saves her life, he promises to help. But the gang, and the charismatic rapper who leads it, is not about to cooperate with him.

Saint Death

John Milton has been off the grid for six months. He surfaces in Ciudad Juárez, Mexico, and immediately finds himself drawn into a vicious battle with the narco-gangs that control the borderlands.

The Driver

When a girl he drives to a party goes missing, John Milton is worried. Especially when two dead bodies are discovered and the police start treating him as their prime suspect.

Ghosts

John Milton is blackmailed into finding his predecessor as Number One. But she's a ghost, too, and just as dangerous as him. He finds himself in deep trouble, playing the Russians against the British in a desperate attempt to save the life of his oldest friend.

The Sword of God

On the run from his own demons, John Milton treks through the Michigan wilderness into the town of Truth. He's not looking for trouble, but trouble's looking for him. He finds himself up against a small-town cop who has no idea with whom he is dealing, and no idea how dangerous he is.

In the Beatrix Rose Series

In Cold Blood

Beatrix Rose was the most dangerous assassin in an off-the-books government kill squad until her former boss betrayed her. A decade later, she emerges from the Hong Kong underworld with payback on her mind. They gunned down her husband and kidnapped her daughter, and now the debt needs to be repaid. It's a blood feud she didn't start but she is going to finish.

Blood Moon Rising

There were six names on Beatrix's Death List and now there are four. She's going to account for the others, one by one, even if it kills her. She has returned from Somalia with another target in her sights. Bryan Duffy is in Iraq, surrounded by mercenaries, with no easy way to get to him and no easy way to get out. And Beatrix has other issues that need to be addressed. Will Duffy prove to be one kill too far?

Blood and Roses

Beatrix Rose has worked her way through her Kill List. Four are dead, just two are left. But now her foes know she has them in her sights and the hunter has become the hunted.

Standalone Novels

The Art of Falling Apart

A story of greed, duplicity and death in the flamboyant, super-ego world of rock and roll. Dystopia have rocketed up the charts in Europe, so now it's time to crack America. The opening concert in Las Vegas is a sell-out success, but secret envy and open animosity have begun to tear the group apart.

Subpoena Colada

Daniel Tate looks like he has it all. A lucrative job as a lawyer and a host of famous names who want him to work for them. But his girlfriend has deserted him for an American film star and his main client has just been implicated in a sensational murder. Can he hold it all together?

Printed in Great Britain
by Amazon